PROJECTIONS

Joshua Danker-Dake

Three Giant Elephants

PROJECTIONS

Copyright 2020 by Joshua Danker-Dake
www.dankerdake.com

Three Giant Elephants

Cover design by David Lange

This is a work of fiction. All names, characters, places, and events
are the work of the author's imagination.
Any resemblance to real persons, places, or events is
coincidental.

For the TNW and TGE

ONE

Juha Karjalainen, who may or may not have murdered his wife, had returned from Mars after two years and moved right back into his old apartment in Portsmith's Aldersgate District.

The building was decrepit—it didn't even have a holographic façade. And the elevator was out. Green Greene took the steps two at a time and was disappointed to find himself pausing to catch his breath when he reached Juha's floor.

Greene steeled himself and knocked on Juha's door. When it opened, a miasma of odor spilled out, bacon and incense fighting for dominance.

Greene didn't recognize the man in the doorway, long-haired in jeans and an undershirt. The man was a head taller than Greene, like Juha, but thin and fit, although loose skin hung from his neck and upper arms.

Greene cleared his throat. "Sorry, I was looking for—"

"That's a hell of a nice suit," the man said. "But you know, I liked you better with the mustache. You don't even look half Indian now. Makes your nose look bigger, too."

Greene blinked. "Juha?"

Juha allowed him entrance. "Green Greene. It's been a while."

Greene stepped inside. The studio apartment was cramped and messy. A bookcase and a threadbare sofa were shoved up against the entertainment wall. All the décor was shabby; certainly nothing here was holographic.

"Juha," Greene repeated, trying to convince himself. "You must have lost thirty kilos."

"Almost forty." Juha went to the kitchen area. "Want some cake?"

"No thanks." Greene hadn't even had his coffee yet.

"It's chocolate. No? I never understood why a person would turn down cake. I'm not sure it's trustworthy." Juha cut himself an enormous piece and sat down at the apartment's small table with his plate and an empty bowl. He motioned toward Greene's Spec-Tron glasses. "Would you mind turning those off while you're here? I haven't brushed my hair yet."

Greene switched off the Spec-Trons' video stream, then removed his jacket and sat down across from Juha in the only other chair in the place. The morning sun shone through the single window and directly into his eyes.

Juha took his phone and scanned the cake. "1,108 calories," the phone said.

"Mark it," Juha said. "I had to lose a bunch of weight to go to Mars. Once I got there, I decided to keep going. Not much worthwhile to eat up there anyhow. You still living with your mom? Your wife's still okay with that?"

"*She* lives with *me*," Greene said. "And Nisha's fine. Besides, it'll be good when the baby comes."

"Congratulations." Juha crammed a giant bite of cake into his mouth.

"Thanks. How was Mars?"

Juha held up a finger as he chewed. Then he spat the entire mouthful into his bowl. "Boring." He ignored Greene's look of revulsion. "There's no crime there yet. It was half accounting, mining inventory and such. People try to get into the food or the booze once in a while, that's all. Give it ten years to grow before they'll need some real security."

Greene didn't find this surprising. But the job must have paid well—and yet here Juha was, back in this dump.

"So what's this all about?" Juha asked. "If you didn't come to eat my cake, you could have just called."

"I need your help."

Juha spat another glob of chewed cake into the bowl.

"Why don't you just buy the diet cake?" Greene asked.

"Because it tastes like chemicals. My help? I'm not a cop anymore. If you knew I was back, you must know that too."

"I'm not a cop anymore either." Greene took out his phone and showed Juha his credentials. "I'm chief of security for Xiong Holonautics."

"Good for you," Juha said without looking at them. "The Bear, huh? Kind of young for that position, aren't you?"

"Yes," Greene said, pride and defensiveness mingling in his voice. "Have you seen the news?"

"I don't watch the news. Nothing but jackasses on the news."

"Our COO was murdered a few hours ago."

Juha shrugged. "It's always some damn thing, eh? Sounds like a job for the cops."

"The killer also stole a prototype from R&D. Getting it back is my job."

"You have plenty of minions over there at Xiong, right? What do you need me for?"

"Because of your special way with holograms."

Juha waved his fork at Greene's glasses. "But you've got infrared, right?"

"Not effective anymore. Our newest projectors cover a broad range of the infrared spectrum."

Juha spat out more cake. "But you think I'll still be able to ... you know."

"Assuming you can, Xiong Holonautics will pay you ten thousand gigayuan to help us recover it."

"Ten thousand bucks to find your MacGuffin? You really are moving up in the world."

Greene leaned back and crossed his arms. He'd forgotten just how much patience Juha required. And he didn't have time to waste. "It's not a MacGuffin. It's a weapon. Potentially."

"A weapon? From a hologram company? Do tell."

"It's top secret."

"Of course it is."

Greene sighed. "It's our first solid hologram projector. It combines our latest holographic technology with a force field structure. Basically, it can create solid objects out of thin air. Not only camouflage but attack and defense—the possibilities are almost endless, as you can probably imagine. You've got to understand, Xiong is five years ahead of everyone else on force fields. Nothing like this has ever been seen before."

Juha drummed his fork on the table as he considered this. "For all of that, you don't seem like you're that concerned. Certainly not ten thousand gigs worth of concerned."

Greene fidgeted, struggling not to let his impatience show. "I'm concerned. I can't even tell you how concerned I am. Anyway, the police are there now."

"You couldn't buy them off? Really? All that Xiong money I've heard about?"

Greene shook his head. "They sold out to the media. A high-profile murder like this ... the conglomerates are really stepping up their game. I— We can't even get in there until nine. But we have the latitude to investigate without interference and we're getting their leads—*that's* the Xiong money you've heard about."

Juha spat cake. "A weapon, huh? And you didn't think I'd help you just for the money? You're appealing to my better nature? Fraternity, the good of humanity and such?"

"Then you'll do it?"

Juha was on his last bite of cake, and this one he swallowed. He took his phone and scanned the bolus in the dish.

"936 calories," said the phone.

"Log the difference." Juha rose and scraped the vile mass into the garbage.

"Juha," Greene said.

"I don't know, okay? It sounds exciting and all, but I'm not really looking for exciting right now. I have a business I'm trying to get off the ground and—" Juha's phone rang. "Excuse me. Hello?" He set the phone in the center of the table and turned on the speaker. "It's Satu," he mouthed.

Juha's younger sister, who'd had a bit of a crush on Greene back in the day.

"... I'm at the store, trying to get your stuff," Satu was saying. "I don't know why you haven't gotten the automated pickup set up yet."

"I like picking my own stuff," Juha said. "What's the problem?"

"A couple things. First, you wrote *butter*, but I don't know if you want the one-gallon tub or the two-gallon, or if you have a preference between *Butteresque* and *The Buttery Tears of Angels*."

"None. Neither. Just real butter. They do have real butter, don't they?"

"Seriously? It's like ten times the price."

"Oh yeah, that's the stuff. Anything else?"

"Just the lotion. They've got all these scents and—"

"Doesn't matter." Juha had a twinkle in his eye. "Pick anything. They all end up smelling like pornography after a while anyhow."

Greene rolled his eyes. Yes, this was Juha all right.

Satu made a disgusted sound. "You're a pig."

Juha put his hand over the microphone. "I shouldn't have said that. Now she's not going to buy any."

Chafing at this waste of time, Greene stood. "Can I use your bathroom?"

Juha jerked his thumb toward the apartment's single bedroom.

The tiny room was dominated by the unmade bed and over-piled bureau. Standing among the heaps of clothing on the dresser were two picture frames, and when Greene saw them, he did a double take.

Each photo was of a different short, buxom woman: a blonde, Juha's late wife, Hana; and a redhead, Marlena, Juha's old unacted-upon love. The latter picture, which showed Marlena in the prime of her considerable beauty, had to be ten years old.

Well, this was awkward, Greene thought—and maybe just what he needed. He had no idea Juha still carried a torch for Marlena. After all these years ...

When Greene returned to the living area, he found Juha washing dishes.

"Listen, Green," Juha said without turning, "it was good to see you, and all the best in finding your MacGuffin, but I don't think—"

"Do you know who was killed?" Greene said. "R. R. Ranga Rao."

"Sounds Indian. Was he family? Look—"

Greene closed the distance between them. "He was Marlena's husband."

"Marlena?"

"Marlena Gary, and don't you even pretend like you don't know."

Now Juha ceased his activity and faced Greene. "Marlena? Really?"

"They got married about two years ago. You didn't know?"

"I haven't kept up," Juha said, and Greene wasn't sure he believed it. "Married, huh? People still get married these days? Any kids?"

"No kids."

"Hm." Juha leaned against the counter, hand on his chin. He stayed that way for what seemed like an inordinately long time.

Greene retrieved his jacket. He wasn't going to beg, wasn't going to tell Juha that he might lose his job over this, lose everything. "I have to go. Are you coming or not?"

Juha's eyes flicked to him, his gaze burning. Then he grinned. "Did you really think I wouldn't help you out? You're my favorite person named after an ancient-ass folk song. Eh, maybe second favorite. Of course I'm coming. Let me get my stuff. It'll be just like old times."

TWO

Diverting the autodriven traffic around it, Greene's car conveyed them swiftly through an endless forest of glistening skyscrapers to Portsmith's Waterfront District. The glare was bad enough that Greene had to pull all the car's shades to review the last hour's developments on the windshield display.

A glut of illegally parked media vehicles clogged the avenue in front of Xiong Tower. Greene's car stopped at the sprawling plaza that lay across from the tower, and they exited.

"Park and charge," Greene said, and the car departed.

On the way, Juha had occupied himself with his own affairs, allowing Greene to get caught up on the police activity in the tower, but now he was ready to make conversation.

"Look at this nonsense," Juha said, nodding at the nearest of the HOLOGRAPHIC ZONE signs that ringed the plaza. "Everywhere in this town gives me a migraine nowadays."

Juha shouldered his pack, and they set off across the plaza.

"Mind the ads," Greene said.

"Happy Wednesday," said a woman's voice over the plaza loudspeakers. "Rain will now begin to fall on your position." A purple ball the size of a melon fell from the sky and landed at Greene's feet, bursting in a spray of water that did not wet him. Balls of all colors fell, splattering throughout the crowded plaza, along with a light holographic rain. Now the balls had legs like spiders, and they skittered away into the shrubbery. A helicopter careened overhead, then exploded. Debris rained down, vanishing when it hit the ground. Greene ignored it all.

"Go to the north," said the woman's voice. "The all-new Blackridge North."

"The hell," Juha said, turning away from the scene. "How is that a car commercial? They didn't even show the car. Haven't you people heard of good taste?"

"We don't sell good taste," Greene said. "We sell 'the actualization of imagination.' It's the opposite of good taste, usually."

Greene crossed the congested street without looking, ignoring the members of the media who called to him, trusting his Xiong credentials to prevent any autodriven cars from hitting him.

The Xiong Holonautics building, that antiquated Art Deco monolith, loomed before them, its hard angles, black granite facing, and ornate gold leaf alien in the midst of downtown Portsmith's reef of streamlined, glittering glass.

Juha paused, his eyes drawn upward to the hologram of the immense golden bear that prowled the sky above Xiong Tower. "You aren't kidding."

They passed through the colossal entrance archway and stepped inside the building. As usual, Greene bypassed the security line and went directly to the executive clearance checkpoint, where he was scanned and admitted in a matter of seconds, but the guards stopped Juha.

"I'm legit," Juha said.

"He's with me," Greene said.

"Sorry, sir, but it's procedure," said one of the guards, a young man named Reich. "Especially with ... with what happened last night."

"Fine. You're right, of course." Greene stepped behind the counter as they X-rayed Juha and his bag. He skimmed the readout. "Duct tape, rope, bottle of water, pills, pocketknife, goggles, notebook, pens, first aid kit, pistol. Is that your old service pistol?"

Juha nodded. "Is there a problem? I was under the impression we were going to be getting into some serious business today."

Greene shook his head. "You should have told me is all. Just keep it unloaded and put away while we're in the building." He turned to the security guards. "Mr. Karjalainen is my guest. Please log him and his weapon as such."

"Sir, that's against company policy," Reich said. "He has to check it."

Greene set his jaw. "I know that. Do you think I don't know company policy on weapons? Do you think I was somehow uninvolved in the determination of that policy? I am *authorizing* it."

Now both guards were stiff and nervous. "No, sir. Sorry, sir. Sorry for the trouble."

Greene tried to relax. "Don't be. You're just doing your job. Speaking of trouble, though, get a team down here to clear the street. The media have got it completely blocked."

"Yes, sir."

Greene nodded. "Juha, let's go."

Smirking, Juha retrieved his backpack. "Haven't been here long, have you?"

"Three months. Why?"

"Oh, no reason."

The five-story lobby was another Art Deco relic, a masterwork of gold, black, and stained glass. A ten-meter mosaic of the Xiong Holonautics logo, an X and an H overlaid to form two narrow triangles, marked the center. Behind it were the reception desk and the elevators; to either side stood large fountains that filled the lobby with the sound of splashing water.

"You work on a cruise ship," Juha said.

Greene called the elevator, and they boarded.

"One hundred eleven," Greene said.

When the doors opened, they were met by a twitchy man with manic eyes and a pencil mustache who fell into step with them and matched their brisk pace down the hall.

"Good morning, Chief Greene. And this must be Juha Karjalainen." He butchered the pronunciation with conventional hard J's.

"Juha Karjalainen"—Greene repeated the name, but correctly, emphasizing the Y sounds—"this is Max Fill. He's going to help get you up to speed.",

Fill peered intently at Juha. "Hm."

"What?" Juha said.

"Oh, nothing, sorry. You don't look Japanese is all."

Confusion flitted across Juha's face. "Japanese?"

Fill clasped his hands together. "I beg your pardon. I didn't mean to offend."

Juha gave him a flinty look. "It's Finnish."

"Get going, Max," Greene said as they turned a corner.

"Yes indeed. Apologies." Max was having trouble simultaneously keeping the pace and speaking. "Mr. Karjalainen, how familiar are you with our company?"

"I'm not."

"Oh, my," Fill said. "Xiong Holonautics is *the* worldwide leader in holographic décor. Has been for fifteen years. We made holograms commercial. We *perfected* the hologram, you see. Color, texture, sheen—wood, glass, stone, metalwork, fabric—you name it. Totally indistinguishable from the real thing to the naked eye, with no glasses, no headset, no apparatus necessary. Odds are you decorate your house with Xiong or perhaps"—distaste crept into his voice—"with one of our competitors' lesser imitations."

"Nope," Juha said.

Greene turned to see a look of disbelief cross Fill's face, but the man adhered to his script.

"Virtual reality? Ha! Anybody can give you a headset, a collar, help you 'escape' into a different world. Xiong doesn't bother with any of that. We're only interested in improving one reality—the real one."

Juha glanced sidelong at Greene. "You stuck me with a marketing guy?"

"Did you want to hear the technical side? The specs?" Greene asked.

"Not really." Juha's phone rang. "Excuse me a second, my sister again. Hello? Yes, of course we're open today. Why would we not be open? 'National Day of Not Prayer'? That's a real thing? Okay, no, I get it, it's fine, but why would we close for that? ... That's what I'm saying. Uh huh. Okay. Oh, and see if you can figure out who clogged the toilet yesterday—give them double burpees. He what? It's always some damn thing, eh? All right, I'll see if I can swing by this afternoon." He said this last with a look at Greene, who had more important things to do than ask what it was all about.

They reached a conference room and stopped. The double doors swung open upon detecting Greene's credentials, and they entered.

Three people sat at a vast table that could accommodate thirty. Nearest them, Garcinia Cambogia, Xiong's elderly head of R&D, worked at a tablet. Across from her sat Brunhilde Burg, Greene's deputy chief of security, a hard, muscular woman fifteen years his senior. At the end of the table was Lord-Is-My Shepherd, Xiong's chief technology officer, looking even sterner than usual.

Shepherd slapped the table with both hands. "Chief! Where the hell have you been?"

Greene stiffened. "I was getting help, as I'm sure Burg told you. Sir."

Shepherd, who had eyes like steel and wore a charcoal suit that was a work of art, rose and took up an aggressive stance in front of Greene. He was middle-aged, of average height and build, but his demeanor added fifteen centimeters and ten kilos of muscle to his presence.

"Help?" Shepherd eyed Juha, in jeans and a leather jacket, his hair in a ponytail on top of his head. "Who is this?"

Juha grinned. "I'm the help."

Greene glared at Juha. "Sir, this is Juha Karjalainen. I believe he can help us. Juha, this is Mr. Shepherd, our CTO."

Shepherd looked Juha up and down like he was a piece of meat hanging in a market. "Is he cleared?"

Burg crossed her arms, her biceps straining the sleeves of her black security uniform. "He's cleared. *Provisionally.*"

Shepherd shook his head. "We've wasted enough time already. Tell me right now why he's in this room or else get him out of here."

"He can detect holograms," Greene said. "With the naked eye."

All heads swiveled as one toward Juha.

Shepherd moved to violate Juha's personal space instead. "How?"

Juha met his gaze. "I don't know. Always been able to. The light doesn't hit them exactly right—it's hard to explain. They give me a headache if I look at them too long."

Garcinia rubbed her hands together and stood. "Oh, my. All that and handsome, too. How remarkable."

Juha gave her a little theatrical bow.

Shepherd's disbelief was obvious. "Even our holograms? Ours are the best."

"Test him, then, sir," Greene said. "I need him."

Shepherd thought a moment. "Fine, we'll test him. Let's run him through the kill house."

Juha raised an eyebrow. "Kill house?"

Fill jumped in. "Yes, it's a training range for close-contact engag—"

Juha waved him away. "I know what a kill house is. Why do you have one?"

"Let's go," said Shepherd. "You can tell him on the way." He stalked out of the room, and everyone scurried after him. Greene brought up the rear.

Fill reattached himself to Juha's hip. "Our top-of-the-line holographic programs enable us to project nearly any scenario you can imagine with unparalleled detail and realism. And not just for urban combat—you can imagine how attractive this would be to most any military, paramilitary, or law enforcement group. Indeed, time in our kill house goes at quite a premium."

"Indeed," Juha said.

Garcinia shooed Fill away, then hooked her arm through Juha's and gave him a sweet smile. "Young man, I'm extremely interested in your abilities, if they do test out. I've been in this business most of my life, and we haven't had a hologram that could be identified as artificial one hundred percent of the time in over eight years. Eight years! And everything we've released commercially in the last three has been rated as visually indistinguishable from real by at least ninety-eight percent of our clients. Never mind that I have never—*never*—heard of someone who could spot *every* hologram, and my boy, you must believe that we have *tried*. And by *tried*, I'm talking *budget*. Would you be open to further study of your abilities once we're through this crisis?"

Juha smiled back at her. "I'm open to discussing it."

Burg dropped back to Greene's side. "How sure are you about this guy?"

"He can help us. I'm sure about that."

"Do you trust him?"

"We have a history," Greene said.

She didn't bother to hide her scowl. She was almost as tall as he was, she was intimidating, and she knew it. "You didn't answer the question. Sir."

It was funny, Greene thought. Here was Burg talking about trust when Greene knew good and well she didn't even really trust him to do his own job—at least not as well as *she* might.

"How much do I need to trust him for this operation?" he said.

She turned her palms up. "Maybe you're right. But if not, then ..."

Greene bit down his irritation. "Then you might end up with my job after all."

They reached the elevators and entered. "One ninety-two," Shepherd said.

Fill wrung his hands. "I can't believe it. A breach here, in our building, and the story's been leaked to the press. Our stock price has taken a big hit already."

"The stock will recover," Shepherd said. "As long as we get that tech back."

"But Dr. Ranga Rao was the greatest innovator this company's ever had!"

"Yes, he was." Shepherd's face was grave. "But one thing at a time, Fill. One thing at a time."

"Yes, sir."

Shepherd turned the superior expression he always seemed to wear to Juha. "So, Mr.—"

"Karjalainen."

"Assuming you pan out and we bring you on board, how shall we remember you in our records? As 'the help'?"

Juha shrugged. "A rose by any other name."

"You seem like a smartass, Karjalainen. I don't have a lot of patience for smartasses." Shepherd snapped his fingers at Fill. "Put 'troubleshooter.'"

"Yes, sir."

The elevator deposited them in the kill house, an open area three stories high encompassing all this level's available floor space. Half the kill house was occupied by an expansive plywood maze; the other half was bare except for a few folding chairs and tables, with a raised control booth at one end and another set of elevators on the wall across from them.

Greene hung back, watching Juha take it all in.

"Goes straight to the roof," Fill said when he saw Juha looking at the far elevators. "Helicopter pad. As you might imagine, that sort of direct access makes things easier when clients visit."

Shepherd snapped his fingers twice. "All right, we don't have all day. Karjalainen, show me the magic." He turned to Garcinia. "Standard tests, quick as you can. You've got the other solid projector hooked up?"

"Yes, sir." Garcinia worked at her tablet, and a wide velvet curtain appeared before them, seemingly hanging from nothing. "Mr. Fill, if you would be so kind. And grab a chair."

Fill obligingly retrieved a chair and went behind the curtain.

She turned to Juha. "Ready?"

"Always."

Garcinia tapped the tablet, and the curtain vanished. Before them, Max Fill stood behind five identical chairs.

Garcinia patted Juha's arm. "Now, dear, please tell me which of the chairs is real."

Greene stared at each of them. The texture of the molded plastic, the grain of the metal, the reflection of the light—they all looked exactly the same to him.

"That one," said Juha.

Garcinia made the four holographic chairs disappear, leaving only the real one—the one Juha was pointing at.

Beside Greene, Burg muttered something he didn't catch.

"Marvelous, marvelous," Garcinia said. "Now, one moment."

She went to work on her tablet. The curtain reappeared.

"Mr. Fill, take your place, please."

The curtain disappeared again, revealing five identical Max Fills, each fidgeting identically.

Garcinia smiled at Juha. "Now, please tell me which Mr. Fill is the real one."

Juha studied them a moment without replying. Greene found this odd—he assumed that a person would be more difficult to get just right and thus easier to detect—not that he could tell any difference.

Shepherd snorted. "And here I thought we might have something."

Juha shook his head. "None of them."

Smiling broadly, Garcinia caused all five Fills to vanish.

"The hell?" Burg said. "Where did he go?"

Juha nodded his head. "Right there."

A hand appeared out of thin air, waving. The air in front of them rippled, and Fill appeared from nowhere. Grinning like an idiot, he picked up the chair and put it back.

Burg had her hands on her hips. "Cloaking? We have cloaking now and nobody told Security?"

"Now, now, it's not as bad as all that." Garcinia tucked her tablet under her arm. "Single-angle cloaking has been around forever and you already know all about that. This is something else. It's not really cloaking ... not yet. Still experimental. Only viable from a very narrow viewing range at this point. It hasn't left this building."

Greene held up a hand. Even after three months with Xiong, he was still struggling to wrap his mind around all the nuances of holographics. "You ... projected an image of the empty room in front of Max? And he stuck his hand through it."

Garcinia smiled at him. "Yes, that's it exactly."

Greene turned to Shepherd. "Sir, are you satisfied? Surely you can see how he can help us find the prototype."

Shepherd, hand on chin, said, "Let's test him with a hard 'gram."

"One moment." Garcinia went to work at her device, and five chairs sprang into existence before them. "Now, dear: all five of these chairs are holograms."

"That's right," Juha said.

"But one of them is a *solid* hologram. It will hold your weight. Which one? Ah ah, no touching."

Juha examined them, first casually, then with greater interest, sticking his nose within centimeters of them. "I can't tell," he said finally.

Fill rubbed his hands together. "Well, that's a point for us, eh?"

"It's the one in the middle," said Garcinia. "Go ahead, sit on it."

Juha looked at her suspiciously. He poked it, then jerked his finger back. Gingerly, he sat on the chair, and it held him. He remained there, an odd expression on his face.

"What?" Greene said.

"It feels weird. Like ... like I'm riding on a bus. Or in a big truck. Try it."

Juha hopped up and Greene sat down. When he came into contact with the chair, Greene felt more than heard a buzz; this feeling became a steady vibration that did indeed call to mind a rough ride in a large vehicle.

Greene rose. "So this is a standard hologram projected over a force field?"

"More or less," said Garcinia. "As far as you boys would be concerned, yes, that's close enough."

Shepherd snapped his fingers. "Kill house. Load the maze."

Garcinia nodded. "If you'll all join me in the control booth."

Greene followed, wondering what purpose continued testing served. Surely Juha had proven himself. Surely it was time to get on with things.

They climbed the steel staircase to the control booth, which comfortably accommodated the six of them. Greene found the many panels and instruments intimidating, but Garcinia seemed right at home as she went to work configuring the program.

When she finished, she touched Juha's arm. "If you'll go down the stairs, you'll see the entrance to the maze. There's a red light, you can't miss it. Please stand at the yellow line on the floor there."

Juha nodded and departed.

Greene hated this maze. Different every time, with holographic plywood walls projected over empty space and illusory pathways projected over solid walls. As far as he was concerned, it was an exercise in frustration and little else, a contest to see who could slam himself into the most walls the fastest.

"What's the course record?" Shepherd asked.

"1:55," Garcinia said. "It was Sonnenschein, I believe, in Security."

Greene's eyebrows shot up. Sub-two minutes? That Sonnenschein kid was practically a ninja. Greene made a mental note to say something to her about it the next time he saw her.

Shepherd now looked genuinely interested. "What's your best time, Chief? Burg?"

"2:33, sir," said Burg.

Greene's best time was 2:49, and he said so. The first time he'd run the maze, he remembered, it had taken him over five minutes. Everybody Xiong hired had to run the maze, not just security people—and Greene had heard about but not witnessed several people who'd had claustrophobic fits and given up. That had to be tough—Xiong policy was that nobody got pulled out before the fifteen-minute mark.

Burg glanced at the monitor. "He's in place."

Garcinia tapped the control booth's microphone. "Can you hear me?"

They watched Juha nod on the screens.

"When the light turns green, make your way through the maze as quickly as you can. There's a checkered stripe across the exit. It will mark your time when you cross it. Do you understand?"

Juha gave a thumbs-up.

"Do it," Shepherd said.

Garcinia pressed a button, the light turned green, and Juha entered the maze at a determined but unhurried pace.

As they watched his progress, Shepherd said, "Now what was this about provisional clearance?"

"He was under investigation three years ago in the death of his wife," Burg said. "While he was a police officer. While Chief Greene was his partner."

"She was murdered?" Shepherd asked.

"The court thought not," Greene said. "They ruled it an accident. He was never charged."

Burg drummed her fingers on the console. "There were suspicious circumstances. With the case and the ruling."

Greene wheeled on her. "Since when are you up on the case and the circumstances, Burg?"

"Enough," Shepherd said. "Both of you. I'll put it to you plainly, Chief: do *you* think Karjalainen killed his wife?"

Greene hesitated. "I—"

The console buzzed and Garcinia shrieked. "He's through!"

Their heads jerked toward the screen as one.

"God damn," said Shepherd. "Time?"

"Twenty-eight seconds!" Garcinia clapped her hands. "How wonderful!"

"And it was legit?" Burg asked. "Nothing glitched out?"

"Seems to be perfectly legitimate." Garcinia pressed the microphone button. "Please come back to the control room, dear."

"Twenty-eight seconds," Shepherd repeated. "Holy shit. That's unbelievable."

"Do you want to run him through again, sir?" Burg asked.

This was too much for Greene. "Sir—"

Shepherd held up a hand. "No, I've seen what I need to see. It doesn't matter who that jackass killed; how can I tell you not to use him? Clear him for this job. Fill, take him to sign all the relevant paperwork."

"Yes, sir."

Shepherd nodded to Greene. "Chief, I had some serious doubts about you when you went off the grid for your friend here, but you've surprised me."

"Thank you, sir." That was as close to a compliment as he'd ever received from Shepherd.

As soon as Juha returned to the control booth, Garcinia grabbed both his hands. "Oh, I'm just delighted!" she said. "That was the most remarkable thing I've ever seen."

Juha gave her a polite smile in return.

"We'll debrief here," Shepherd said. "That'll be simplest."

There were only four chairs in the control booth, so Greene remained standing.

Shepherd did as well. He leaned back against a console and crossed his arms. "Around 4:30 this morning, Dr. Ranga Rao, our COO, was murdered here, in the kill house." He waved a hand vaguely toward the window behind him.

"4:30?" Juha glanced at the wall clock. "It's not even ten, and you've got the body and the cops and everything out of here already—that's impressive."

Shepherd scowled at this interruption. "We're Xiong Holonautics."

Greene himself would have been hard-pressed to provide a more concise or more comprehensive explanation.

Shepherd brushed a speck from his lapel. "After murdering Dr. Ranga Rao, the killer, who we suspect is a recently terminated employee, disconnected the solid projector prototype and escaped the building with it."

"Do we know who it was?" Greene felt unsettled. He was accustomed to giving these briefings, to being the one in the know. But he'd relinquished that privilege when he'd taken the risk to go recruit Juha.

Shepherd held up a hand. "I'm going to say no right now and clarify in a moment."

"We're operating under the assumption that the prototype was the target, correct?" Greene said. "That killing Dr. Ranga Rao was incidental to getting it."

"For now, yes," said Shepherd.

Juha held up a hand. "Two things. First: access? How does somebody you fired get in here and get their hands on your latest tech? Second, how does somebody get the MacGuffin out of the building without being detected, or at least without showing up on your surveillance?"

Shepherd sighed. "If you would stop talking for five minutes, maybe you wouldn't have to ask so many questions."

Juha, unperturbed, only shrugged.

"Dr. Ranga Rao was never much of a sleeper," Shepherd said. "It was not uncommon for him to be here so early, working alone. He liked to keep his hand in on the development side. We don't yet know how the killer gained access to this room. However, if, as we suspect, it was a former employee, then there are several ways it could conceivably be done, especially if it was someone in IT."

Greene switched on his Spec-Trons and consulted his records on their display. "Dr. Ranga Rao entered the kill house at 4:03. The log says William Rubin came up at 4:27. Rubin was IT. He was fired two weeks ago. His access was revoked then, SOP." The thought that the man had gotten through anyway was galling. "Maybe he had inside help."

"Burg has been exploring that possibility, and we will continue to do so, but thus far, we have no evidence of that," Shepherd said. "Until we do, we are treating this as a straight security breach."

Greene's jaw clenched. This was beyond bad. This was an unmitigated disaster. How could this have happened?

Shepherd caught Greene frowning. "At the moment, I am more concerned with recovering our multi-billion-gigayuan piece of technology than assigning blame for holes in our security."

Burg bristled, and Greene felt his stomach knot.

Shepherd seemed oblivious to both their reactions. "The security records show Rubin in this room, show him killing Dr. Ranga Rao."

Juha tugged absently at the loose skin of his neck. "So he's the guy. How is he not the guy?"

"Karjalainen, shut the fuck up," Shepherd said, and Greene winced. Juha, however, appeared unfazed. "Out. Everybody out. Down the stairs. I'm going to show you the footage, and I don't want to hear one more goddamned word until I'm done. Not one! Understood? Good."

They filed out of the control room.

"Since it was done in here, not only do we have video, we have a full hologram," Garcinia said. She tapped at her tablet, and an unassuming man of fifty of average height and medium build appeared in their midst. Wearing shirtsleeves and a loosened tie, he stood before a thick plastic cylinder, which he ran his hand over in various places.

"Raj—that is, Dr. Ranga Rao—was working on the solid holograms," Garcinia said. "Trying to make them more natural to the touch."

A second man, thin and haggard—Rubin, according to Greene's records—appeared, brandishing an enormous two-handed longsword that looked to Greene like something out of a fantasy movie.

"That sword's a nice touch," Juha murmured.

Ranga Rao turned toward Rubin, who thrust with the sword, burying it in Ranga Rao's chest. Fill gasped, and Garcinia looked away. Soundless, Ranga Rao fell backward.

"I have it muted," Garcinia said, her voice almost a whisper. "Sorry. It didn't seem ... necessary."

Rubin departed the scene, leaving only the prone Ranga Rao twitching in an expanding pool of blood. The sword was still embedded in his chest, the hilt sticking upward.

"Jesus," Greene said. Holographic blood reached his shoe and he reflexively jerked his foot away, then felt silly for doing so.

A moment later, the sword disappeared. Blood spurted from the wound, and then Ranga Rao lay still.

Garcinia switched off the program. Juha shut his eyes and massaged the bridge of his nose.

"The sword was a hologram," Shepherd said. "A solid hologram. It disappeared when the killer disconnected the projector. Now listen very carefully. Dr. Ranga Rao wasn't killed with a sword—he was killed with the projector. You need to understand that. As to the killer, there are several possibilities. The first is that it was Rubin. That's rather obvious, of course, and there's nothing in Rubin's file to suggest that he's anywhere near that stupid. The second is that it was an entirely holographic killing. A completely solid person is currently beyond our capabilities, as I understand it, but a standard hologram would suffice in that respect; all you'd need is the force field plane of the sword blade. The third is that someone projected the image of Rubin over him- or herself to carry out the murder. So which is it? As far as you're concerned, it doesn't matter. Let the police worry about that right now. Job one is to get the projector back. In any case, Rubin is our first suspect, and he'll be your first target, Chief."

"Yes, sir."

"However, we don't have any video of him entering or exiting this building. Nor of anyone leaving with the device. Garcinia?"

Garcinia obligingly conjured up a hologram of the prototype projector. Equal parts metal and black plastic, it was a squat box about the size of a mini-fridge, with lenses on each side.

"It's extremely heavy, too," Shepherd said. "Trying to lug it out of here would be very conspicuous. Because it has to generate both light fields and force fields, this prototype is extremely energy-intensive—even with Xiong Tower's ambient wireless power, it couldn't possibly function for more than two minutes out of ten without an external power supply. Correct?"

"That's right," Garcinia said.

"However, that *might* be enough time to get it out of the building on a dolly if it were disguised," Shepherd said. "If the killer projected a hologram over it—as, say, an ordinary-looking parts crate."

"The tracker," Greene said. "The prototype has a tracker, right? That's standard procedure."

Shepherd nodded. "It was disconnected within three kilometers of here, less than ten minutes after D-. Ranga Rao was killed. Which means that whoever took it knew not only that it was there but also exactly how to go about disconnecting it."

"Failsafe?" Greene said. This was getting ridiculous.

"Standard prototype: disabling the tracker disables device functionality. Given enough time, however, I'm sure that could be overcome."

"How much time?" Greene asked.

Shepherd looked to Garcinia, who frowned. "I don't know," she said. "Perhaps hours. Less if it was an inside job."

"Assuming it's functional," Juha said, "what's the range on the prototype?"

"About fifteen meters," said Garcinia.

"And how do you know the projector is even still in Portsmith?"

"We don't," Shepherd said.

Burg chewed her lip. "If it's not ..."

"If it's not, then we're fucked, aren't we?" Shepherd snapped. "Yes, it could be on a ship, on a plane—it could be five hundred kilometers away by now. Nevertheless, I honestly think there's a good chance that it's still here. We only have a few competitors with enough capital to make a real play for the projector, and each of them is headquartered in Portsmith: Crestridge, Pleasant Valley, Algary Applications."

"Korin," Fill added.

"One of those companies could have it already," Greene said.

"A smart man would hold out, drum up a bidding war," Shepherd mused. "One Algary would almost certainly win. But if Algary or one of those other companies does have it, then your job is to prove it. Prove it and we will completely bury them."

Juha held up a hand. "What does Mr. Xiong have to say about all this?"

"Mr. Xiong has every confidence in my ability to oversee the investigation and recovery," Shepherd replied.

Juha grinned. "You mean he doesn't know you lost it. I'm right, aren't I?"

Shepherd set his jaw and motioned to Garcinia. "Here are your primary leads." Three holographic faces appeared before them. "First, William Rubin, IT. Fired two weeks ago. Caught trying to take copies of proprietary work home. Second, Unique Bonsegundo, R&D. Fired last week for selling betas of holographic programs to Algary. Litigation in progress. Third, Lewis Clark, IT. He's still with the company. Was written up last week, has a history. Called in sick today."

"I thought Unique was in HR," Burg said.

"That's Unique Taylor," Fill told her.

"The data have been sent to your devices," Shepherd said. "Chief Greene is going to track down these leads with his little sidekick here. Burg is going to give support from the tower and continue to explore the possibility that the killer had inside help from a current employee. That's it. Go."

Burg opened her mouth, saw Shepherd's expression, and closed it again.

Shepherd drew conspiratorially close to Greene. "Chief, it is not possible for you to lean on these people too hard," he said. "Xiong Holonautics is behind you, remember that. You have the authority to do *whatever is necessary*. Do you understand?"

Greene nodded. "Yes, sir."

As Greene turned toward the elevators, Garcinia touched his arm and pressed a fist-sized device into his palm.

"It's a force field jackhammer," she said. "That's what we call it, anyway. Brand new; this is the only one we've got, just finished it this week. Not much range; less than a meter. But if the prototype is operational, this ought to be able to break through whatever it's throwing at you in just a few seconds."

"Thank you."

"Good luck, dear."

Greene made his way over to Juha, who was trying to extricate himself from a one-sided conversation with Max Fil. "Time to go, Juha."

Juha gave him a look of gratitude and followed. "You let them tell you how to run your investigation like that? Don't give me that look, I'm the only one in here not telling you how to do your job. I tell you what, though, that's a hell of a murder weapon ... no fingerprints, nothing to trace. Should be a good time."

"I'll meet you in the lobby in five minutes," Greene said. "Let me go change into something a little more tactical."

THREE

Greene, dressed in a short-sleeved Xiong security uniform, black with gold piping, zipped up his light tactical vest as the elevator opened onto the lobby. He felt more comfortable now, and more confident, even with the boots, which he hadn't fully broken in yet. Anyone who looked at him now saw not the man Greene, but the powerful megacorporation he represented.

He found Juha draped over the reception desk, apparently deep in conversation with a plump, attractive woman there.

"... No judgment at all, I promise," Juha was saying. "I've been there." He glanced up at Greene. "I've got to go. But here, think it over. Only if you're interested." He handed the woman a card.

"Meeting women?" Greene asked. "That was fast."

Juha gave Greene a card that bore an unflattering photo of Juha at his absolute heaviest. A word balloon read, *That goodlooking guy who gave you this—that was me. I can help you reach your health and fitness goals—at FatAss.* Underneath was contact information.

"FatAss?" Green said. "You're running a gym now?"

Juha pocketed the rest of his cards. "I am. Shit, look at you, I feel underdressed now."

"Do you want a vest?"

"What do I need a vest for when I've got you to protect me? Wait, where's your gun?"

Greene patted the primary-red grip of his sidearm.

Juha shook his head. "That's not a gun. It looks like a toy. What the hell is that?"

"Active denial." Greene headed for the front door. He tapped his phone. "Car: Xiong front drive. Immediately. Map the addresses from my dashboard."

Juha followed. "A heat ray. You're serious."

"It's non-lethal and near-silent, plus no reload."

"You work for Xiong. Why should non-lethal matter?"

Greene hesitated before responding. "It matters to me."

Juha shrugged. "Same old Green. Well, it's your show; if you want to live life on hard mode, that's your business—as long as you don't get me killed. You ever shoot anybody with it?"

"Not yet."

"Those glasses—you're recording everything you see, aren't you?"

"Yes, I am." Greene was less than pleased with the admission, although it really wasn't a secret.

"How does that work when we're looking at all this classified stuff?"

"It transmits securely through my phone to the department. There's no recorded footage on my person."

"Good thing I have nothing to hide then. Oh, that old lady pinched my ass on the way out, you know that? And that other one, Burg—she really wants your job, doesn't she?"

Greene sighed. "She almost had it."

"And they tried to chip me while you were gone, too."

"That's standard procedure. You didn't let them?"

"No chance in hell."

"I'm surprised they let you get away with that. Usually, they—" Greene saw who'd entered the lobby, and he stopped abruptly.

There was a sharp intake of breath from beside him. "Marlena ..." Juha murmured.

Marlena Ranga Rao walked toward them, her hair a copper blaze amidst the lobby's golden glory. She wore an expensive suit that did not fully succeed in downplaying her substantial curves.

Even though she'd put on a few kilos since the photo on Juha's dresser had been taken, she'd lost none of her beauty, except that her eyes were bloodshot and she looked exhausted.

"Chief Greene," she said. "It's good to see you."

Greene nodded to her. "Mrs. Ranga Rao. I'm so sorry for what's happened."

"I'm on my way to meet with Deputy Chief Burg. It's so terrible. I can't believe—" Marlena's formal veneer cracked. "Chief, I know your main job is to get the technology back, not to find the killer, but I hope you do find him, and I hope you nail him to the wall. Promise me you will if you get the chance."

Greene gave her an awkward smile. "We'll do our best."

She nodded at Juha. "Who's your friend?"

Juha stepped forward and took her hand. "Your friend still as well, I hope."

Marlena cocked her head, studying him.

"It's Juha Karjalainen," Greene said, seeking to speed things along. This might turn sappy in a hurry if he let it.

She gripped Juha's arm, as if to confirm he was real. "No! Juha! Look at you, you're like a different person!"

"It's good to see you," Juha said.

The two of them just stood there, looking at one another, updating their mental files.

Greene cleared his throat. "I'm sorry, but we're on our way out. You understand. I can bring him by later and you can get caught up."

"Of course," Marlena said. "I look forward to it." Businesslike, she strode away toward the elevators. Juha stared after her.

Greene pushed Juha toward the front door. "She works here, you know."

"I didn't know."

"She's our vice president of IT."

"Huh. Good for her."

They stepped outside. The Xiong security team had partially cleared the street. All the media were still present, but they'd been spread out enough to free up one lane of traffic each way.

Good enough by far. Greene's company car idled just in front of them, and they headed toward it.

When the reporters saw him, they immediately began shouting questions—so many that Greene couldn't identify any particular one of them.

He focused on the car and didn't turn his head, although out of the corner of his eye, he spotted Juha smiling and waving.

Greene opened the car door, got in, shut it, and let the silence wash over him.

Then Juha opened his door, and the clamor returned briefly as he climbed in.

"Oh, man," Juha said. "You've got to love that attention."

Greene made a concerted effort not to roll his eyes. He buckled his seatbelt, and the car pulled out.

He turned on the car's traffic credentials. "Rubin co-owns a hologram boutique. That's our first stop."

"Can I see the addresses?"

Greene pulled them up on the car's windshield display. "What's the matter?"

Juha had a peculiar expression on his face. "I need to stop by my gym."

"You're joking."

"No. For real, I'm sorry. I have some paperwork I have to get in today. We just opened—permits and such. It'll take five minutes, I promise. I just have to sign it and send it."

"Juha ..."

"It's important. Five minutes. I'm not jerking you around. I was anticipating going in today and taking care of that stuff, not playing buddy cop action movie with you."

"Let's hope it doesn't come to 'action movie.'"

Juha grinned at him. "Where's your sense of adventure? Look, this second address is only three kilometers from FatAss."

Greene sighed. "Fine. *After* that stop."

"Thank you. I gratefully accept your generous terms." Juha put his backpack between his knees, rummaged for his pistol, and loaded it. "Has it occurred to you that whoever took the projector may not be trying to sell it to one of your competitors? That they might try to take it up a level, to a government? Not the Zaibatsu, probably, but what about the Islamist Bloc, or Los Estados?"

"Yes," Greene said, "it has occurred to me. But that doesn't change anything." He leaned back in his seat and closed his eyes. In all the commotion, he still hadn't managed to get any coffee.

The car took them well south on the Waterfront Highway. Greene watched the sunlight sparkle on the waves, contemplating by what miracle he might recover the prototype, keep his job, and avoid utter ruin and disgrace.

The car turned off into an upper-middle-class suburb. Greene switched on his Spec-Trons' display and pulled up the relevant files.

He instructed the car to park illegally in front of Erliquin's Holographix Emporium, a one-story brick-and-glass building that had previously been an independent bank, the glasses told him.

They climbed out. Greene told the car, "Logos on, credentials on," and glowing Xiong Holonautics emblems appeared on the hood and doors.

"That'll be good for business." Juha tucked his pistol into the back of his pants.

"I'd prefer to avoid any trouble," Greene said.

Juha glanced around at the clean streets, manicured boulevards, and well-kept buildings. "In this neighborhood?"

"Come on." Greene pulled Erliquin's front door open, and they entered.

The building's interior was an assault on the eyes. On Greene's left, a heatless flame crackled in an immense baroque marble fireplace—the sort that was so trendy right now—flanked by Caravaggios in ornate gold frames. To Greene's right was a sandy ocean beach: the tide rolled in gently, and gulls wheeled in the distance, keening. There were twelve more such alcove displays in what had formerly been the bank's lobby, and no customers.

Juha had his head down, was shading his eyes. "It's too much."

Greene strode down the main aisle toward an antique desk at which a man sat watching what sounded like sports highlights on his phone. Greene checked his files. This was the other owner: Chongololo Jones.

When he saw them, Jones jumped to his feet, warding them off with a hand that Greene saw had six fingers on it. "I already talked to the police, all right? I *cooperated*." He spoke with an African accent that Greene immediately decided was affected.

Greene showed his credentials. "I'm not police. I'm Xiong Holonautics. I need you to shut the programs down for me."

"Uh huh. The Bear." Jones sneered. "Shut them down for what? I'm trying to run a business here. A *legitimate* business."

Greene turned his back to the desk, looking out over the cavalcade of gaudy décor. "How many of the programs you sell are from Xiong, I wonder? Thirty percent? Fifty? I can revoke your Xiong license permanently, and I can do it right this minute. How long are you going to stay in business offering a much more limited selection?"

"All right, you bastard, just a minute." Jones went to work on his computer. After a moment, all the displays vanished and all the sounds ceased, leaving only bare walls and rows of ceiling- and wall-mounted projectors. Jones's fancy desk was now a folding table.

"Thank you for that," Juha said.

"We're looking for William Rubin," Greene said.

"Yeah, the police were, too. But Billy ain't here." Jones sat back down, put his feet up on the table, and spread his hands. "As you can see."

There was a set of blacked-out glass double doors on a side wall. Juha tried them; they were locked.

"Open it," Greene said.

Jones tossed him a red rabbit's foot keychain that looked like a lump of raw meat. "Let me know if you see anything you like."

Greene unlocked the doors with the single key and pulled them open. "The porn."

"Man, 'porn' is such an ugly word," Jones said. "What does it mean, anyway? 'Porn.' It's so hard to define."

Juha laughed. "No, it's not."

"Why you gotta be like that?" Jones said. "What did adult entertainment ever do to you? Most of the best stuff in there is Xiong, too. The strippers, the dancers ... the nude beach is my favorite, though."

"Shut it down," Greene said.

Jones flipped him what would have been the middle finger on an ordinary hand. "I got customers in there, man. You seem a little uptight—you could probably stand to spend some time in there yourself. You can pay by the hour if you're not ready to buy, you know. But I guess you probably get it for free, being a company man."

"Shut it down. I'm not going to tell you again."

Sighing the heavy sigh of the persecuted, Jones complied. "You might want to give them a minute."

Greene entered immediately and found more bare walls and two uncomfortable-looking men sitting in folding chairs. Neither was Rubin.

"How you guys doing?" Juha asked, taking a pass around the room.

"Nothing," Greene said. Disappointment washed over him, but he wasn't sure what he'd hoped to find.

"Don't get yourself down," Juha said. "The day is young."

They returned to the main showroom, and Greene tossed the key back to Jones. "We'll have to try Rubin's apartment," he said to Juha. "That'll be trickier."

"Just a minute," Juha said. "Jones, is it? What's behind this door?"

Jones rolled his eyes. "That's the supply closet. Mops and shit. Go nuts."

"No." Juha was now standing in front of a bare stretch of wall. He rapped his knuckles on it, and the sound was as against glass. "*This* door."

"I don't know what you're talking about," Jones said unconvincingly.

Greene shook his head. "Do you really need me to tell you again?"

Jones looked close to panic. "How in the hell did he— Shit, man. Oh, shit, I'm going to be in so much trouble."

"However much it is, I promise I can make it more," Greene said.

"Fine! Okay! Just a minute!" Jones punched at his computer. The hologram of the wall vanished, and a blacked-out glass door appeared.

Juha tugged on the handle. "Locked."

"Open it or we'll smash it," Greene said.

Jones looked like he was going to be sick. "He'll have to open it from inside."

Juha drew his pistol and tapped on the glass. Greene drew his sidearm as well and took up position on the other side of the door.

"No need for all that," Jones moaned.

Juha nodded to Greene. "Your lead."

The door opened inward and Greene lunged forward, gun raised, jamming his foot into the doorway lest it close again. He shoved against the door with his shoulder, knocking down the man who had opened it.

An instant later, Greene and Juha were standing in a small office, looming over a prone Billy Rubin. He looked just as worn-down as he had in the hologram.

"Oh, God." Rubin's hands were up in a pathetic defensive posture. "Please don't kill me."

Greene made a disgusted sound and holstered his weapon. Juha lowered his pistol but kept it in his hand.

"Get up," Greene said. "Sit in the chair." If Rubin had wanted to attack them, he figured, he would have done it already.

"But roll it back against the wall," Juha said, and Rubin obeyed.

Rubin was scowling, pouty, like a child called on the carpet for misdeeds. "What's this all about?"

"That's what you're going to tell us, mister hidey-man." Juha sat on top of the desk, his legs in Rubin's personal space and his pistol in his lap. He was clearly enjoying himself.

Greene closed the door and turned the lock. Let Jones do what he wanted. He glanced around the room, which contained only a desk, a chair, and a bookcase, plus an adjoining toilet— nowhere something the size of the projector could be hidden.

"Any holograms?" Greene asked.

Juha shook his head.

Greene turned to Rubin. "Do you know who I am?"

Rubin tugged at his ear. "Xiong security."

"Good enough. 'What's this all about,' you said. If you really don't know, then why are you hiding in here?"

Rubin chewed his lip. "The police were here earlier, asking questions. And Dr. Ranga Rao was killed— I saw that on the news. I knew somebody from the company would be along eventually."

Greene leaned against the wall and crossed his arms. "Sounds like you have a pretty good idea of what it's all about. Keep going."

"I don't! I was fired weeks ago, you must know that. I haven't been back in the building since."

"Surveillance footage places you in the building this morning."

"What— How could— A hologram!" Rubin was nearly frantic. "It must be!"

"Maybe. Either way, you know I've got to take you in."

"No! Wait!" Rubin tried to jump up, but Juha shoved him back down with his foot.

"Where's the prototype?" Greene said.

"What prototype?" Rubin almost shrieked.

Greene lunged forward and slammed his hands on the desk. "The prototype you stole after you murdered Dr. Ranga Rao!"

"I don't know what you're talking about!" Spittle flew from Rubin's lips.

Juha shrugged. "I think I might believe him. In any case, I don't think you're going to get much more out of him. Unless you want to exercise that Xiong authority."

"No, please," Rubin whimpered.

This made Greene feel dirty. "No, that's enough. I'm not my predecessor, and I don't intend to be." He opened a pocket on his vest and pulled out a small injector, which he placed at the base of Rubin's neck. He pressed the button and the device hissed.

Rubin winced. "What was that?"

Greene returned it to his pocket. "A tracking chip."

"You can't chip me! I don't work for Xiong anymore!"

"Unless you negotiated otherwise, we have the right to re-chip you for a year after the termination of your employment," Greene said. "Plus this is probable cause."

"Damn it!"

Greene shrugged. "We're going to go now; someone else from Xiong will come and take you back to the tower. If you wait in this building, you'll be all right, I promise. But if you try to run, you're going to have trouble—more than I could possibly help you with. Do you understand?"

"Yes." Rubin's voice was almost a whisper.

"Has he got a phone?" Greene asked.

Juha frisked him quickly and handed Rubin's phone to Greene, who took out his own phone and pulled the data.

"Anything else?" Greene asked.

Juha hopped off the desk. "Nothing leaps to mind."

Greene went to the door and put his hand on the lock, then paused and turned. "You didn't whip this door hologram up this morning," he said. "You're used to hiding in here. Yourself, or some*thing*."

Juha was already rifling through the desk.

Rubin shrank into his chair. "Oh, no."

"Oh, *yes*." Juha plunked a container the size of a shoebox onto the desk.

Greene came over. "What have we got?"

Juha upended the box, spilling about thirty squarish cartridges across the desk. He picked one up and examined the written-upon masking tape stuck to it. "Hologram programs. Bootlegs, I'd guess. Unlicensed? Jailbreakers? Look at him, I'm right."

Rubin had buried his face in his hands.

Greene began to replace the cartridges in the box. "We'll take these. This changes things, as you might imagine. Still, you'll stay here if you know what's good for you."

Rubin didn't respond.

Greene tucked the box under his arm and nodded to Juha, who raised his pistol and yanked the door open.

But Jones was still seated at his table. When he saw the box Greene was carrying, he said, "Shit. You assholes done now? You want one of my kidneys before you go? Hell, Xiong Holonautics—you'd probably take both of them."

"Just need to pull your computer and phone records," Greene said.

"Like hell," Jones said. "The police don't even get to do that."

Greene shrugged. "Might be your only chance to keep your license."

Jones handed over his phone as if willing it to explode in Greene's hand.

Greene pulled the information and handed the phone back. "Now we're done."

Jones immediately switched all the holograms back on. Juha hurried to the exit while Greene maintained a more dignified pace.

As he stepped outside, a customer emerged from her car.

"Buy while you can," Juha told the woman. "I don't know if they're going to be around much longer. Tell them Xiong Holonautics said you could have a discount."

Greene popped the trunk of his car and deposited the box of illegal programs inside. "Logos off," he told the car.

They climbed inside, and Greene sent the car toward the next address.

"Well, I had fun," Juha said. He took a bottle of pills from his backpack, popped a capsule into his mouth, and washed it down with water. "That was a good bust."

"Thanks to you," Greene said. "It's nice to see you're still handy to have around."

Juha snorted. "And it's nice to see you haven't gone totally soft at your cushy job, that you've still got a little streak of badass in you."

Greene smiled at this, but unease tugged at him. He didn't like using the strong-arm tactics, but he wasn't about to tell Juha that. Not now or ever.

Juha probably already knew.

A message from Nisha appeared on Greene's Spec-Trons—she was putting together the day's shopping order and wanted to know if he needed anything. Greene responded in the negative, then turned his attention to the windshield display. He had to request a retrieval team from Burg and send the Erliquin records to Shepherd before their next stop.

The bust was nice, Greene thought, but it meant nothing without a lead on the prototype. As far as he was concerned, this stop had amounted to little more than strike one.

FOUR

Unique Bonsegundo's apartment stood across from a raised hypertube, upon which was mounted a billboard that proclaimed PORTSMITH—THE WORLD'S NEW HONG KONG! The apartment building had a façade of large, rough-hewn gray-green stones covered with flowering ivy, like something out of a fairy tale. Greene had no trouble identifying this hologram without Juha's help.

Juha glanced up at the billboard. "I still miss the old Hong Kong."

They entered the building, and as the elevator took them to the forty-second floor, Greene reviewed his files. Bonsegundo was about his age—early thirties—and athletic. She'd been fired for selling programs to Algary Applications. Xiong Holonautics had initiated litigation, which meant that she probably wouldn't be in this apartment much longer.

Her hallway had bad motel-style carpeting, a green and cranberry floral pattern. The walls were pasted with vertically striped tan wallpaper.

"Blew all the money on the exterior, I guess," Juha said. "Terrible. Think she's home?"

Greene nodded. "She's chipped pending the resolution of her legal issues, so we know she's in there."

"What are you expecting here?"

Greene found Bonsegundo's door. "Not much. Given her legal issues and everything else, I don't think she's going to want to talk to us."

"You can at least search the apartment, right?"

Greene knocked on the door. "Not legally."

Juha gave him a knowing look. "But you *can* search it, right? Whether or not she answers the door?"

Greene sighed.

The door jerked open. A knife flashed out, snagging in Greene's vest. A second knife caught Juha in the arm, and he grunted. Then Bonsegundo was in the doorway, feinting at Greene. His move for his heat ray gave her enough time to kick Juha squarely in the groin.

As Juha went down in a heap, Bonsegundo darted back into her apartment and slammed the door. Greene heard the lock turn.

All of this had taken perhaps five seconds.

Juha was writhing, bleeding on the ugly carpet. "Ugh ... what the hell just happened?"

Greene crouched beside him. "Where is it? How bad?"

Juha rolled over and scowled. "It's always some goddamn thing. I'll live. You go get her."

Greene rose. He pointed his heat ray at the lock, activated it, and held it there for several seconds until the metal glowed red. Then he judged the door, committed, and kicked it.

The door popped open. Greene was a little surprised at his success; it had been a while.

He ducked, and a knife whistled over his head and clattered against the wall in the corridor. Weapon raised, Greene advanced into the living area, where he was confronted by four identical knife-wielding Bonsegundos.

Holograms—and with Juha out of action.

Each of the four had a knife cocked by her ear, ready to throw; in each off hand was a leather bag presumably filled with more projectiles.

They eyed each other. A standoff.

These were live copies, Greene realized, not pre-programmed duplicates. From across the room, he had no way to tell which was the real Bonsegundo—not without trying to touch them. Greene didn't suppose she'd just stand there while he used his phone to check exactly where the tracking chip was.

Now what? He had his heat ray pointed between the middle two, which were far enough apart that if he took a shot at a false image, there was a good chance he'd be wide open for a knife reprisal. Probably he was still fast enough to shoot at two of them.

But maybe he could get her to give herself away by her voice.

"You attacked us without provocation," Greene told the four Bonsegundos. "That's five years in prison at least. Labor. Surely you know that." He took one hand off his gun and tapped his glasses. "We've got the footage. That's nothing but trouble for you. Especially given your current legal situation with the company."

She didn't bite.

"Maybe it doesn't have to be that way," Greene continued. "If you help us, we might be able to make a deal. You don't have to let this ruin your life."

"Xiong already ruined my life!" screamed the real Bonsegundo, and Greene shot her.

She shrieked and staggered sideways, dropping the knife and the bag. Greene kicked her buckling legs out from under her, and she landed hard on her back, falling as one with the three holograms.

Greene was on top of her in an instant, pinning her with a knee. "Calm down. It's just a heat ray. You're not hurt."

He frisked her quickly, found the remote to her projector but no more knives, and switched off the duplicates.

"You ruined your own life," he said.

Juha lurched in, face pale, clutching his arm. "Damn, Green, that was cold-blooded. Well done."

"You all right?" Greene asked.

"Peachy. Looks like you had all the fun without me."

Bonsegundo struggled to free herself, and Greene pressed down on her harder. When she quieted, he took a pair of handcuffs from a pocket of his vest and secured her hands behind her back.

Juha produced his roll of duct tape and knife, then bound her ankles together. "Better safe than sorry."

Greene hauled her up, not roughly, and deposited her in an armchair.

Bonsegundo's eyes flitted between the two of them. The anxiety was plain on her face. "What are you going to do?"

Greene sat down across from her on the sofa. "We just want to talk to you, believe it or not."

"And check the apartment," Juha said. "Can I check the apartment?"

Greene sighed. "Check the apartment."

Juha touched his arm where he'd been cut and brought his hand away bloody. "Damn it to hell, look at my jacket," he said, in a tone anyone else might use to remark upon the weather. "This was a nice jacket. Let me clean this up." He vanished into the bathroom.

Bonsegundo spat at Greene. "A deal, you said. Xiong doesn't make deals. I'll be dead in a gutter next week—that's the kind of deal The Bear makes."

Greene was coming to understand. "You thought we were here to kill you."

Juha soon returned, jacket off, wrapping a bandage around his biceps. "That's last year's Xiong, haven't you heard? All those gestapo tactics were bad for the stock price, so they hired squeaky-clean Greene here to give the iron fist a polish."

Greene opened his mouth to refute Juha but found himself unable to. How was it that he had never considered his position within the company that way before?

He forced his attention back to Bonsegundo. "If you cooperate with us, I'll do my best for you. I promise. That's the only promise I can make. I'm not going to pretend I can keep the full wrath of Xiong off you. One way or another, you're almost certainly going to prison."

"Fine, what do I care?" Fire burned in Bonsegundo's eyes. "I can't get work in this town anyway—Xiong saw to that."

Greene was surprised. "You aren't working for Algary? After the 'favors' you did for them?"

"No." She looked embarrassed. "They said I was untrustworthy, didn't have integrity."

Juha laughed. "You've got to appreciate the irony. On a couple of levels. Listen, I'm sure you're going to cooperate with my friend here, going to tell him nothing but the truth, but I've got to go ransack your apartment in any case, all right? I'll try not to make too big of a mess." He went into the bedroom.

Bonsegundo opened her mouth, closed it, then gave up and turned back to Greene. "What's this all about?"

Greene leaned forward in what he hoped was a non-threatening manner. "You were in R&D. Did you know about the prototype?"

"I can't talk about anything like that. You're not going to get me on video breaking an NDA."

Greene sighed. He pulled off his glasses, held them up, and made a show of switching them off.

She gave him a piercing look. "We had a lot of prototypes."

"I'm specifically referring to the one that was stolen this morning after Dr. Ranga Rao was murdered."

Her expression of shock was either genuine or extremely well done.

"Oh, God," she said finally, and her voice broke. "Dr. Ranga Rao. I can't believe it." Tears welled in her eyes.

Juha came out of the bedroom and handed Greene her phone and tablet, and Greene pulled her records.

"Wow," Juha said, seeing her face. "What kind of guy was this Ranga Rao?"

Bonsegundo jerked against her bindings as she reflexively tried to wipe her eyes.

Greene rose and removed the handcuffs, but he left her legs bound. "You'll behave yourself, I trust."

She nodded her thanks and composed herself. "What kind of man was he? He was one of the very few people running that company who wasn't a complete asshole."

This got a chuckle from Juha, who was into the closet now. "I love it. What do you think, Green? I've just about been through the whole place."

"I didn't steal any prototype," Bonsegundo said.

Greene thought he believed her. "Do you have any idea who might have done it? Who might have been sufficiently ... *motivated* to commit murder and steal from the company?"

She looked Greene in the eye, then at the glasses in his lap. "Last week—the day after Xiong fired me—a man approached me. He asked whether I'd be interested in acquiring some Xiong tech for him. I didn't want to talk to him—I thought the company had sent him, trying to entrap me. I told him no, I wasn't interested. He offered me money. Kind of a lot of money. When I told him I'd been fired, though, he lost interest right away."

Juha leaned against the couch. "Who was he?"

She shook her head. "I don't know. I never saw him before or since. He was a big guy. Huge. All muscles. Blond hair."

"Name?" Greene said.

Her brow furrowed. "Wheat, I think he said."

"No first name?"

"Er ... Bavarian? He might have said Bavarian Wheat."

"Is he from Bavaria?" Juha asked.

She looked at him sharply. "How the hell should I know that?"

Juha held up a hand theatrically. "Undoubtedly an alias in any case. That's it?"

She shrugged.

Greene looked up Wheat in the database. "I've got nothing," he said.

"Sorry," Bonsegundo said. "If he's the bastard who killed the Doc, I hope you get him."

Greene sent his contact information to Bonsegundo's phone. "Call me if you think of anything else." He turned the Spec-Trons back on and replaced them on his face.

Juha retrieved his gashed jacket. "Leave her legs taped. Don't take any chances. She'll get free the minute we're out the door anyway."

Bonsegundo's nostrils flared. "This guy is a real jackass, you know that?"

"It's actually one of my better qualities," Juha said.

Greene rose, considering the knives scattered across the floor. He shrugged apologetically at her, and they left.

"So what do you think?" Juha asked as they walked down the hall.

"I don't know. She gave us next to nothing. A name? An alias? All of this, and where are we? She could have the projector stashed somewhere for all we know. Rubin could have it. And we're looking for one man in a city of twelve million?"

Juha thumped him in the arm. "That's no kind of attitude to have. Assume she was telling the truth. One: she turned Wheat or whoever down. Two: somebody stole the MacGuffin. Logically, in between those two points, Wheat approached somebody else. Assuming they're connected."

"Maybe."

Juha motioned toward Greene's glasses. "Anyway, you were still taping, right? You got all that?"

"No."

Now Juha looked genuinely surprised. "You might be the last honest man on earth. I'm going to need stitches. Have you got sutures in your first aid kit?"

"I don't think so."

"Man are you ill-prepared. Anyway, there's none in mine, either. It's cool, I'll take care of it at FatAss."

While they were in the elevator, Burg called. "Your feed cut out there for a few minutes."

"Everything's fine," Greene said.

She was undeterred. "Why did your feed cut out?"

"Because I switched it off." He was in no mood to get into it with Burg over her lack of respect. But someday ...

"Why?"

Greene clenched his teeth. "Because it helped put Bonsegundo at ease. And because as *chief* of security, I have that right."

Juha had a tiny smile on his face as they exited the elevator. "That's the way. Don't take any guff. Show her who's boss."

Greene rolled his eyes. "Give me a report on the Erliquin records."

"Yes, *sir*." Those two words carried more feeling, more antipathy than Greene wanted to process. "Erliquin's phone and mail records are clean. In terms of the prototype ... and in terms of the bootlegging." This last was added grudgingly.

"Thank you, Burg," Greene said. "I'll send you Bonsegundo's records momentarily." He ended the call.

Juha fingered the gash in his jacket. "You know what this reminds me of? You remember the time that four-armed gorilla escaped from the genetics lab and attacked those vagrants down by the docks?"

"Yes." Greene sighed. He knew where this was going.

"And then when we responded, those drunk hobos came after us with knives?"

"Yes."

"And then one of them stabbed you in the ass, right?"

"Yes."

"Man, that was hilarious."

Greene climbed into the car, trying not to let Juha's carefree attitude bother him. But this was strike two, or near enough to it. He could feel the clock ticking, could think of no more terrifying prospect than returning to Xiong Tower empty-handed.

FIVE

The Xiong car parked in front of FatAss, and Greene activated his logos and parking credentials.

"Must you?" Juha said as he exited the car. "That's not good for business."

"We're making this quick, remember?" But Greene sent the car off in search of a more distant parking space.

Juha's gym occupied half of the ground floor of a glass-covered high-rise that seemed to reflect the sun into Greene's eyes no matter where he stood even though his Spec-Trons were on full tint.

Directly across the street, on the ground floor of an equally blinding high rise, was Morbid O'Beefity's Triple Bypass.

"Interesting location," Greene said.

"That's a great restaurant," Juha said. "They have ranch dressing and nacho cheese sauce fountains at every table. But I know what you mean. I don't think they're all that happy that I'm here."

FatAss was small and simple. To the left of the front desk was a set of glass doors leading to a mirror-paneled room containing a row of treadmills, a floor area that could accommodate perhaps twenty-five people, and several racks of free weights. Prominently displayed beside the desk was an enormous picture of Juha at his largest, with FATASS emblazoned across the bottom. Several people were stretching and chatting in the floor area of the workout room.

"Come on," Juha said. "If you want to get out of here quick, it needs to be before the one o'clock class starts."

Greene followed him to a small office behind the front desk. The walls were bare except for a before-and-after picture of Juha and three photos of his sister competing in track and field events.

Juha shut the door behind them, tossed his ruined jacket onto the loveseat in the corner, and pulled the first aid kit off the wall. He rolled up his bloody sleeve and gingerly peeled off the red-soaked paper towels he'd taped on at Bonsegundo's apartment, revealing an ugly laceration across his upper arm. He opened the first aid kit and rummaged until he found a suture.

"You want some help with that?" Greene asked.

"Nah. I'm a badass and I live life on the edge, you know that," Juha replied. "Thanks, though. So what do you think of my place?"

Greene sat in the chair behind the desk—the only one in the room—half afraid that it would inspire Juha to take longer. But he needed to patch himself up, there was no doubt of that.

"I like it. What made you buy a gym? I didn't know you had an interest."

Juha clapped alcohol-soaked gauze over his wound and hissed. "Son of a bitch, you never get used to that. I turn forty-five this year, Green, as your glasses well know. And you know what I used to look like, how ridiculously fat I was—I had to get my shit together before I ate myself to death or decrepitude. Once I did, I figured maybe a gym would help me stay on the straight and narrow. Even so, I almost bought a farm instead."

"You? A farm?"

Muscles clenched against the pain, Juha began stitching his wound closed. "Yeah, a pig farm, actually. It was a really good price. Special pigs, too—the new kind they use for kosher and halal bacon and ham. They've been taking over all the farms since the lab-cultured cell meat got so cheap."

Greene marveled, not for the first time, at Juha's tolerance for pain. "How does that work? Are you sure you don't want a hand?"

Juha shook his head. "I'm good. It's pretty cool, actually. The pigs are genetically engineered to have a four-compartment stomach—they chew the cud and everything. That makes them kosher. And then they're also halal because from a certain point of view, they're not pigs anymore, strictly speaking. There's big money exporting that stuff to the Islamist Bloc, but the farm was in Los Estados, so I passed."

"What's wrong with Los Estados?"

"This was last year, while I was on Mars—you know, when we were all wondering if we'd ever be able to come back to Earth."

Greene snorted. "That 'zombie apocalypse' was the most anticlimactic event the world has seen since Y2K. Los Estados lost Florida and that was it."

Juha shrugged. "Nobody knew at the time, and the land prices there were in the toilet. Now? Of course. And they'll be able to reclaim all that land in, what, twenty, thirty years? However long it takes for the environment and the wildlife to kill all those feral things off. And it surprised everybody how fast they built that wall across the panhandle. So after all of that, plus with all those coastal patrols, it even turned out to be good for Los Estados's economy. But I messed up even bigger than that—I had a chance to get in on that illegal zombie safari action. I missed out, Green. I could have been a rich man."

"Sorry."

Juha finished his stitches and admired his handiwork. "They had a couple at the zoo here. Zombies, I mean. People ones and alligator ones." He put the first aid kit away. "Until it closed. You people and your holograms put it out of business."

Greene rose from his seat, hoping to speed things along now that the first aid had been completed. His stomach rumbled. "You don't happen to have any food, do you?"

"Nah." Juha commandeered the chair the instant Greene was out of it. "You could run across the street real fast while I handle my business if you want."

"That wouldn't be my first choice."

Juha opened a desk drawer and handed over a bottle of capsules. "This is all I got."

Greene examined it. "Slim Balloonz?"

"Man, those are fantastic. They inflate in your stomach, make you feel full. It's all-natural. Breaks down after about six hours."

Greene handed the bottle back. "No thanks."

"Aren't you picky. I might be able to scrounge up a couple of bananas. Probably science bananas, not real bananas—Satu buys them."

"Doesn't matter."

"Head on back out to the front desk, then. My sister ought to be around; she's teaching a class here in a few minutes. I'll be out as quick as I can."

Greene left the office, and sure enough, Satu was standing behind the front desk. Fit, pretty, and dressed in tight-fitting workout gear, she was stunning. Juha might get more business if they put her picture on the door instead of his, Greene thought.

"Hello, Satu," he said.

She turned, and when she recognized him, she smiled her dazzling smile, and Greene suddenly remembered the crush she'd had on him so many years ago.

"Greene! I knew Juha was running around with you, but I didn't expect to you to come here today. It's good to see you. You look well."

Greene smiled. "Thanks. So do you. So ... a fitness center."

Satu shrugged. "Yeah, it's turned out to be a pretty good fit for us. No pun intended. And it's a pretty good living, too, or it should be once we get everything going. Permits, you know? We're trying to get the food vendor license so we can do shakes and things, but if you don't know how to do everything just so, those bureaucratic sons of bitches over there want a kickback for helping you through it."

"Your brother's in the office now; that might be what he's working on." Greene elected to say nothing about Juha's injury.

"If anybody can make headway with those bastards without caving, it's Juha." Satu turned toward the floor area, whose glass doors had been propped open, and hollered, "Two minutes, you guys!"

"I'm sorry to mooch, but Juha said you might have some snacks out here," Greene said. "We've been so busy, I haven't had a chance to eat today."

"Hm? Oh, sure." Satu handed him a small cooler bag. "Help yourself."

The bag was full of fruit. Greene selected a banana and an apple.

Juha emerged from the office in a fresh shirt, tying his ponytail up anew on top of his head. He nodded to them. "Hey, kid. Green, you ready to get the hell out of here?"

Satu put a hand on Juha's chest. "Just a minute. I've got one of the new classes starting right now. First session. It would be great if you could say a few words to them."

With feigned reluctance, Juha said, "I'd love to, but Green's in a hurry. We've got to go."

Satu's eyes met Greene's. "Please? Two minutes."

Against his better judgment, Greene said, "Fine. Two minutes."

Juha sighed. "Always so uptight." He went over to the floor area to address the fifteen workout-attire-clad people there, all of whom were varying degrees of overweight.

"He pretends like he doesn't like it," Satu said to Greene in a stage whisper, "but I think this is actually the most fulfilling part of his life right now."

Looking uncomfortable, Juha addressed the group. "Hello, everyone. My name is Juha Karjalainen, and that is my fat ass over there." He pointed at a picture of his old corpulent self on the wall. "I'm glad to see you here. It means you're among those who have decided to improve your health through relatively natural means, those who have elected not to have three-quarters of their stomach removed. There's something to be said for that. Namely: this way actually works."

Juha appeared to settle down as he went into his spiel.

"At FatAss, we're not just focused on thin versus fat, although that's certainly part of it. We also want you to think about yourself in terms of healthy versus unhealthy. I'm going to tell you a hard truth, but I know you can handle it, because you already paid your money."

There was a smattering of laughter from the group.

"Here it is: none of you are fat by accident. You chose to be fat. It's easier to choose to be fat than to choose to eat carrots—I know that from experience. I chose—somewhat inadvertently—to be fat for most of my adult life. Now, I'm not here to embarrass anybody or shame you like all those places that peddle their chemical fixes and get-thin-quick bullshit. You aren't any less of a person for being fat. If you're good with it, I'm good with it. But if you were good with it, you wouldn't be *here*, would you? I know it's true, because I've been where you are, and you can get to where I am—but it's going to take time, and hard work, and discipline. You have goals—we're here to help you reach those goals. I've talked enough; I'm going to turn you over to the capable hands of my lovely sister, and I look forward to seeing each of you again next time."

The instant he'd finished, Satu, beaming sunshine and energy, bounded up to the front of the room to take over and begin the workout program.

Juha made his way back to Greene. "How was that?"

"I feel motivated," Greene said.

Juha rolled his eyes. "Let's just go find some bad guys to shoot or something, huh?"

SIX

Juha put his feet up on the dashboard as the car sped them toward their next destination. "So is Xiong actually a real person?"

Greene looked at him, confused. "What do you mean?"

"Mr. Xiong. Is he real? Have you met him? I heard a rumor he was an AI."

Greene shook his head. "I've never met him. Never even seen him."

"Interesting."

A message from Nisha came in on Greene's Spec-Trons: Mother was cooking, and did he want rice or idli with the sambar tonight? Greene replied that he didn't care—and at the rate the day was going, the odds that he'd be home for dinner were close to zero anyway.

Juha yawned and stretched. "So who's this next guy?"

So now Juha was showing a greater interest. Getting stabbed could do that to you, Greene supposed. Better late than never.

Greene pulled the file up on the car's windshield display. It included a photo of a thin, sneering middle-aged man. "Lewis And Clark. That's one guy, 'And' is his middle name. He's one of our mid-level IT people. Got a history of being arrogant, having a bad attitude, getting into conflicts—but he does good work. Kind of like you."

This made Juha smile. "I missed you, Green, I really did."

Burg called again, and Greene put her on speaker. "We've picked up Rubin," she said. "He's not cooperating. Yet. And we've got nothing on Bonsegundo."

"We're on route to Clark now," Greene said.

"Still?"

Greene chose to ignore this. "What does Shepherd want us to do after we talk to Clark? Assuming he's not helpful."

"I don't think you're going to have that problem," Burg said. "Rubin's access credentials were reissued last night from Clark's workstation. We just now got in. Clark's got all kinds of non-standard security on there. It took most of the morning to break through. We're not sure what flavor yet but he's been up to some real shit."

"Good work."

"Shepherd says to bring him in. *Alive*. If he doesn't have the prototype, he knows who does."

"I always bring them in alive. Any reading on his chip?"

"None," Burg said. "He's probably jamming it. I don't know if he's dumb enough to still be in his house, but in either case, bring back all his devices. Odds are you won't be able to pull all his data with the standard breaker program."

"Understood. Thanks."

When Greene ended the call, Juha said, "Well, that sounds exciting. Are you ready for a good time? I'm ready for a good time."

Greene checked the charge pack on his heat ray. "Maybe it's a good thing we stopped at your gym after all. If Clark is smart, he'll have skipped out, but if not—if he thinks he can deal with us—we might have walked into an ambush."

"We're still walking into it, though, right?" Juha said. "Just a little more tactically is all."

Greene removed his Spec-Trons and cleaned them. "That's one way to look at it."

"Come on, that's no kind of attitude to have. You're a young man, you've got to enjoy your work."

Greene opened his mouth to say that he was just trying to do—and keep—his job, but instead he instructed the car to let them out down the block from Clark's address.

They were now well away from Portsmith's city center, in a primarily commercial district. The block was lined with shops and restaurants. Post-lunch, the foot traffic was relatively light.

"You're a little conspicuous in that gear," Juha said.

"Then I guess I'll draw his fire for you," Greene said.

Juha smiled and clapped him on the shoulder. "See, that's why we always made such a great team."

As they made their way down the block, Greene became increasingly uncomfortable. Every pedestrian yielded as if he magnetically repelled them. He received uneasy looks from dozens of people, and he made a point not to return eye contact. Juha, in contrast, smiled at everybody and handed out FatAss cards to heavier passersby.

Their destination came into view, and Greene pointed. "There."

"I'll be damned," Juha said. "He lives there?"

It was an ancient-looking edifice—gray stone, arching leadlight windows, tall steeple.

"An interesting choice," Greene said.

Juha shook his head. "It's not a hologram."

"What?" Greene consulted his files. "Ah. It was converted into apartments when it closed a few years ago. Used to be Free Wi-Fi Separatist Methodist Church."

They went up the front steps, Greene hauled open the massive wooden door, and they entered. The narthex had been converted into a lobby. Walls had been built down the center aisle of the church, dividing the nave, chancel, and transept into seven residential units. The entire place was whitewashed and bright.

Greene stood to one side of the lobby's interior archway and drew his heat ray. "Unit C. Any holograms?"

"Looks clear. Wait." Juha stood in the archway and looked upward. "Huh. Bunch of fuzzy spots on the ceiling. There, there, there, and there. My guess is projectors hiding each other. But what are they—" He drew his pistol and stepped into the hall. "Does your floorplan for this place have the apartments numbered?"

Greene checked. "No."

Juha went to the first door on his left, which had a brass B affixed to it. He reached out and ran his fingers over the letter. "I'll be damned. That's got to be the smallest hologram I've ever seen. This is A." He touched the door across from it. "And A is B."

"Odds are he knows we're here, then. Or that we're coming."

Juha went to the D door and put his hand on it, then gave Greene a thumbs-up. They took up breach positions on either side of the door.

"Want to knock?" Juha asked.

Greene shook his head. He used his weapon to heat the lock, then kicked the door in. Guns raised, they stepped into Clark's apartment.

The layout of the residence was completely open. Most of the exterior wall's large stained glass windows had been replaced with traditional clear glass, enabling light to flood the dwelling. The furnishings and décor were sparse, the hardwood floors were waxed to a blinding sheen, and every bit of the place, from the walls all the way up to the vaulted ceiling and beams fifteen meters overhead, had been painted white.

All was quiet. They began a search of the ground floor.

Juha went to the kitchen. "When are you guys going to invent something to disrupt all the holograms in an area? That would save us all a lot of hassle."

Greene peered into the unit's large bathroom, the exterior wall of which was comprised almost entirely of elaborate translucent glasswork depicting Christ, holding a lamb and a staff, surrounded by sheep.

"They're working on it, I'm sure," he said. "As I understand things, to do it with software involves overriding programs from a dozen companies. To do it with hardware ... well, thus far, it's just more efficient to shoot the projectors with a gun."

"If you can find them." Juha grinned. "There are a gang of them in here, you know that? Not doing anything but cloaking each other, though, as best I can tell."

Greene nodded toward the staircase. "Let's see if he's left any tech."

They ascended to a loft area with a bed, desk, and closet. The large circular window, enlaced with elaborate armature and still containing the original stained glass, occupied the bulk of the wall. Afternoon sunlight filtered through leaves outside, turning the light-colored carpet into a dappled rainbow sea.

Greene pillaged the desk and found a tablet, a phone, and several data cards. A search of the rest of the loft turned up nothing further.

Juha sat on the bed. "Are we getting somewhere?"

Greene ran a finger along the loft's waist-high railing, surveying the living area. "Maybe. I don't know how much more we can expect—" He broke off when he saw Juha scrutinizing a blank wall intently, but Juha shook his head and motioned him to continue. "—to find." He looked at Juha expectantly. "Maybe we should head back?"

Juha nodded and winked. "Yeah, let's finish checking downstairs." His route toward the staircase hugged the wall. "Just one sec."

Juha surreptitiously touched the wall with his foot, and Greene saw the edge of his shoe disappear. Juha plunged his arm through the holographic wall and dragged a man out, then threw him to the floor.

Greene was ready. He pounced on the man, pinning him face-down, checking for weapons.

Juha squatted and peered at the man's face. "It's Clark."

Clark writhed like a cat, and Greene dug his knee into the man's back.

Clark yelped in pain. "I don't have it! He took it already!"

"Well now that sounds like progress," Juha said. "I'm having a wonderful time, Green, I just want you to know that."

Greene cuffed Clark's hands behind his back, then brandished his heat ray. "Get up and go sit on the foot of the bed, or I'm going to shoot you."

Clark staggered to his feet and obeyed.

Greene waved his pistol at the holographic wall. "Juha, see what's in there, please."

Juha disappeared through the wall and reappeared a moment later with another phone, which he added to the small pile of tech on the desk.

Greene nodded his thanks, then turned his full attention to Clark. "Where's the prototype?"

The sneer was gone—Clark looked terrified. Maybe he could work with this, Greene thought. He leaned on the desk and lowered his weapon. Juha, following his lead, took up a less threatening position near the stairs.

Greene held up a hand to Clark. "You don't have to be afraid of us. We're not going to hurt you."

Clark laughed, a nervous titter. "I'm not afraid of you. I know all about you, Chief Greene."

"Then you probably know I'm your best bet out of everyone in the company, and that if you don't cooperate, I'm going to take you back there. This can be as hard or as easy as you make it."

"You're going to take me back regardless," Clark said. "Isn't that right?"

"That's right."

Clark stamped his foot. "Then let's just go."

This was not what Greene had expected. He glanced at Juha, who shrugged.

"We'll go," Greene said. "After you tell me what happened to the prototype."

"He took it!" said Clark, anxious again. "I told you that already!"

"Who? Who took it?"

Clark shook his head spasmodically. "You weren't supposed to find me! He'll kill me. He'll kill me. If he even finds out you've talked to me, he'll kill me."

"We'll protect you," Greene said. "We'll take you back to Xiong Tower. We can keep you safe there. You know that."

Clark let out a burst of maniacal laughter. "If you even could. I know Xiong's idea of safety. Especially given what they think I did."

Juha stalked over and slapped Clark hard, rocking his head sideways. "Settle your ass down and tell the man what he wants to know."

Here was Clark's famous sneer. "Go to hell."

Juha, face placid as ever, hit him again. "Tell him. You killed the big cheese with the MacGuffin that everybody's all up in a dander about. Tell him that."

"Fuck you!"

Juha just smiled.

Clark kicked Juha in the shin, sent him stumbling back. Clark leapt from the bed, and Greene shot him with the heat ray. Clark spun sideways as if jerked by strings, collided with the railing, and went over.

"Oh, shit," Juha said. He vaulted over the railing after Clark, hair flying behind him.

Greene dashed for the stairs, afraid of what he'd find below.

He found Clark lying on the floor in the living area, thrashing in pain. "My shoulder!"

Juha crouched beside him, pistol out. "Amazing flip, couldn't stick the landing. Five out of ten."

Greene put a hand on Juha's back. "Are you okay?"

Juha nodded. He grabbed Clark by the arm and jerked him to his feet, making him shriek.

Greene took custody from Juha. "Can you grab the tech from upstairs?"

Juha gave him an amused smile. "Sure thing, boss." He trotted back up the stairs.

"Last chance," Greene said to Clark.

"I can't," Clark said in strangled tones.

Shrugging, Greene called the car, and when Juha returned, they marched Clark out of the building.

The instant they were outside, Clark's attitude seemed to change. The afternoon sun hit his face, and he seemed almost surprised to see it.

He chewed his lip and looked at Greene, pleading. "You don't understand. He was here. Today. Wheat. They could be watching, listening."

"We're going to take care of you," Greene said, knowing it was a platitude.

As they stood at the curb, Clark asked, "Do you really think you can protect me?"

Greene was in wonder. Clark was more afraid of this Wheat than of what Xiong might do to him to recover the prototype. It was inconceivable, absurd.

"I'll do my best for you," Greene said. "We'll take you straight to Xiong Tower. Whoever you're afraid of, they can't get in there."

Clark looked despondent. "He did this morning."

"Wheat, you mean. With your codes."

"Yes."

"We've gotten into your system. That access has been revoked."

Clark raised an eyebrow. "So quickly? That's impressive."

Greene peered down the street, looking for the car. "Does Wheat have another way into the tower?"

"Not that I know of. But knowing him ..."

Now what? Greene wondered. How were they supposed to get the prototype back with Wheat gone and Clark of seemingly little further use?

Here was the car—Greene saw it approaching from down the street. He was so intent upon it that it took him a moment to realize that Juha was saying something.

"Green. Green. Green." Juha thumped Greene in the arm, and Greene snapped to attention.

A white van, moving fast and weaving sharply through traffic, had overtaken Greene's car and was heading toward them.

"Green."

"I see it." Greene began backing Clark quickly toward the church. There was no cover. His car was stuck behind a delivery truck midway down the block.

"Wheat!" Clark cried. "Oh, God, it's Wheat!"

Juha, retreating with them, raised his pistol. "You were right, Green, I should have borrowed a vest."

Greene tapped his phone. "Car, to me, *now*, emergency protocol, disengage all safety protocols."

Down the street, his car pulled out and tore down the center lane, sideswiping the delivery truck.

The white van stopped in front of the church. A back window slid down, and a bright light flashed. Greene moved to yank Clark back inside the building, but he collided with an unyielding, shimmering wall that blocked the doorway and buzzed with a vibration he felt throughout his entire body.

Juha took aim at the window. "I think I found your MacGuffin."

Greene leapt sideways and almost knocked himself down on another wall of energy. "We're boxed in."

Juha put a hand to one of the force fields. "I look forward to seeing how you get us out."

Greene tapped his phone again. "Car, ram the white van!"

Juha fired two rounds into the van's window, but the force fields remained.

The Xiong car slammed into the back of the white van, shoving it forward. The force fields moved with it, throwing the men to the ground even as they dissipated.

"Get to the car!" Greene called as they scrambled to their feet.

With his hands bound, Clark stumbled. Greene grabbed the man's collar and half-dragged him.

There was another flash from the van. A twinkling plane of light shot forth, waist-high.

Juha tackled Greene around the waist, driving him to the ground, and Greene lost hold of Clark. Greene's Spec-Trons flew off his face and clattered on the pavement. The force field plane crackled over their heads.

Behind them, Clark cried out, and Greene was spattered with warm blood. Hugging the concrete, he looked back. The plane had cut Clark in two: his top half lay facedown near his legs in a rapidly expanding pool of gore.

Juha was up, pulling Greene toward the car. "He's dead, Green. Let's go, or we're dead too." His blood-spattered face, Greene marveled, was almost serene.

The car was at the curb, barely ten meters away. It seemed like a kilometer. Greene hunkered down and ran, waiting for the next blast from the projector to tear him apart.

Instead, the van peeled out, maneuvering recklessly through traffic.

Greene and Juha climbed into the battered car. The windshield was shattered; bits of broken glass covered the car's interior like a snowfall.

"Think it still runs?" Juha tried with little success to wipe Clark's blood from his face.

"Pursuit!" Greene ordered. "Intercept protocol! Credentials! Logos!"

The car sprang obediently into motion, accelerating quickly until it was going double the speed of the vehicles around it.

"Engine's in the back," Greene said, nonetheless relieved. And the front axle, thank God, was undamaged.

The car accelerated to well over 100 kilometers per hour on the city street, and the wind whipped in their faces. Greene's eyes watered profusely; he could barely keep them open.

Juha, who was likewise squinting, pulled off his backpack and rummaged around until he'd produced a pair of round reflective motorcycle goggles, which he strapped on.

Greene looked at him in surprise.

"Always be prepared!" Juha shouted over the wind.

Wheat's van was now in sight, still well ahead of them, still barreling straight ahead.

They were now going 140 kilometers per hour on this four-lane street, and were closing only slowly. The rush of air was blinding, forcing Greene to keep his head down—although this had the benefit of preventing him from seeing most of the near-collisions they'd had. The car had long since decided that even though its signal was diverting the autodriven cars around it, driving down the center line was generally more efficient than weaving through traffic. Greene took the opportunity to buckle his seatbelt, wondering idly how many accidents this chase had caused thus far.

"Any idea where he might be going?" Juha bellowed.

Greene shook his head. He felt naked, ill-equipped without the Spec-Trons, without his heads-up display and constant feed of information—and the car's display was gone, too.

Ahead, Wheat's van jerked from lane to lane, sideswiping a small sedan and sending it careening through a plate-glass storefront.

Greene thought about the brief delay between the van stopping and the appearance of the first force fields. And there had been that same brief delay between the last force field—the one that had killed Clark—and the van driving off. The van was certainly moving as if it had a human driver. Did that mean that Wheat was the only one in the van?

Gradually, the Xiong car closed on Wheat's van. The car moved into Wheat's lane; there were perhaps thirty meters between the two vehicles.

Wheat was heading for the highway, Greene decided. He leaned over so Juha could hear him. "Can you shoot out a tire?"

Juha beamed. "At this speed? Holy shit, that would really fuck him up. Hell yes, I'll try."

The car continued to close. Juha brushed glass from the dashboard and leaned forward, lining up his shot. At last, he fired.

His aim was true. Energy sparked over the right rear tire.

Disgusted, Juha threw himself back in his seat. "Force field protecting the tires. That bastard."

"Hold this distance," Greene instructed the car. He pulled out his phone and called Burg, hunching over to minimize the roaring of the wind.

Burg answered immediately. "We just got a wreck signal. What's your—"

"Burg! We're in pursuit of the prototype! Visual confirmation! I need you to patch me through to Garcinia right away!"

The noise was such that he only caught about half of what Burg said, but he thought he caught an "All right."

Juha tried another shot, this time at the left tire, but was again thwarted by the force field. Scowling, he raised a middle finger at the van.

They'd reached the Waterfront Highway. Still at high speed, the van jerked into a hard turn. Staying upright against all known laws of physics, it barreled up the entrance ramp.

"Did he just use a force field to prevent a rollover?" Juha said. "That's a hell of a trick."

Finally, Garcinia came on the line. "Yes, Chief Greene?"

Greene had to strain to hear her. "We're pursuing the prototype!" he shouted. "He's using the force field to protect his van! I need to know how strong it is!"

"Well, assuming it has full power—from a fusion battery, most likely—it should be rated for up to twenty gigapascals, assuming that—"

"Gunfire!" Greene shouted. "Can we penetrate it with concentrated gunfire?"

"Small arms, you mean? Oh dear me, not a chance—you would have to have multiple projectiles simultaneously striking *precisely* the same spot. Let's see, how many would it take—"

"Thank you!" Greene ended the call.

He sat and pondered, the ocean on his left, the palm trees on the boulevard to his right flying by so quickly they were little more than a green and brown blur. He seemed to have become inured to the countless near-accidents his car was so deftly avoiding.

What next? They had to do *something*, or they'd end up wherever it was Wheat was headed, somewhere Wheat wanted to be, where they'd no doubt be outmanned and outgunned. They had to stop him from getting there.

"Oh, hell." Greene realized what he had to do. He nudged Juha. "Give me your goggles."

Juha handed them over without question. "Your piss-ass heat ray isn't going to do shit against that force field, but you're welcome to try. Oh. *Oh*." Juha shook his head, and a wry smile crossed his face. "You magnificent bastard."

Greene fastened the goggles over his eyes. "You probably want to buckle your seatbelt."

"I have a lot of regrets in my life, you know that?" Juha said, strapping himself in. "Oh well, too late now. Let's do it."

"Manual drive!" Greene told the car. A steering wheel emerged from the dashboard in front of him and pedals descended near his feet.

"Switching to manual in three, two, one," said the car.

Greene mashed the accelerator down as control transferred to him. He tugged the car over into the next lane, nearly sending them into the concrete median. A compensatory jerk on the wheel to put the car back on course threw them sideways in their seats.

"Drive much?" Juha shouted.

"It's been a while!"

Greene accelerated until they were alongside Wheat's van.

Juha rolled down his window and tried a shot at the black-tinted driver's window, but was again rebuffed by the force field. He shrugged, stowed his pistol in his backpack, and braced himself. "The hell with it. Okay, let's get this over and done with."

But Greene waited, looking for the right moment. The van was no doubt substantially heavier than the Xiong car; brute force would likely do more damage to them than to Wheat—and if Greene destroyed the car but not the van, they'd lose the prototype for good.

Seconds passed like minutes as Greene, white-knuckling the wheel, pulled back behind the van, awaiting his opportunity.

It came at last. Wheat swerved at the last instant toward the exit ramp, bashing a tiny hatchback into the guardrail.

Greene was ready. He wrenched the wheel and pressed the accelerator to the floor, and the car rocketed down the exit ramp. Greene navigated onto the shoulder, once again drawing alongside the van.

"Here we go," Greene said.

"Shit," Juha said.

Greene flung the car across the front of Wheat's van. The force of the impact shattered Greene's window—he felt the crackle of energy and the sting of glass on his face and arms—and sent the car airborne.

Airbags exploded into being all around them. The car landed on its passenger side, then went wheels-up, its momentum sending it scraping down the road with a horrific noise.

Greene, disoriented, couldn't see what had happened to the van. Something hard struck his head, and his last thought before he blacked out was that he hoped it had been enough.

SEVEN

"Green. Green, wake your ass up."

At a painful pinch on his cheek, Greene opened his eyes. His pulse pounded and his head throbbed. On top of that, he felt ... strange. Then he realized why.

He was upside down, still strapped into his seat in the car. He touched a throbbing spot on his head and felt a welt. On the ceiling of the car below him was the stainless steel water bottle that had caused it.

Juha was crouched outside Greene's open door, an ugly gash across his chin. He was cutting away the deflated airbags with a knife.

"Can you support yourself?" Juha asked. "I'm going to pop your seatbelt."

Greene raised his arms—toward the ground—and nodded.

Juha set him free and Greene worked his way out of the car, shredding his bare forearms on the carpet of shattered glass. The car was in the middle of an intersection; traffic wended its way around them on all sides.

Greene stood up too quickly, and pain flashed in his head. "Wheat, you think?"

"He's in there," Juha said.

The van was turned over some ten meters away, broadside to the car, its undercarriage facing them.

"You tangled him up pretty good," Juha said.

Greene drew his heat ray. "You take the front, I'll take the back."

Juha, weapon out, backpack on, face as placid as if he were going for a walk in the park, nodded.

As Greene approached the van, the rear doors opened, and he fell back a step.

The air hissed and hummed around him—solid holograms. Greene dropped to the ground and rolled back toward the car.

An enormous man with short blond hair emerged, blood trickling from his ear. He carried a massive machine gun that looked too heavy to lift. Wheat pointed it in Greene's direction, and Greene dove behind the upturned Xiong car.

Greene heard the sound of several impacts against metal, but the gun itself was silent—it was a solid hologram, he realized.

Juha was caught in no-man's-land between the two vehicles. After an instant of hesitation, he dashed back to the car.

"God damn it," he said as he slid in next to Greene. "I should have gone for the flank. Rusty. I'm sorry."

The top of the car's trunk was nearly flush against the pavement, and they squirmed to both fit behind that space as Wheat's silent gunfire pounded the car like a rainstorm on a tin roof.

Greene put his head down and peeked through the car's broken windows. Wheat had stopped midway between the car and the van, seemingly content to bombard the car interminably with holographic bullets.

"He could definitely be Bavarian," Juha remarked.

Greene wondered how much power Wheat had for the projector. The fire was nonstop; real bullets would have surely penetrated the car by now. But Wheat would have run out of ammo by now, too.

Juha seemed to be thinking along the same lines. He looked at Greene and said, "Why are we not dead?"

Greene mentally grasped for his hologram briefings—he'd never really been that interested before today. "The force field is projected rapidly, but not anywhere near the velocity of a real bullet. It would be plenty fast to kill you in the open, but if that holographic gun's projected ammo is the diameter of a bullet but flat rather than conical, he's not going to have the force to get through."

"It cut that other asshole in half," Juha said.

"Because that force field was paper-thin."

"So we're the beneficiaries of half-assed programming? This is like the chain gun beta? The hell with this, before he figures it out." Juha dropped to his belly and wormed his way to the front window of the car, where the glass was smashed, and squeezed off two shots at Wheat's legs.

Wheat bellowed.

"Suck on that popsicle." Juha launched himself back as Wheat sprayed that part of the car with fire.

Wheat backed toward the turned-over van, still firing in a wild pattern. Then he threw down the machine gun and disappeared into the van.

Juha reloaded. "Want to rush him?"

Greene shook his head. "Could be a trap. He could conjure up a new attack before we got there and we'd run right into it. But let's get ready for him."

"You think he's going to make a move?" Juha asked.

"What else can he do?" Greene said. "Wait there until backup comes, or the cops? The minute the airbags deployed, Xiong sent out a team. All we have to do is hold out."

At Greene's direction, he and Juha took up positions on either side of the car, weapons trained at the van. The afternoon sun was in Greene's eyes, and he wished again for his Spec-Trons.

The machine gun vanished. On the ground immediately in front of the van's rear doors, a revolver and a riot shield appeared.

"Not very imaginative, eh?" Juha said. "I'd have gone with something creative, you know, like ... like a bear with a ninja sword, or a dragon. Something badass. This kid needs to step up his game."

"He's limited to the programs loaded onto the projector." Greene realized it even as he said it.

Wheat dove out of the van, rolling, and they each got a shot off. Juha missed; Greene was slow—Wheat got the holographic riot shield up in front of him.

"It might be time for us to stop sandbagging," Juha said.

Greene snorted.

Wheat picked up the revolver and advanced toward them, limping, shield raised. He began firing, and they ducked back behind the car.

After a moment, Juha started to jump up.

Greene yanked him back down. "Are you trying to get killed?"

"What. That was six shots."

"It's a holographic revolver," Greene said. "It doesn't run out of bullets."

Juha considered this. "By golly. There ought to be a law. Now what?"

Wheat reached the car, and suddenly there were two Wheats, identical in every way, standing side by side. One began to work his way around Juha's end of the car; the other, in perfect step, was coming around Greene's side.

Both were firing solid holographic bullets as they came, forcing Greene to keep his head down and preventing him from getting a good look at their timing.

"Which one is real?" Greene demanded.

Juha backed toward Greene, seeking better cover. "Um ... yours!"

Greene dropped to his belly and tagged Wheat in the ankle with the heat ray.

Grunting, Wheat spun to one knee behind his riot shield and ceased firing, and the duplicate Wheat did as well.

What was Wheat doing? His head was down and his attention seemed to be on a device in his enormous hand. Ordering up something new, Greene realized.

"Juha, flank!" Greene called.

Juha leapt up, and as he did, total darkness descended upon them. It was tangible—Greene could feel the solid hologram buzzing above him, making his hair stand on end. The dark force field slammed Juha to the ground, audibly knocking the wind out of him. Then all was silent except for their breathing.

The blackness was total—Greene couldn't even see his hand in front of him. The smells of asphalt and dirt filled his nostrils, and a wave of claustrophobic panic swept over him.

"The hell just happened?" Juha said, and there was a buzz. "Ow! A force field box. I'm going to kill that bastard when we get out of here."

Greene fumbled for his phone and activated the light, bathing their confines in a piercing white glow. The box extended barely beyond them, and they didn't have room even to sit up.

"What now?" Juha asked. Numerous shards of glass embedded in his cheek twinkled in the phone's light. "Just wait for the cavalry while that asshole escapes?"

Wheat, escape? That would mean abandoning the prototype. Greene didn't dare get his hopes that high.

The force box began shrinking, flattening, contracting around them on all sides.

"Dirty pool, I say." Juha, already on his hands and knees, was forced onto his belly. "Is the force field strong enough to crush us?"

"Probably." And if it wasn't, they'd likely suffocate.

Juha smiled wanly. "My fury is boundless."

Greene fought down his panic and thought. He opened a vest pocket and pulled out the "jackhammer" Garcinia had given him. It looked undamaged. He thumbed it on and placed it on the ground by the nearest force field wall, hoping Wheat wasn't standing right outside with a real gun this time.

The jackhammer gave off a high-pitched squeal that made Greene's ears ring, and the black holographic walls flickered and vanished. The afternoon sun was blinding. Wheat was nowhere in sight.

Greene pocketed the jackhammer, raised his heat ray, and moved quickly to the van. His heart skipped a beat as he looked inside. Could it be?

Wheat was gone. But the projector was there, wired to the van's front console and mounted on a pneumatic arm to move it from window to window.

Greene let out a breath he hadn't realized he'd been holding and sank against the side of the van. "It's here. We've got it."

He reached out to touch it, to assure himself that it was real, and a vibration buzzed through his hand. Wheat had surrounded it with a force field.

Or was this projector an illusion? No—it had to be the real thing, or else where was the force field coming from? Greene reached for the jackhammer.

"There he is!" Juha cried. "Look at him, just walking down the street like a smug bastard, trying to blend in. He didn't think we were going to get out of his box."

Exhaustion swept over Greene. "Let him go. We've got it."

"Nope," Juha said. "Catching that clown has become my primary goal in life."

"Juha—"

Juha glanced back at Greene. "That's got a force field around it, right? So we're good to leave it until your people get here. Come on, it'll be fine." Tucking his gun into his waistband, Juha adjusted his backpack on his shoulders and set off at a brisk walk in Wheat's direction, maneuvering deftly through the slowed traffic.

Greene's eyes lingered on the projector. Would it be safe to leave? The jackhammer was the only one of its kind, Garcinia had said, so nobody was going to come along and break through the field ... at least not quickly. What about the van's power source, though? Did the force field cover it? Would Wheat have thought of that?

Juha was fifty meters away now—Greene could see his absurd ponytail bobbing up and down in the crowd. Greene didn't know how well he liked Juha's chances against Wheat in any case, and Juha was badly torn up. But as stubborn as always.

Greene sighed and went to his upturned car. He managed to get the trunk door open far enough to pull out the surveillance drone. He activated it, and the black plate-sized contraption took to the air on four tiny propellers.

"Follow," he told it. Then he called Burg. "Have you got a lock on me?"

"Yes, we're en route by air," Burg said. "About five minutes away."

"We've got the prototype. But don't come to me; come to the car."

"What? Why would—"

Greene ended the call, turned his back to the projector, and ran after Juha, wondering whether he might yet get fired today.

EIGHT

The drone trailing above and behind him, Greene jogged down the sidewalk, evading passersby as best he could while maintaining his pace. He scanned himself with his phone as he ran: no concussion, not that it would have changed his course of action.

At last, he caught up to Juha, who had closed to within thirty meters of Wheat. They had entered a market district. The afternoon foot traffic was heavy, both on the sidewalks and in the narrow streets. The expression of slight amusement Juha had worn all day had been replaced by something more serious, and those pedestrians not preoccupied with their phones gave way before his bloody visage.

Greene finally fell into step just behind him. "Are you okay? You look terrible."

Juha turned his head to be heard. "Glad you could make it. I might not be able to stand up straight tomorrow, but I've got enough left in the tank to take this fool down."

Wheat, more than a head taller than most everyone else around him, was easy to tail, at least.

"He's going to be hard to bring down in this crowd," Juha said.

"I don't like the idea of letting him get where he wants to go, though."

"True. Can you get him with your heat ray?"

An oblivious man slammed into Greene, spilling hot coffee on his arm and then swearing at him.

Greene shoved him aside. "Xiong Holonautics, get away from me."

The man's eyes widened, and he backed away.

Greene trotted back up to Juha, who hadn't stopped. "Not from here. Not in this crowd. We'll have to get closer."

Juha snorted. "The crowd? You've got a sissy-ass non-lethal weapon and you're worried about the crowd?"

Greene resisted the urge to thump him in the back. "If I hit him, I don't know if we can close in time. If I miss, I'm going to hit someone else, and he's going to know we're after him. What, do you think you can shoot him in the head from twenty-five, thirty meters?"

"I'm willing to try," Juha said, clearly delighted at the prospect.

Greene took a deep breath. The street-level shops with their garish neon signs, the high-rise apartments looming over the cramped street, and the press of the crowd around him were suffocating.

A woman coming toward them actually stopped at the sight of Juha's bloody face and mangled cheek, recoiling in horrified disgust.

Juha leered at her as they passed. "What's the matter, lady? You never had a bad day? It's diamonds. Diamonds in my face. It's the trend now, you better ask somebody."

"Stay the course a minute, will you?" Greene said. He rested a hand on Juha's shoulder, letting him pull the two of them through the crowd, and took out his phone. He pulled up the local map. "There's a mall up ahead. This street runs right into the Galleria Arcade."

Juha shook his head. "That'll be a holographic apocalypse. We've got to take him before he gets there."

"Okay. You get across the street and see if you can pull even with him, maybe get where you can cut him off. I'll tell the drone to stick with him, and then I'll try to get as close as I can and bring him down from behind."

"Fine," said Juha. "As long as I get to kick him in the kidneys afterward."

"He's got to be armed. Be careful."

"I'm touched at your concern."

"I'm also worried about the safety of all these people."

Juha shrugged. "Just do your best. They'll get over it."

Wheat looked back then. They reflexively put their heads down, but Wheat undoubtedly saw the drone.

"Shit," Juha said. "He's running."

Wheat began to shove his way forward through the herd of people, a one-man stampede.

"Ass crackers," Juha muttered. "This freaking guy." He dashed off, and the crowd swallowed him.

Greene sent the drone ahead, managed with his phone to get it locked onto Wheat, and then followed, pushing—but not as roughly as Juha.

Wheat was obviously headed for the mall. All those exits ... it was his best chance to lose them.

Greene hopped over a prone woman Wheat had trampled. He was falling behind. It crossed his mind that he could use the heat ray on the people in his way, soften up the pack. He dismissed this thought, and not primarily because there was just as good a chance he'd create a pileup in front of him.

Keeping both hands free, he pressed forward on his toes, turning sideways and half-swimming through the mass of people.

He reached the Galleria, which seemed to be squeezed in amongst the high-rise apartments. It was—whether truly or holographically, Greene had no idea—a four-story, glass-vaulted double arcade. There were no exterior doors; a towering archway admitted him.

The path before him was decorated with mosaic scenes and lined with haute couture shops, whose stucco façades were covered with ornate reliefs. The cast-iron and glass roof cast a bluish tint over everything within.

Greene spotted the drone, still bearing straight onward, with Wheat beneath it.

The foot traffic here had thinned sufficiently for Greene to sprint, and he began to gain ground. He spotted Juha's ponytail bouncing some distance ahead of him.

The mall's avenue led to an octagonal plaza topped by an ostentatious glazed dome. At the center of the plaza, where the Galleria's two perpendicular avenues intersected, stood an immense marble fountain done in a classical style.

Wheat veered toward the right-hand path, with Juha closing.

Greene took the most direct route toward them, which was through a sidewalk café on the edge of the plaza. He threaded his way clumsily through the dense cluster of tables and chairs, leaving a trail of spilled drinks and swearing customers in his wake.

Clearing the restaurant, Greene found himself perhaps thirty meters from Wheat, with Juha about halfway between them. Greene again broke into a full sprint and immediately felt a stitch developing in his side. He gritted his teeth and maintained his pace, cursing himself for going soft at thirty. Juha, in contrast, looked like he was ready and able to run all day.

They ran down the avenue, the three of them. This promenade looked much like the first—shops with displays of designer clothing, purses, shoes, and jewels, of the sort Greene had never set foot in. He saw no opportunity to take a different angle, to cut Wheat off. But Juha was gaining, backpack and everything. Greene marveled that if he had been told of such a thing yesterday, he would never have believed it.

Still running a weak third, Greene reached the archway, which opened onto a sunken open-air courtyard filled with more conventional stores. They were, relatively speaking, on the third— and topmost—floor. The avenue's composition changed from tile to clear acrylic but continued straight across the top of the shopping bowl, with railings on either side.

Greene found himself slowing. The shooting pain in his side could no longer be overruled, and his lungs burned. Juha was close. Greene fumbled for his heat ray. Catching up to Wheat was now a task for Juha alone, and Greene meant to be ready when he did.

A food cart stood just outside the archway, on the paved ring around the top of the courtyard, directly in Wheat's path. Juha tackled Wheat, his arms around the huge man's waist, and they both collided with the cart, sending hot dogs and eggrolls flying. Their momentum slammed the cart into the railing: Wheat slid across the top, Juha still clinging to him, and then they both went over the rail.

Greene's heart skipped a beat. "Oh, hell."

He sprinted to the railing, nearly running over the startled vendor, and looked down, afraid of what he'd see.

The three levels of the shopping ring were tiered. Juha and Wheat had landed in a large box planter on the second level, with Juha on top.

Wheat was struggling to rise. He shoved Juha, then punched him in the face, knocking him away.

As Wheat stood, Greene aimed and fired. Wheat pitched sideways and fell down behind the planter.

Greene cast about for the stairs, then dashed for them, finding it hard to get his exhausted muscles moving again. His feet ached in his new boots.

By the time Greene reached the second level, Wheat was moving again, and Greene found himself beginning to question his ethical reasons for not using a standard-issue firearm.

Nose bleeding, Juha climbed to his feet, brushing leaves and soil from his torn jeans. Tattered, bloody, and swollen, he was a horror.

The two exchanged a glance. "Hey, I got him once too," Juha said. He lurched after Wheat, pistol in hand, and Greene followed.

Wheat vaulted over the second-level railing and landed on the roof of a phone kiosk, then dropped to the pavement on the bottom level near a small and well-populated children's play area. Greene's blood turned to ice.

Juha gamely followed Wheat by the same path. To Greene's relief, Wheat kept going, ignoring the kids.

Greene made his way around the second-level ring in the direction Wheat was heading—a longer route, but one that just might give him a chance to cut Wheat off.

The drone still buzzed above Wheat's head. The giant man stopped short and whipped out a pistol. He quickly fired twice, barely seeming to aim, then began running again without waiting to inspect his results.

The drone crashed to the pavement. Wheat's trick shot had cost him very little ground.

"Jesus." Greene forced himself into a sprint, wondering whether he'd be able to get out of bed in the morning.

There, ahead—another kiosk.

Greene leapt over the railing—and sailed right through what had appeared to be a sturdy awning.

Damned holograms, he thought as he smashed through what turned out to be a thin plastic table laden with sunglasses.

Greene fought to get to his feet. His left arm was in the kiosk's projection space, making it look like he was embedded in the display, and it was disorienting.

And here came Wheat, moving full-tilt in his direction. If Greene could only tag him with a tracker ...

Out of energy and ideas, Greene timed his move, then simply hurled himself into Wheat's path.

As planned, Wheat tripped over him and went sprawling across the concrete.

"Hell yes, well done," Juha remarked as he vaulted over Greene.

But Wheat, apparently indestructible, was already up and going again. He had to be buffed on some kind of drug, Greene thought.

Greene rose once more—it was getting progressively more difficult. Searching Clark's apartment felt like yesterday.

Juha had flanked Wheat, and now they had him practically pinned up against the plate glass window of a department store. At last, Wheat had stopped running.

Greene raised his weapon, ready to shoot Wheat again on general principle, but held his fire, mindful of the bystanders.

Wheat had his pistol in one hand, a phone in the other. Thus far, the massive man had proven resistant enough to the heat ray that Greene didn't trust that another shot wouldn't just provoke him.

Juha had his gun pointed at Wheat as well. Bleeding, panting, he said, "Put it down and be cool, huh? I'm tired as hell, and I'm more than ready to shoot you in the face right here and now."

The behemoth's eyes went to Juha, then to Greene, then back to Juha. Wheat was a little sweaty, but he looked scarcely fatigued. What on earth drug could he be on?

But Wheat didn't move; his gun remained pointed vaguely at Juha's legs.

"Put it down," Greene told him.

Greene was so intent on Wheat's gun that it took him a moment—too long—to notice that the big man was working the phone in his other hand without looking at it. He knew immediately what Wheat was doing, and in the instant his muscles tensed to fire, to open his mouth to warn Juha, a pulsing wall of vertical lines of colored light appeared between them and Wheat.

"Get down!" Greene shouted, flinging himself to the pavement.

Juha followed suit as two shots cracked in front of them.

Wondering but not daring to turn to check whether anyone behind them had been hit, Greene fired blindly into the black where Wheat had been standing.

Another shot came, followed by the sound of breaking glass.

Greene wormed his way to the dizzying holographic wall, steeled himself, and poked his head through, half-expecting it to be the last thing he ever did.

But Wheat wasn't there. The department store window was smashed in.

Greene jumped up. Wheat was in the store already, heading away down an aisle. Some shoppers fled; others stood gawking.

None were between Greene and Wheat, so Greene shot Wheat in the back with the heat ray, and he went down again.

"Juha, let's go!" Panting, Greene climbed through the window, trying to avoid the broken glass without taking his eyes off Wheat, who was, at last, taking a gratifyingly long time to rise.

Juha, who looked like he shouldn't even be able to stand up, was already there beside him, hurdling the window frame with minimal regard for his own flesh and passing through a holographic model in a trendy miniskirt and halter top.

They found themselves in the women's section. Juha nodded at a spatter of blood on the floor inside the window. "Did you see that fool's gun hand? All bloody. Cut his fingers on the glass shards in my face when he hit me like a dumbass."

Greene hadn't noticed. He was watching Wheat now. The big man had crawled out of the aisle and was crouching in a forest of clothing racks.

Juha wiped his nose. "This reminds me of that time we got called to that department store in Estadostown to subdue a Holiday Day riot and you got hit in the head with a mannequin and a toaster. You remember that?"

Greene moved behind a pillar. He took a deep breath, trying to slow his pulse. "You see him?"

Juha positioned himself behind a shelf opposite. "Yep. Why isn't he shooting at us?"

"Waiting for us to make a move, probably."

"Oh, good." Juha made a cursory inspection of his pistol. "That means he's given up on trying to get away. I, for one, am tired of running, so let's go shoot this jackass and be done with it."

Greene checked his own weapon. "Yes, let's."

"But before we do, can I tell you something? As a friend? Your gun really sucks, you know that? You shot him, what, four, five, twenty times? And that dude didn't give a fuck. Not a single one."

Greene rolled his eyes but couldn't argue the point.

"He's just playing on his phone," Juha said. "We going to sit here and let him check his mail, look at porn, whatever the hell?"

"He's getting into the store's holographics system."

"Lovely," Juha said. "This is going to become a goddamn funhouse if we give him enough time."

Greene glanced around. On the ceiling was mounted a full grid of the projectors that generated the virtual models standing on the raised displays around them, whose attire had been programmed to change every ten seconds or so. Perhaps they generated even more of the store's décor than that; Greene had no real idea.

"All right, let's take him," Greene said.

As if on cue, the clothing models vanished from their pedestals, and a shimmering rainbow curtain descended from the ceiling, spanning the store from wall to wall. So many colors, changing rhythmically, hypnotically, gave Greene the beginnings of vertigo.

On the bright side, Wheat shouldn't be able to see them either—and at least they didn't have those damned solid holograms to worry about anymore.

Fixing his gaze on the floor, Greene circled around Wheat's position before plunging through the kaleidoscopic curtain. Greene saw the look of confusion on an elderly shopper's face a split second before he plowed her to the ground.

"Sorry," he called over his shoulder.

Wheat had moved. Greene had holographic walls of color on all sides now, and he became unsure of his direction—one rack of ladies' clothing looked much the same as another to him. The hair on the back of his neck stood on end.

Then he heard the gunshot. It came from somewhere to his left, in what he thought was Juha's direction.

Greene dashed that way, passing through several holographic panels, upending a clothing rack and causing an explosion of sundresses.

He found himself shaking his head as he ran. It figured that Wheat would go after Juha—Juha had the *real* gun.

Greene crossed through another colorful wall, then pulled up short to keep from colliding with a tall, almost comically thin young man in a dress shirt and slacks who, seemingly oblivious to the optical nightmare around him, was straightening up the racks.

When Greene saw he had a nametag on, he grabbed the man's arm. "Baylor? You work here. Can you shut down the hologrid?"

Baylor looked at him blandly. "I'm sorry, sir, I guess we're having some technical difficulties with it. If you'll bear with us, I'm sure they'll have things sorted out properly in just a minute or two."

Greene blinked. Was this man an idiot? Was the sound of gunshots a common feature of malfunctioning holograms?

He whipped out his credentials and shoved them in Baylor's face. "I need you to shut down the hologrid *right now*. Can you do it?"

Baylor's eyes nearly crossed as he struggled to read Greene's too-close ID. "I ... I suppose, sir."

"Then do it. Do it now."

"Okay." The lanky man shrugged, then turned away.

Greene clapped a hand down on Baylor's shoulder before he could take two steps. "Wait! What other exits does this store have?"

Baylor stopped and turned with a slowness that rankled. "We have an exit on this floor and one on the second floor, sir."

"They exit to the courtyard?"

"Yes, sir."

"Any others? Fire exits?"

Baylor screwed up his face in thought. "Yes, sir."

Greene forced himself to stop chewing his lip. "Where do they exit to?"

"To the courtyard."

"There are no exits that go anywhere other than the courtyard?"

"I *think* so."

Greene shook him by the shoulder. "A delivery entrance? There's a delivery entrance, right?"

"I— I don't know. I'm kind of new."

Useless. Greene shoved Baylor away. "Okay, go!"

Greene tried to reorient himself and pressed on. He had little confidence that Baylor would come through for him.

Finally, Greene found Juha and Wheat, and not a moment too soon. And he'd caught a break: Wheat had his back to Greene and hadn't seen him.

Wheat was on top of Juha, a meaty hand clapped around the smaller man's throat. Blood trickled from a bullet wound in Wheat's shoulder as Juha struggled ineffectually to free himself.

Here was Greene's chance. Moving quickly, he hooked his left arm around Wheat's neck and squeezed. With his right, he jammed his heat ray into the small of Wheat's back and fired, holding the trigger down.

Wheat jerked upright, releasing Juha. He'd gone completely rigid. Wheat roared with pain and thrashed from side to side, trying to shake Greene loose.

Greene held on and continued firing, giving Wheat a sustained blast. It must have been agony—at least, Greene hoped so.

Still on his back, Juha managed to free one leg. Coughing and hacking, he lifted it toward his chest, then kicked Wheat squarely in the balls.

Bellowing like an animal, Wheat launched himself backward, throwing Greene to the floor and then landing on top of him.

The man's weight was crushing, but Greene kept the heat ray's trigger down even as he lost his hold on Wheat's neck.

Greene grasped wildly as Wheat struggled to escape the heat ray's blast, found an ear, and twisted. Wheat's now-constant roar of pain was deafening, but he gave no sign of submitting.

Juha was up on one knee, still struggling for breath, fumbling for his pistol. "Green, get clear."

But Greene was still pinned, still firing, still redeeming the honor of the heat ray.

Then, faster than Greene thought possible, Wheat twisted, tearing free of Greene's hold and coming face to face with him. Utter fury on his face, he swatted the heat ray from Greene's grasp.

Greene didn't see where it landed because Wheat locked both massive hands onto his vest and jerked him upright.

Greene scrabbled to plant his feet but failed entirely to find the floor. Wheat flung him headlong into Juha, sending them both tumbling. As Greene worked to extricate himself, Wheat disappeared again into the holographic ether.

Juha lay there on his back, awkward on top of his backpack, a bloody mess.

"Are you all right?" Greene asked, knowing he couldn't possibly be.

"I just need a minute," Juha said. "You go ahead. I'll be along."

"Are you sure? I—"

"Just go, man!" For the first time, Juha's voice rose, and he sprayed blood-flecked spittle. "If you let that bastard get away after all the shit I've endured, I will kill you my fucking self."

Greene forced himself into motion, snatching up his heat ray from a pile of dresses and heading toward the rainbow wall Wheat had vanished through.

There was nothing he could do for Juha now anyway, Greene told himself. But backup was on the way, had to be: once Burg and the Xiong team had secured the projector—which they should have done by now—they'd come after him, following his chip.

So abruptly that it took Greene a moment to realize what had happened, all the holographic static vanished, leaving only an ordinary store.

Baylor had come through.

And ahead was Wheat, in a firing stance, pistol pointed at Greene, squeezing the trigger.

At this point, Greene was running purely on adrenaline, willpower, duty—he didn't know what. The bullet ripped through his left triceps, sending searing pain through his arm. He grunted but didn't break stride.

This was clearly not the response Wheat had been expecting. He fired again. To Greene's surprise, he missed—Greene dared to hope that maybe they were finally wearing him down—then turned and dashed for the escalators. In his rush, Wheat found himself going up the *down* escalator.

Greene leapt onto the unoccupied *up* escalator and gained some ground.

Wheat fought his way up. An obese man was descending, blocking his path. Wheat tried to shove past him but didn't have room. He bashed the man in the face with the butt of his pistol, grabbed him by the belt, and flung him over the divide onto Greene's side.

Greene saw the man tumbling toward him, headfirst and arms flailing. In the instant he had, he considered trying to vault over onto Wheat's side, but didn't trust himself, didn't trust his burning, weakened arm.

Instead, he leapt over the tumbling man, inadvertently stomping on his back and very nearly becoming entangled with him.

"Sorry," Greene muttered.

He ascended past Wheat, who, too close to bring his gun to bear, tried to punch Greene in his wounded arm.

Greene took a retaliatory swipe, dealing Wheat a glancing blow on the chin with the barrel of his gun.

They emerged into the children's section—which was, thankfully, free of kids as far as Greene could see—and then separated. Greene ducked behind a pillar as Wheat drew aim again.

But it was a feint—Wheat was running again, heading for the second-floor exit.

Greene followed, lungs burning, pulse pounding, arm throbbing, wondering how much longer he could keep pace with this untiring, indestructible juggernaut.

Where was Xiong? They wouldn't hang him out to dry, abandon him as he had abandoned the projector, would they? It was a ludicrous thought, he knew, but he couldn't shake his insecurity—not now, when he needed them so desperately.

Greene followed Wheat out to the second level of the open-air shopping ring. Without his auto-tinting glasses, he was momentarily blinded by the unexpected brightness of the sun. Still moving, he reflexively raised his left hand to his eyes for shade. The pain of movement made him wince.

And there was Wheat, still fleeing.

Greene shot him again, and it was the last of his charge.

Wheat barely stumbled, but it was enough for Greene to close most of the distance between them. He threw his spent pistol at Wheat. It bounced off his shoulder with all the impact of a tennis ball.

Still Greene ran, fumbling at a vest pocket for his injector. If he could just get a tracker into Wheat, he could stop, sit, rest.

Or maybe Wheat would stop running then and try to kill him—if so, Greene was confident there wouldn't be much he could do about it.

The injector was in his hand. Greene flung himself onto Wheat's massive shoulders, clinging there like a small child trying to wrangle a piggyback ride from an unwitting parent.

Wheat stopped running. He clawed at Greene's head and shoulders, trying to shake him free.

Greene grabbed Wheat's ear with one hand and ground the injector into the bullet wound in Wheat's shoulder. The giant went rigid long enough for Greene to inject a tracker into him.

Greene's profound sense of accomplishment was short-lived, however. Before he could let go, Wheat slammed him into the railing. Greene lost his grip, and he flailed to keep from toppling over and falling to the lower level.

It was Wheat, ironically, who kept Greene from dropping—he grabbed Greene's vest with both fists.

Greene noted fleetingly that a good number of shoppers were standing nearby, watching—at this point, he wasn't certain whether he'd prefer them to get to safety or try to help. But they did neither; many took video with their phones, heedless of the danger.

Wheat jerked Greene up and held him over the railing. Then he clapped a massive hand over Greene's face and began to squeeze.

Clutching at Wheat's wrists, Greene fought to free himself, fought to breathe, but his strength was gone.

This was the end, then, Greene thought, trying and failing to find any purchase with his legs.

As consciousness began to leave him, even as he began to clench and spasm because of the lack of air, Greene felt strangely at peace. He had done his best, he had completed his mission—or near enough to it. He thought of his wife, of his unborn daughter ...

From behind and below Greene came a pistol shot, and shrieking from the bystanders. Wheat grunted, and Greene was suddenly free—and falling.

By some miracle, he managed to grab the railing with his good arm. He braced his feet on its base and hoisted himself up, clinging there, sucking air greedily.

Another gunshot sounded, and Wheat collapsed.

Greene looked down. There in the courtyard was Juha, battered, swaying on his feet, his pistol in his hand. He met Greene's gaze and gave a little salute.

Greene hauled himself over the railing and collapsed on top of Wheat, who was trying again to rise. Under Greene's weight—at last—Wheat stayed down.

Lightheaded, Greene retrieved Wheat's handgun. Then he pulled a pair of handcuffs from a vest pocket and secured Wheat's hands behind his back. He would have liked to put his second pair on the man, too, just to be safe, but it was on the other side of town, still fastened to Clark's corpse.

Still panting, heart pounding, Greene turned Wheat over and inspected his injuries. Wheat appeared to be breathing normally. Juha had put two rounds into the man's left thigh; there were no exit wounds. The entry wounds bled freely, but not so much that Greene was urgently concerned for the man's life.

Greene moved just out of Wheat's reach and unbuckled his tactical vest. He removed it, opened the wide, flat pocket on the back, and took out his first aid kit. The bandages it contained were thin, inadequate.

Greene drew his knife and cut away Wheat's blood-soaked pant leg. Wheat glared but didn't struggle. The expression on his face was pure disgust.

While Greene was applying the bandages, the crowd edged closer. More had their phones out now, recording.

Juha rode up the escalator and staggered over, looking like death. "Look at you wasting your time with this Good Samaritan shit. You always were a pussy. Let him bleed." He kicked Wheat in the hip. "If you limp for the rest of your life, it'll be better than you deserve. I ought to shoot you in the face right now, you King Kong Third Reich motherfucker."

"Are you all right?" Greene had finished taping up the bandages. The work was crude but serviceable.

"I don't think I'm going to die imminently, if that's what you're getting at." Juha glanced around at all the spectators. "The hell is this? You kids never seen a pro takedown? How about a little personal space?"

When no one moved, Juha snatched the phone from the hand of the nearest videographer and flung it over the railing to the courtyard below. The sound of it shattering carried up to them. The man began to take umbrage, but when he saw Juha's pistol and bloody face, he appeared to think better of it.

Juha looked at the bystanders again, pistol pointed at the ground. "If the rest of you clowns don't back the hell up, you're going to get the same or worse. Come on now. I want a good ten meters."

Now they complied.

Juha shrugged off his backpack and sank down against the railing. He pointed his pistol at Wheat's head. "Try something else. I wish you would. Green, you forgot his shoulder."

"Do you have any more bandages?" Greene asked.

Juha gripped one strap of his backpack tight. "Yes I do. For me."

Greene let the matter drop. He felt no particular malice for Wheat—victory was sufficient—but he had no great compulsion to aid the man further. He turned to Juha. "You want me to help you get patched up?"

Juha put two fingers to the cheek under his black eye, swollen almost shut, and winced. "Your people are coming, right? I assume you all employ a proper doctor? Plus I think I might want to be drunk when they start picking the glass out of my face." He peered at Greene. "Oh, shit, what about you? That's your own blood, isn't it? You didn't tell me you got shot. Here, this is for you only."

Juha opened his backpack and tossed Greene his first aid kit. Greene opened it and wrapped his arm with only slightly more care than he had used on Wheat.

Seeing that Juha still had his pistol aimed at Wheat's head, Greene rose and retrieved his spent heat ray. He inserted a fresh energy cell, then returned to Juha.

"Hey, let me see that a minute," Juha said.

"Why?"

Juha's one good eye radiated innocence. "I just want to cook him a little bit more while we're waiting."

Greene holstered the weapon.

Juha sighed. "You're no fun." He stuck out his leg and prodded Wheat, who was still lying facedown. "Hey. Jackass. Are you Bavarian?"

Wheat curled his lip and spat at him, and Juha shrugged.

Greene sat down next to Juha, fatigue washing over him. He took out his phone and called Burg. As he waited for the call to connect, he turned to Juha and said, "Thank you."

"Don't mention it." Juha took a deep breath and let it out in an exhausted huff. "That was the most fun I've had in a long time. Oh, and you owe me ten grand."

NINE

Not two minutes later, Greene heard the approach of the Xiong helicopter. The low *whup-whup-whup* of its quieted rotor blades was a lullaby, an assurance.

Greene watched in an exhausted reverie as the helicopter descended toward the bridge above. It stopped, hovering, and two of his security officers rappelled down. They cleared the bridge of foot traffic with an efficiency that satisfied Greene, and then the helicopter landed.

A team of five made its way down to them. Four were in Xiong tactical gear—Burg was in the lead. The fifth was in a suit—it was Shepherd.

Greene started in surprise, and pain shot up his arm. Shepherd, in the field? And not at the crash site, with the projector, but here? He couldn't think of any reason Shepherd would be here himself—except maybe to fire him on the spot.

Greene dragged himself to his feet as they arrived, assuming as straight a posture as he could. "Suspect secured," he said to them. "Alive."

"Get this crowd cleared out of here," Burg told her team, and they went to work. She looked at Greene, then at Wheat, then back to Greene. "Nice work, Chief," she said, grudging respect in her voice.

Greene recognized a high compliment when he heard one. "Thank you, Burg. You have the prototype?" If by any chance they hadn't managed to ...

It was Shepherd who answered. His face was hard and unreadable. "We do. It's on its way back to the tower as we speak. Although God damn, I can't believe you left it. What the hell were you thinking, Chief?"

Greene looked at Juha, mentally commanded him not to say anything. Juha obeyed.

Meeting Shepherd's burning gaze, Greene said, "We had a chance to apprehend the man who had it, sir." He prodded Wheat with his foot. "We took it. He's a murderer, and probably the man who killed Dr. Ranga Rao."

Shepherd turned his piercing stare to Wheat, his lips thin. Wheat stared back.

"So this is the man with the balls to take on Xiong Holonautics," Shepherd mused. "And look where that's gotten him." Shepherd nodded to the security staff, and they pulled Wheat, still glowering at anyone who would make eye contact with him, to his feet.

Shepherd turned to Greene and seemed to see his wounds for the first time. He snapped his fingers at Burg. "Get the doctor down here right away." Then he put a hand to his pocket, held up a finger to Greene, and stepped away to take a phone call.

The doctor was already halfway to them—Burg had already called for her.

This was Mainprize, a small, efficient young woman. She locked eyes onto Greene's bloody arms and made straight for him.

Greene held up a hand. "I'll live. See to Mr. Karjalainen first, please." He nodded toward Juha, who still had his pistol in his hand, still pointed unmistakably at Wheat.

Mainprize obeyed. Cracking her chewing gum loudly, she knelt beside Juha, who looked surprised when she tried to take the pistol out of his hand. But he allowed her, and he didn't resist her attempts to scan him.

With Juha, it no doubt helped that she was pretty, Greene thought—but Juha wasn't watching her; he was watching Wheat being led away to the helicopter.

"Burg, did you deactivate my Spec-Trons?" Greene asked. "I lost them."

She nodded. "Revoked the credentials as soon as we realized you'd left them behind. *As per procedure*."

He hadn't meant to suggest she didn't know how to do her job, but this wasn't the time to get into it. "Of course," he said. "Thank you."

Now Mainprize returned to scan Greene.

Shepherd came back, pocketing his phone. "I'm told our armored transport has just delivered the projector safely to Xiong Tower. Well done, all."

This news brought Greene an unexpectedly large measure of relief.

Shepherd peered down at Juha, a bloody, bruised mess, in a way that made Greene wonder whether he hadn't been deliberately ignoring Juha's presence up to this point.

"Now there," Shepherd said, "is a man who earned his paycheck today."

Juha smirked through his pain. "You're goddamn right."

Mainprize cracked her gum. "He and the Chief are going to be fine, but I'd like to fix them up properly at the tower."

Shepherd looked them all over. "You don't want to do any more for them right now? I don't want any blood in my helicopter. That was a joke," he added, although Greene certainly couldn't have guessed from his face or his voice.

Small-framed though she was, Mainprize pulled Juha to his feet almost by herself, and they began to make their way up to the helicopter.

Greene moved to follow, but Shepherd took him by the shoulder in a firm grip, jerking him to a halt.

"God damn it, Greene." Shepherd's voice was like gravel. "Force field or not, I am not at all happy you left the prototype behind. And for what? To chase that thug?"

Greene bristled, tried to pass it off as pain. He was exhausted, frustrated. "Sir, Wheat is obviously a trained killer. We saw him murder Clark. Plus I thought that the company would want to ... *talk* to him about our security breach."

Shepherd's eyes bore into Greene's. Then he softened. "You're right, of course. I'm sorry. The bottom line is, you did a hell of a job. A hell of a job."

Greene allowed himself to embrace the peace of mind that tugged at him. "Thank you, sir."

Shepherd shook his head at his own thought. "I'm going to be honest with you, Chief. You know I haven't been your biggest supporter in the company. You probably know I wanted Burg in your place when you came on board."

Greene had heard the rumors, had suspected. He said nothing.

Shepherd began walking toward the escalator, and Greene followed.

"In fact," Shepherd said, "this morning, when I heard about what had happened, I had no real expectation that you would get the projector back, never mind catch Dr. Ranga Rao's killer. I didn't believe in you, Chief—I thought you were too soft. I expected you to prove that to me today. I was wrong about you. Completely wrong."

This "praise" hit Greene like a slap to the face, but at the same time, the knowledge that his status within the company had improved immeasurably in the last twenty-four hours did not escape him.

Greene didn't know what to say. For him, another "Thank you, sir" would be vacuous and, worse, a validation of Shepherd's low expectations. At the same time, Greene didn't want to come across as unappreciative.

So he said nothing, and they rode up the escalator in silence. This didn't appear to bother Shepherd—now that Xiong's golden egg was back in the fold, the man no doubt had better things to do than chitchat with the rank and file. And it remained to be seen whether Greene would yet get a reprimand or worse for the company's loss of the projector in the first place.

As they ascended, Greene looked back at where they'd waited and was surprised by how much blood he could see—his, Juha's, Wheat's.

He and Juha had bled across half the city today, Greene thought.

They reached the top level of the shopping bowl. Burg and her team were in front of the helicopter, making ready to secure their prisoner aboard. Wheat stared vacantly into the sky. Mainprize was still fussing over Juha, apparently trying to get him to take his backpack off. Juha's own eyes were still locked onto Wheat; God only knew what he was thinking about.

As Greene walked toward the helicopter, his thoughts shifted to the tasks ahead of him. With the projector secured, the next order of business was to figure out exactly how Clark, Wheat, and whoever else had gotten into and out of Xiong Tower. They had the broad strokes of this already, and Greene didn't anticipate undue difficulty on this front—the challenge would be to ensure that such a thing never happened again. At the rate Xiong's progress with holography was going, it was going to be challenging to keep—

The rifle shot reverberated throughout the shopping bowl, startlingly loud even over the low drone of the idling helicopter's rotors.

Greene reflexively threw himself on top of Shepherd, knocking them both to the ground. With a fresh burst of adrenaline, Greene bounced up again almost immediately, half-dragging Shepherd toward the cover of the helicopter and then shoving him roughly aboard.

There was no second shot—at least, not yet.

Greene thought he'd seen a red flash of blood in his peripheral vision, but in the chaos of panicked shoppers and with the Xiong security team spread around the shopping bowl, he wasn't sure what had happened.

His instinct was that Shepherd was the target—a belated rescue operation by Wheat's associates, perhaps, or an escalation of hostilities against Xiong's upper echelon.

With Shepherd secured, Greene quickly took in the situation. Weapons ready, Burg and two team members had taken up strategic positions around the helicopter. Wheat lay facedown in a rapidly expanding pool of blood—one Greene realized he'd just tromped through—and Mainprize was kneeling over him. Juha was still leaning against the helicopter, looking up into the cityscape with an expression of curiosity on his face.

Shoving Juha clear of the helicopter, Greene turned to the pilot and jerked his thumb upward. "Get Shepherd out of here!"

Shepherd, who now had Wheat's blood on his shoes and Greene's on his once-immaculate jacket, clapped the pilot on the shoulder. "Don't you do it! I'm not going to leave my people in danger. I've had enough of being pushed around by these fuckers. Give me a gun!"

Greene was taken aback. "Sir!"

Grabbing the pilot's sidearm from him, Shepherd shoved his way off the helicopter.

Greene set his jaw and followed. If Shepherd got killed on his watch ...

But no second shot came, and after a tense, interminable minute, Greene ordered the team to stand down.

"Wheat is dead," Mainprize told them. "The bullet went through his jaw, then his neck. Tore through the artery. There was nothing I could do. I'm sorry."

"God damn it." Juha took several steps away from the helicopter, turned his face upward, and flipped two middle fingers to the sky. "After all the ludicrous shit we just went through. What a goddamned waste of my time."

Greene found a bottle of water in the helicopter and guzzled it in one draught. Then he looked up at the forest of towering buildings above them, which obscured all but a thin corridor of sky. Thousands of windows.

"Burg, did you see where the shot came from? Anybody?"

Nobody had. Not that it would do them any good—the shooter was undoubtedly long gone.

Shepherd gripped Greene's arm and jerked his head at the bystanders accumulating around the helicopter, many of whom, of course, had their phones out and were recording. "Get this body covered up right away. And it's probably too damn late, but have your people do a phone sweep. We don't need this kind of publicity. Not again."

"Yes, sir," Greene said, and gave the order.

Having given Shepherd a broad-strokes recap of the day's events, Greene tried without much success to make himself comfortable on the flight back to Xiong Tower. He was wedged awkwardly between Shepherd and Juha; Shepherd's shoulder rested uncomfortably against his wounded arm, and Greene made his best effort to ignore it. The vibration of the aircraft lulled him, but it wouldn't do to fall asleep on top of his boss.

Juha clearly had no such compunctions. He leaned against the side of the craft, eyes closed, hugging his backpack on his lap. It didn't seem to bother him that his feet rested on Wheat's tarp-enshrouded body.

And why would it? Greene very nearly smiled to himself. God, he was tired. He took a deep breath and adjusted the bag of confiscated phones between his legs. These would be purged of any photos, videos, and other media relating to Xiong's operation and then returned. Eventually.

The material already posted online, though, would be more difficult to expunge. The law was on Xiong's side, of course—their army of lobbyists saw to that—but chasing all of it down was like trying to capture a hundred ants after overturning their rock. The media conglomerates were a heavyweight opponent—they made everything more difficult.

Feeling thankful he wasn't actively involved in Xiong's PR, Greene shifted in his seat, trying to avoid touching Wheat's cadaver. But his eyes kept returning to the black tarp.

He felt regret for Wheat's death in a general, casual way, as he would for the death of any man who'd been murdered in cold blood. But he remembered how Wheat had nearly killed him, how Wheat had butchered Clark, cut him in half ... Greene struggled to force the image from his mind. But mostly, Greene couldn't help but think that Juha was right—after everything they'd gone through, it really was a waste.

Shepherd leaned close to be heard over the noise of the helicopter, pressing painfully against Greene's arm. "When we get back, the press is going to want to talk to you."

Greene nodded. That was standard whenever Xiong had to come out of the tower and make a mess, and one of the least enjoyable parts of his job.

"I'm not going to let them," Shepherd continued. "Because you look like hell. And not in a way that would get us any popular support—more like a 'we don't have our shit together' kind of way, and we can't have that. I'll have you talk to them tomorrow, after you get cleaned up. We'll get a statement written for you."

"Yes, sir." Greene would just as soon have skipped the whole thing.

In the past, before Greene had come on board, it had been easier. But the press had caught Xiong giving them holograms to talk to a few too many times, and Xiong had spent hard to shed the label of an unscrupulous corporate titan—however apt that descriptor was.

Shepherd seemed to be thinking along the same lines. "Those ungrateful bastards need to learn to be happy with what they get."

"Yes, sir."

Shepherd smoothed his hair. "At least there were no civilian casualties. That's a real break. Very well done on that front, Chief."

"Thank you, sir."

Shepherd closed his eyes and took a deep breath. "We don't always have to be rivals with them, why don't they understand that? I don't know why they get so bent out of shape about talking to holograms. The message isn't any different. Much as I would love to run you out there today, I can't. But someday we'll be able to give the solid projections a more natural feel."

"What about projecting a hologram right over you?" Greene asked. "One that looks like you? Then you could be there and look put together."

"We're working on it, believe me. It's not ready yet, though. Ghosting's a real problem. We can solve arm movement issues with a motion-capture suit, but we haven't gotten the mouth right yet. That split second of difference between the man and the projection—talking can get blurry, odd looking. And that's what everybody would be focused on, obviously. You put a man and a hologram side by side, and you can't tell the difference, but you overlay them and it doesn't look right. That's a top-secret project right now, of course."

"Yes, sir."

Shepherd turned his attention away from Greene and lapsed into thought.

Greene tried again to get comfortable. He was just starting to drowse when Shepherd pressed into him again.

"Chief, what do you think about the shooter?"

Greene sat up straight. He hadn't, really—not in the way Shepherd meant. He stared out the windshield and collected his thoughts. The tremendous golden bear that kept watch over Xiong Tower loomed directly ahead.

He could think of only one possibility. "Someone sent by Wheat's employer. Somebody who didn't want him to talk to us."

"Drastic. Why not extract him before we got there?"

Greene shook his head. "We chased Wheat halfway across town. We had him off-plan. Wheat was on his phone in the shopping center just a few minutes before it happened—he was probably calling for help."

Shepherd sneered at the tarp-covered body. "And look at the help he got. It makes me happy. Teach these assholes to fuck with us."

The helicopter descended toward the roof of Xiong Tower. An army of Xiong staff awaited them—R&D technicians, medics, and armed security. Greene spotted Garcinia, who looked inordinately pleased.

The instant the helicopter had settled on the landing pad, Shepherd was out of his seat and opening the door.

"Get yourself fixed up," he said to Greene. "Then we'll talk some more."

"Yes, sir."

Juha was snoring. Greene nudged him.

"Five more minutes," Juha muttered, not opening his eyes.

Greene raised his hand to thump him on the leg, but stopped. Let him rest; let the medics coax or drag him out.

Greene picked up the bag of phones, then stepped out of the helicopter. His muscles were starting to stiffen. He went down the steps to the roof and handed Garcinia the force field jackhammer.

"Thank you for taking care of it, dear," she said. "I hope it was helpful to you."

"Oh, yes." Greene thought again of the claustrophobic, crushing force fields Wheat had trapped them in. "It probably saved my life."

Garcinia clasped his hand with hers. "Wonderful. But are you all right? You look like you've had quite a rough day."

"I'll be all right. I—" Greene heard the snap of Mainprize's gum behind him and felt a tug on his vest. "I'm sorry, excuse me."

"That's quite all right, dear. It's good to have you back in one piece, that's all."

Greene nodded his thanks, then turned and surrendered himself to Xiong's swarming medical team.

TEN

Greene let the quiet solitude of his office wash over him. He removed the holster from his hip and dropped the heat ray onto the desk. Then he sank into his chair and stared out the window.

The sun was just beginning to set over the glittering cityscape, sending rays of glare into the office. The plate glass window tinted automatically in response.

Greene scratched at the bandages that swathed his glass-shredded arms. Medical wanted him to come back down in the morning for bioprinting.

He shuddered. Bioprinting—he could scarcely bear to sit through it, and he certainly wasn't going to go through that agony for any of his superficial injuries. Plus the new skin they'd grow for him would be pale and hairless—his arms wouldn't look right for two weeks at a minimum.

He crossed his arms without thinking about it, and his bullet wound reminded him of its existence with a lance of pain through his arm. For that, at least, he could probably endure a little bioprinting.

Greene turned to his console and pulled up the sizable quantity of paperwork accrued from the day's events. He worked for a while, but when he realized he'd been staring blankly at the screen for several minutes, he switched it off. The work would keep. Right now, he wanted to go home, see Nisha, and have a cup of tea.

He was in the act of mustering the energy to stand when there came a knock on the half-open door.

Greene pivoted in his chair, was on his feet immediately. "Mrs. Ranga Rao."

Marlena wore the same clothes she'd been in—dear God, had it really been this morning?—but with her expensive jacket over one arm. Her hair was mussed, and she looked exhausted.

Even so, her presence seemed to make the room shrink around them. It was no wonder Juha carried a never-ending infatuation with her.

She stood in the doorway. "I'm sorry to disturb you, Chief."

"Not at all. Come in. Please sit down."

Greene motioned to a chair, and Marlena sat, draping her jacket over his other chair. She waited until he had returned to his seat before she spoke.

Her lips were thin and her eyes were hard. "I wanted to thank you. For getting the man who killed my husband. Wheat."

Greene gave her a polite smile. "Just doing my job."

"You don't have to use clichés with me, Chief. I know how you left the projector to go after him. And you got him. Thank you."

All that had been in Greene's mind at the time was Juha's safety, not whatever promise he'd made to Marlena this morning or any noble lust for justice.

"Chief, this man who died at the Galleria Arcade—Wheat—you're sure he's the one who killed Raj?"

Greene took a deep breath and let it out slowly. "We believe he killed Dr. Ranga Rao, yes."

"You're not sure?"

Greene leaned back in his chair, smoothing the bandages on one arm. "If it wasn't him, then it was an associate of his, but I'd like to think it's only a matter of confirming our suspicions at this point. We know he was directly involved in the theft of the prototype. We believe he was in the building; if so, then he was directly involved in the death of your husband. The man who helped him get inside, Clark, is dead as well."

"Clark? I know Clark. Knew. You mean to tell me—" She shuddered. "That son of a bitch." Her face grew pale.

Greene leaned forward. "Mrs. Ranga Rao, are you— Should you be here right now?"

She studied him a moment, then turned her palms up. "Probably not. But what am I supposed to do? It's so horrible I can't stand to think about it. I've just been trying to work, to stay busy. To keep my mind off of it. Better to be here, where so many people are, than to go back home to an empty house and be alone."

Greene was reasonably certain this wasn't the healthiest course of action, but he wasn't sure how best to respond, or whether he even should.

"Do you have anywhere you can go?" he finally asked.

"I don't have any family in town, if that's what you mean. Don't worry, I'm not the hand-fluttering, fainting type." She straightened in her chair. "I'll manage. How are you? Are you all right?"

Greene wasn't at all sure that was so, but he decided not to push the issue, allowed her to change the subject. "I'm fine. I'll live. I've been hurt a lot worse."

"And Juha? Is he okay?"

"Did you see him?"

"Only in passing. He looked like he was in pretty bad shape."

Greene tried to inject some warmth into his smile. "Today beat him down from start to finish. But I'm told he'll make a full recovery. He's still down in Medical, I think, getting all that glass picked out of his face."

"Chief ..." she hesitated. "You have a reputation for being honest. You have as long as I've known you. May I ask you a question?"

"Of course."

"What happened with Juha? With his wife, I mean."

Perhaps because of his fatigue, the question took Greene by surprise.

"I never expected I'd see him again," Marlena said. "And now he's like a completely different person."

No, Greene thought, the change was only skin-deep. Beneath his startlingly different appearance, he was the same old Juha.

He tried to deflect. "Surely you've read up about it already."

"Sure. I know what the old news articles say about it. I want to hear your take. You were his partner then, right?"

"Right."

"Do you mind?"

"No. I don't mind." Greene dredged up memories he'd left alone for years, difficult memories. "Three years ago, almost four, Juha and Hana went out to Square Lake to spend a week, just the two of them. Cabin, mountains, forest, fishing, nature, the works."

"Sounds nice."

"On the morning of the third day, she went missing. Juha said that they'd had a fight, that she'd gone out in a canoe by herself to do some fishing and get some space—she was a real nature type, you know. The rescue drones tracked down the canoe that afternoon. They found her body in the lake two days later."

"Oh, God."

"Juha and I had just solved the Hollow Hills case, and we'd been in the news a bit, so the media jumped all over this."

Greene paused. He didn't mind sharing these things with her, but he had reservations about telling her about them *now*. It couldn't be good for her grief process. But she'd already read the news archives, she'd said, and he didn't know how to extricate himself otherwise, so he continued.

"Hana drowned, the coroner said. But she also had a head wound consistent with being struck with a blunt object—a paddle, some theorized—and a piece of fishing line was wrapped around one of her ankles. Something like twelve times. The media ran down the field with the idea that he'd murdered her. There were plenty of other ideas, from the reasonable—that the canoe hit a log and capsized—to complete speculation—that she'd used the fishing line to tie a weight to herself and then committed suicide. One station even decided she'd been murdered by eagle poachers. Would you like a glass of water? Something else?"

"I'm fine, thank you."

Greene nodded. "The investigation was public, and ugly. Ultimately, it was ruled an accidental drowning. Juha was cleared completely. But he'd been suspended with pay the whole time this was going on, and he was unequivocally convicted in the court of public opinion. When it was over, he didn't want to come back to the department, and they didn't really want him back either. So he went to Mars."

Marlena seemed to be hanging on his every word. "What about his motive? Your opinion."

Greene puffed air through his cheeks. "He was dealing with a lot of stress then. Hollow Hills was tough on him. It was a high-profile case, and he was in charge of the investigation. He was under a lot of pressure. You know he internalizes all his emotions. He was drinking a lot then, too—never on the job, though—but he did a good job keeping it from most everyone. At some point during the case, he became convinced that Hana was having an affair."

"Was she?"

"I don't know. He never had any hard evidence that I knew about, but he seemed very sure. The media circulated that story, too, afterward, but most of it was just the worst sort of conjecture."

Marlena processed this. "And what do you think?"

"I don't know. She never really seemed like the type, although of course that doesn't really mean anything. I guess it's possible. I know they'd been having a rough time—they went to the lake to try to make things better."

"How long were they married?"

"Almost five years."

Marlena chewed on this a moment. "Chief ... do *you* think he killed her?"

There at last was the question he'd been waiting for. And he didn't have an answer ready.

Greene sat in silence. His hand went up to touch the welt on his head. He stared at a spot on the desk right in front of him. Finally, he raised his head and looked her in the eye. "I don't know."

She raised her eyebrows. "Really, Chief?"

"You asked. I'm being honest."

"Maybe. You're also prevaricating. If you had to bet?"

Greene shook his head. "I wouldn't want to. Mrs. Ranga Rao, why are you asking about all this?"

She got a faraway look in her eyes. "You know that Juha and I go way back. He was always so charming, in spite of his flaws. When we were in school, I always wondered if he—" She waved a hand. "I never imagined I'd see him again. And today of all days."

Greene thought of the old photo of her on Juha's dresser, wondered what she would think of it.

"We wouldn't have gotten Wheat without him," Greene said. "Or recovered the projector. There's no way."

"I'm grateful to him. And to you."

Greene couldn't come up with a reply that wasn't a platitude, so he simply said, "You're very welcome."

They sat in silence together for several moments.

Finally, Greene cleared his throat and straightened in his chair, wishing there were some papers on his desk for him to shuffle. He hated to abandon her, but ...

"Mrs. Ranga Rao, is there something else I can do for you?" he asked.

She looked up as if from a reverie. "Oh, I'm sorry, Chief. I don't mean to keep you." She stood and retrieved her jacket.

Greene rose as well. "Can I call someone to give you a ride home?"

"Certainly not. I'm bereaved, not an invalid." Marlena moved toward the door, and he followed.

They stepped into the hallway, and Greene locked his office. "Then let me walk you to your car, at least."

"No thank you. As I said, I'm not too keen on the idea of going home right now."

Was she going to stay here all night? It would have been impolitic to ask. Greene gave up. "All right. But if you need anything at all, please let me know."

Marlena gave him a smile, warm and genuine. "Thank you, Chief. For everything."

Greene nodded, then turned away from her and walked toward the elevators, using his phone to summon a company car to take him home. As soon as the elevator deposited him in the lobby, he was accosted by Max Fill, who inserted himself immediately into Greene's personal space.

Fill, grinning, had an energy that made Greene feel somehow even more tired. "Hello, Chief! I was hoping to catch you."

Greene headed for the exit, willing the man to vanish. "I'm heading out for the day, Fill."

"Yes, well, PR never sleeps, you know. Especially on a day like today. A phoenix from the ashes today, Chief, thanks to you. Victory from the jaws of defeat! I'm putting some promotions together to celebrate today's company triumphs, and I require your participation."

"Not today, Fill."

Fill switched to his ingratiating smile. "Of course not, Chief. Off you go to your well-earned rest. Tomorrow."

Greene thought of the work that lay ahead. "Probably not."

"Friday, at the latest, then." Fill's tone became petulant. "It needs to be soon, Chief."

Greene stopped at the security checkpoint. "Use the hologram and the voice modulator."

Fill's lip curled. "Now, Chief, you know it's just not the same. I need some spark! Some pizazz! And those bandages on your arms are a wonderful touch, we must use them. How long are you going to be wearing them? Never mind, doesn't matter—we can always put some fresh ones on you."

"Goodnight, Fill," Greene said, and left.

* * * * *

Greene bulled through the horde of media standing between him and the elevators in his apartment lobby. The reporters were undaunted, however, by his refusal to make eye contact with any of them, and they bombarded him with questions they must have known he wouldn't answer.

"Mr. Greene, would you give us a statement on the murder of—"

"What was the technology stolen—"

"Who was the man killed today at the—"

They gave way before Greene, knowing they weren't allowed to touch him, and he reached the safe haven of the elevator without so much as a "no comment." When the doors closed, he still had his back to them, was still ignoring their inane questions.

Greene rode the elevator up, and when he saw the front door of his apartment, he began to relax. He completed the retina scan, then the chip scan, and the bolt retracted.

He pushed the door open and stepped inside. The spartan entryway, which featured a small wooden bench and plain white walls, upon which hung only one simple cross, was a welcome respite from the relentless sensory overload of Portsmith and Xiong Holonautics.

Greene sat down and pulled off his boots and socks. His sore feet blessedly free of their confines, he went into the windowless living area. Mother's favorite program was running.

The living room—the only one in his apartment equipped with projectors—had become a balcony overlooking the hill station of Munnar in southwest India. On three walls and the ceiling, the bright moonlit and star-spangled sky—the program followed Portsmith's day/night cycle—cast its light on an undulating valley covered with tea plantations, whose concentric lines formed mesmerizing geometric designs. The valley ran up on either side to thickly forested hills. In the distance, a single mountain loomed over the valley. A parade of elephants foraged on a far-off hilltop.

The projection of the balcony itself incorporated Greene's actual furnishings. The balcony was mounted high on a massive fortress, all turrets and bastions. The fourth wall, the one holding the doorway that led to the rest of the house, was ancient red sandstone.

In addition to the lifelike animation of the animals and breeze through the tea plants, the program featured sound effects that included the rustling of leaves, the cawing of birds, and the occasional cry of a monkey. In all, it was an exquisite presentation from Xiong's latest line.

Greene sank into his armchair and propped his legs up on the coffee table. He gazed into the starry sky, listening to the leaves rustle. A flock of birds flew across the moon.

The sealed door to the kitchen hissed open, and the potent scent of frying onions was upon him immediately, enticing. Greene's stomach clenched violently, and he realized how little he'd eaten today.

The door hissed closed again, and Nisha appeared on the balcony. She came to his chair and handed him a cup of tea. "Hi, Green."

He took it. "Hi, baby. Thank you." Nisha had her hair up in a bun, the way he liked it, and she was wearing an outfit he hadn't seen before—another new piece of maternity wear, no doubt—that flattered her slender frame but accentuated just how large her belly was growing.

Greene put his tea down, rose, and took her in his arms.

Nisha returned his embrace. "Was your day that bad?"

Chuckling, he released her. "Pretty bad."

"Want to talk about it?" Then she saw his arms. "What happened? Are you okay?"

"I'm fine. Really. It's nothing serious."

She studied his face, believed him. "Do you want to talk about it, or do you need a few minutes?"

"Maybe I'll decompress until dinner."

"It won't be long. Your mom's been in a cooking frenzy all day. She even sent the maid home because she kept getting underfoot. Do you want some Pain-Kill?"

"Maybe just one."

Greene settled back into his chair, and she brought it to him, then left him in peace.

Heavy on milk and sugar, his tea was an elixir for his exhaustion. He sipped it, watched the scenery, and tried to unwind. Working together, the visuals, the sound effects, and the gentle breeze from the ceiling fan almost made him feel like he was outside—almost. Greene typically found this program relaxing, but tonight it wasn't sitting well with him. The stars were a bit too bright, the landscape a bit too stylized, the wildlife a bit too conspicuous. The real Red Fort was 2,500 kilometers from Munnar. It wasn't a problem he typically had, but tonight, his disbelief would not suspend.

Max Fill would be utterly horrified to hear such a thing, he realized.

Greene switched off the program. The white walls and static framed art were much more to his liking, if only for today.

His thoughts went to tomorrow's tasks: getting to the bottom of the security breach and getting it fixed, and chasing down Wheat's employer. Pending the completion of the analysis of Clark's data, the former seemed decently straightforward, but Greene felt uneasy nevertheless, and would until all the holes were sealed.

The theft of the projector had been so clean ... *too* clean. Could Clark have done all of that himself? It was certainly within the realm of possibility, but Greene wasn't sure. No doubt the IT and software people would have something to say about that in the morning.

If not, then what? Another of Wheat's associates, someone on the inside, another Xiong employee they didn't know about— someone else owned by one of Xiong's competitors, who might be even now working to cover his or her tracks.

Greene realized his worrying mind was roaming much too far afield, and he attempted to reel it in. Xiong had a lot of good people, loyal people—the company's generous pay and punitive contract terms saw to that. A widespread infiltration of Xiong by one of its competitors was a ludicrous proposition.

The kitchen door opened again and stayed open, and he heard his mother's shuffling footsteps. The complex aroma of her cooking wafted forth: garlic, onions, chicken, curry.

"Green-kutty! Are you here?"

"In here, Mom."

He heard her laying plates on the dining room table, and he got up and went to her.

His mother was a tiny woman, and while she was somewhat heavier and slower than she used to be—although with the baggy salwar kameezes she liked to wear, how much heavier was something of a mystery even to him—she was by no means infirm. She smiled at him, the way she did every day when he came home, as though seeing him was the highlight of her day.

"Hi, Mom."

"Hello, Green-kutty. Come, let's have food. Oh! What's happened to you, Pacha?" In an instant, she was upon him, clutching his wrists and scrutinizing the bandages with the diligence of a physician.

"I'm fine, Mom, it's nothing. I just fell on some glass." That was all the explanation he planned to give her. His hair covered the bump on his head. He'd passed his concussion test, so he didn't see the need to tell her he'd been in a car accident. And he had no intention of telling her that he'd been shot, today or ever.

"Glass! Why were you falling on glass? This new job of yours is supposed to be safe!"

This dance between them was inevitable, part of the cost of having her in their home. "*Safer*, Mom. And I'm fine. Worse things happened when I was a cop, you know that."

She clucked her tongue. "Yes, I remember. How terrible it was. Come and have food."

Keeping him well fed was one of the few areas where Greene still allowed his mother control over his life, and she exerted this power to the full. It seemed to keep her from worrying about him, at least outwardly.

Greene obediently sat at the dining table, eagerly anticipating his dinner.

But the expression on his face apparently wasn't right, because his mother said, "Green-kutty, are you troubled?"

"No, Mom. I'm fine. I just have a lot to do tomorrow."

She patted his hand. "I'll bring the food and then you'll feel better, Pacha. Tomorrow will worry about itself."

Yes, Greene thought, it certainly would.

ELEVEN

"Green. Green."

Someone was shaking him. Greene was doing a fine job of ignoring it when the lamp went on, painfully bright even through closed eyelids.

"Green." A poke in his side made him flinch.

He clawed his way up from fuzzy oblivion and found himself in his bed, with Nisha sitting beside him, wry amusement on her face, and his alarm blaring.

He peered at the alarm, then switched it off. "6:03? It's really been going off for three minutes?"

Nisha nodded. "Full blast."

"Oh. Sorry." Greene rubbed his face. He couldn't remember ever having been so tired. Consciousness was proving as difficult to maintain as it had been to achieve.

"I was going to try to shove you out of bed next," Nisha said. "I was already up. I forgot my morning sickness pill last night."

"Sorry." Greene swung his legs over the side of the bed and stood—approximately. He was a mass of cramped and knotted muscles wobbling on over-used and damaged hips and legs. His stiff lower back kept him from straightening fully, and his hamstrings felt like rigid plastic.

"Another minute or two of that and we probably would have your mom in here worried that you'd died in your sleep," Nisha said.

With an amused grunt, Greene dragged himself to the bathroom. His eyes were gummed half shut. He splashed cold water on his face, but it didn't really help.

"Don't worry, I'm fine now," Nisha said from the bedroom. "You, on the other hand, look terrible. Can you take the day off?"

Greene examined himself in the mirror, and what he saw matched how he felt. A patchwork of bruises covered his neck, chest, arms, legs, and torso ... the worst, of course, was his left arm, which was purple-black from the shoulder to the elbow.

"No. I can't. As appealing as that sounds." He didn't dare. All the eyes of Xiong would still be on him today, of that he had no doubt.

He opened the medicine cabinet and took two Pain-Kills and a Pain-Flex. "Do we have any A-Gone-Y?"

"I don't know. It would be in there."

He didn't see any, but he found a Power-Through inhaler, and he took several puffs from it. He pulled off his shorts, slapped a waterproof patch over his bullet wound, and climbed into the shower, wondering not for the first time whether there was enough space for him to get a tiny coffee maker for the shelf in here.

Nisha came into the bathroom. "You know, I think I'm doing a pretty good job of keeping it together, but I'm worried about you. I'm trying to have a baby here. I can't have you getting killed on me. When you took this job, you said it wasn't going to be dangerous."

Greene distinctly recalled having told her that it was *much less* dangerous, but this wasn't a hill he cared to battle her on.

"Yesterday was an extreme outlier," he said. "In the three months I've been there, the worst thing that's happened was when Pendarvis Wisconsin accidentally shot me in the back with a rubber slug during training."

Greene hadn't thought of Wisconsin in months. In spite of Greene's attempts to mitigate Xiong's disciplinary actions against him, Wisconsin had been reassigned indefinitely to maintenance, where he still languished. Wisconsin's contract prevented him from quitting, or he undoubtedly would have long ago.

"All right," Nisha said around her toothbrush. "But how do I know this isn't going to happen again?"

"It happened because we had a breach," Greene said. "It's completely out of the ordinary."

"Is it? How do you know you won't have another breach next week or next month?" Her tone was mostly calm, only slightly accusatory. She gargled.

Greene found himself clenching his teeth, although none of his frustration was directed at her. "Obviously, I don't. I guess whether we have another one depends on how well I do my job, doesn't it? I do have a vested interest in ensuring my personal safety, you know."

Nisha spat. "So ... how close did you come to dying yesterday?"

Greene opened his mouth, then closed it again. If the shower curtain hadn't been between them, he would have given her a look that would only have increased the amount of grief she was giving him. In recounting yesterday's events, he'd glossed over the worst of it, but of course he couldn't hide the damage to his body from her.

"What kind of question is that?" he finally said, because he wasn't sure of the answer himself.

"Did you almost die? Was there a chance?"

There's always a chance, every day, he almost said, but that would have been foolish. "A much better chance than most days," he admitted.

"And how do you feel about that?" She was facing the shower now.

"I was a police officer in this town for long enough that it's not an entirely unfamiliar feeling."

"You didn't answer the question."

Greene had finished washing and was leaning against the cool wall, immobilized by the comfort of the steaming water cascading over him. She wanted to talk about feelings, to give him an opportunity to open up about how scared and angry and vulnerable he felt. He appreciated the sentiment, but he was going to pass. Even if he'd had the inclination, he didn't have the energy.

"I don't know how to answer the question," he said. "It's part of the job. We knew that coming in. It's one of the reasons I get paid so well. You know that."

"I know. It's just ... I haven't had to worry about you in this job, and now I do."

"Good thing we have plenty of life insurance."

She let out a sound of exasperation. "Green!"

No, all of this was because *she* was scared and angry and vulnerable, he realized, and she was looking for him to affirm that.

"Nisha, I'm sorry. Yesterday was a one-time deal, honest. I know it's not easy for you. It's not easy for me either. I know you worry about me. I worry about you. And the baby."

This seemed to appease her, and she didn't press him further.

Turning off the shower required a supreme act of will. Greene climbed out, still stiff but feeling better—the meds were kicking in.

He dressed in a suit, forgoing the tie today, and went to the kitchen, where he threw back a cup of too-hot coffee and fixed himself another for the road. Then he went down to the garage and got into his Xiong loaner car, which was nearly identical to the one he'd destroyed yesterday. All his user preferences had been ported over, but the seat was harder, not quite as broken in.

As the car drove him to work, new files popped up on the windshield display for his review. But in spite of the coffee and his attempts to focus, he found himself waking from a doze when the car stopped in front of Xiong Tower. Greene rubbed the crust from his eyes, climbed out, and dismissed the car.

As was customary, Greene bypassed the line for the security checkpoint. He went to the executive clearance station and stood on the scanner with his arms raised.

"Hell of a job yesterday, Chief," said the guard at the console. "Everybody's talking about it." This was "Thick" Rich Lather, an amateur bodybuilder, far and away the largest man in Xiong's employ.

"Thanks," Greene said. "I could have used somebody your size yesterday."

Lather grinned. "It's never too late to start lifting, Chief."

"You're right." Or to start taking steroids, Green thought. Quicker, easier. Might have come in handy yesterday. "Wait, what do you mean 'everyone'?"

Lather raised his eyebrows. "You didn't see the video?"

Well, that was no surprise. The only mystery was what stage in the process of Greene receiving a sound thrashing from a man twice his mass had been preserved for posterity.

Greene shook his head. "No, I went home and went straight to bed."

Lather laughed. "I don't blame you. Here, I'll show it to you. You're clear, by the way."

"Thanks."

Lather held out his phone, which was playing a decently stable but distant video of Greene and Juha taking cover behind their wrecked car as Wheat advanced toward them with his silent holographic machine gun.

"So badass that you took that guy down," Lather said. "I mean, look at him."

Greene handed the phone back after scarcely a glance.

Lather's brow furrowed. "You don't want to watch it?"

"Rich, I was *there*."

"Ha ha, I guess so, Chief."

Greene walked through the Xiong Tower lobby, thinking again about what else might have made it online, what might be out there that would make him look undignified. Plenty, probably. Or worse—he wouldn't want Nisha or his mother to see, for example, video of Wheat dangling him over the railing and crushing his head. He thought about going over to PR for the rundown on the amateur videos released from yesterday but decided against it. He couldn't do anything about it in any case, and then Fill would pester him to shoot those promotional clips.

As Greene rode the elevator up, he sent Nisha a message to keep his mother away from the news. That probably wasn't a significant danger; while his mother watched a lot of TV, she was interested almost exclusively in game shows and soap operas.

She particularly liked *Dead Money*, a quiz show where you could pass on as many questions as you wanted and walk away at any time, but if you missed a question, you were executed right there on television, typically in some grotesque manner. Not only was it in extremely bad taste, it was also completely fake: the contestants were all holograms—Xiong holograms. The majority of viewers, Greene thought, surely knew this, but his mother was convinced it was real, and he'd never seen the virtue in trying to tell her otherwise.

Greene's first stop was the armory. The massive steel door with *J. Kingjack - Quartermaster* emblazoned on it hissed open before his credentials. He stepped inside, and the heavy door thudded shut behind him.

A young woman in black Xiong coveralls sat at a small desk piled with boxes and digital clipboards. Greene recognized her but couldn't recall her name, nor see her name tag.

Greene cleared his throat, irritated at his lapse and at the realization that he relied too heavily on having a constant information feed at his disposal. His memory had suffered as a result. And he had come to the Armory for the sole purpose of enabling himself to perpetuate that weakened memory, he thought.

The young woman looked up from her pad, and now Greene saw her nametag: Dasgupta. Of course.

Dasgupta's first name still escaped Greene, much to his annoyance. Then he realized he'd left his coffee in the car. He resigned himself to the fact that it was going to be that kind of day. Still, he thought, likely a good bit better than yesterday.

"Hello, Chief," Dasgupta said. "What you did yesterday—that was amazing."

Greene stopped himself from shaking his head. It amazed him that so many people thought he'd done something great just because he'd gotten outside, gotten some action. But any sort of excitement tended to be big news around here, especially if it happened outside the tower.

"Thanks," Greene said. "You should have a new set of Spec-Trons for me, with all of my clearances loaded."

"Uh ... right." Dasgupta tucked a lock of hair behind her ear and began to sort through the pile on the desk. "Um ... I'm showing we should have it, but I don't see it here. I'll look for it right now if you want to wait."

Greene managed not to roll his eyes. "Bring it to my office as soon as you find it. Please."

"Yes, sir. I'll get right on it. You know, it's possible it was delivered up there already."

Sloppy. Glasses with access to that much sensitive data just floating around the building? They'd better not be. The Armory wasn't Security, wasn't directly under him, and, not for the first time, he thought that maybe it should be.

"I think that's unlikely," Greene said. "Just bring them up when you find them. Or have someone from Security bring them. No interoffice couriers."

"Yes, Chief," she said, then added defensively, "I know the protocols."

He made his face soften. "All right. Don't worry about it. Is Kingjack around?"

"He's in the magazine, Chief."

"Thanks." Greene started down the hall behind her.

The thick vault door to the magazine was open, which was a breach of protocol Greene was inclined to forgive if Kingjack was within.

With shielded and concrete-reinforced walls, floor, and ceiling, this small ammunition dump was a bunker in the midst of Xiong Tower, one designed to store primarily small arms and riot control equipment. One wall was lined with firearms; two others bore shelves containing boxes of ammunition and various types of lethal and non-lethal grenades. In the center of the room, squatting between two weapons crates, was the quartermaster.

"Hello, Jack," Greene said.

Kingjack, an older man with a bristly gray beard, was worn-looking from decades of paramilitary life but still all lean muscle. The sleeves of his coveralls were rolled up, revealing his large and veiny forearms.

Kingjack looked up, removing his Spec-Trons and massaging the bridge of his nose. "These things always give me a headache. Morning, Chief. Glad you survived your ordeal."

"Thanks, me too. What are you working on?"

Kingjack flipped open a crate, revealing a dozen black shotguns with canary-yellow stocks and fore-ends. "These are supposed to be the good ones. But we've heard that before."

"Range?"

"It'll go a hundred feet with respectable accuracy." Kingjack handed Greene one of the black-and-yellow guns. "It's a shotgun—range isn't the problem. Never has been. Eight-plus-one capacity, just like you're used to. But that's not the problem either."

Greene examined the gun, found it unremarkable except for its coloring, and handed it back. "The shock rounds."

"Naturally." Kingjack opened the other crate, fished around, and held up a barbed and finned projectile with circuitry visible within. "Now, this looks pretty much like every shock round I've ever seen, although it's supposed to give us over thirty seconds of muscle paralysis. They assure me that the failure rate is much lower."

"Fewer fatalities?"

"That too, although that's not what I meant. I don't care about the fatalities. I care about when you shoot somebody and the round doesn't do a damn thing. Penetration, consistent delivery of the shock ... and now they've got the voltage so low ... Chief, you could stop this round with a decently full purse, maybe even a respectably thick leather jacket."

"Jack, it's for crowd control and fleeing suspects, not a home invasion."

"Still a bunch of PR bullshit if you ask me," Kingjack replied. "Oh, the fun new grenades came in, too—plasma. Have you seen them in action? Those babies will make you redefine the word 'cover.' Come by later and I'll arrange a demonstration. Anyway, what can I do for you?"

"I came by for my new Spec-Trons. My pair got smashed yesterday."

"Yeah, I heard about that. Too bad. Would have been nice to see that action from your point of view. Suchi should have your glasses."

Suchitra—that was Dasgupta's first name. Of course. Greene wondered how he could have forgotten.

"She's looking for them. I had something else I wanted to talk to you about, too. Yesterday was the first time I've ever used the active denial pistol in the field. It works great in training, but yesterday, it really underwhelmed me."

Kingjack shook his head. "All this non-lethal bullshit. I don't know why we bother sometimes."

"Public image, stock price, you know," Greene said. He could have added "morality," but then Kingjack would have laughed at him.

"Yeah, I guess. The steady paycheck is nice. So what was the problem?"

"I couldn't bring him down."

Kingjack sat on top of the ammo crate. "You know the heat ray is designed to have a repel effect, not to incapacitate."

"I know that," Greene said. "It wasn't doing a good job of either. Wheat was a big guy—it hardly seemed to faze him at times."

"I don't think his size would have played much of a role," Kingjack replied. "You've got the Zenon III, right? You could drive a bear away with that gun, if there were any bears left. Was he on any drugs, do you know?"

"Don't know yet."

Kingjack smoothed his beard. "Probably was. A pretty heavy dose of Power-Through can give you an irresponsible resistance to pain—that includes heat. I've heard about a new version of Ligaf—you know, the street drug. It's stronger, more dangerous than Power-Through, but with much less loss of control if it works like it's supposed to. No doubt there are others."

Ligaf itself wasn't all that new, as Greene could attest from his time with the Portsmith Police Department. It was quite a drug: an assailant on a heavy dose of Ligaf was a near-unstoppable force of single-minded destruction. But if there was a new version that offered all the benefits without the berserker rage and the ripping off of one's clothes, it might fit what had happened with Wheat yesterday.

"One other thing," Kingjack said. "You might check your focus. Do you know what you've got the beam set on?"

Greene shrugged. "Max focus, probably."

"There's your problem right there. Used to laser weapons, aren't you, where you want that really tight beam. But this heat ray technology was originally developed for use in area-of-effect cannons."

"Bystanders, though," Greene said.

Kingjack rolled his eyes. "It's non-lethal. What are you worried about bystanders for? No, don't you tell me 'stock price' again. Look, Chief, the problem with a narrow-beam heat ray is that if you shoot somebody, odds are they're going to run or fall out of your line of fire, and then they're going to be more or less fine in a matter of seconds."

"So what do you suggest?" Greene asked.

"To solve your personal problem?" Kingjack scratched his jaw. "A good old-fashioned gun that shoots good old-fashioned bullets."

"Jack ..."

Kingjack held up a hand. "I know, I know, you already have one. Chief, I understand that the move toward all this non-lethal crap came from upstairs, and that it's for the Xiong bottom line. I also understand that you're a big non-lethal guy, although maybe not quite the bleeding-heart tissue-soft liberal some of us were led to believe when you came aboard. Funny how those two things happened right at the same time, huh?"

Greene wasn't sure if he'd just been insulted or not.

Kingjack rose from his crate and clapped Greene on the shoulder. "What do I suggest? Chief, if you want to run after professional killers with a heat ray, a stun gun, a water pistol, that's your business. But next time, at least take a real gun with you too, eh? Even the cops do that."

Greene left the armory feeling vaguely foolish. If he'd had a conventional firearm yesterday, they might have ended the conflict with Wheat sooner—by the time they'd reached the department store, at least. And Wheat himself would be just as dead now—but by a different hand. That mattered to Greene. Yet it had all worked out, somehow.

When he arrived at the Security offices, he was flagged down immediately by Sonnenschein at the front desk.

"Morning, Chief. I've got your Spec-Trons here. Need you to sign for them."

Greene obligingly pressed his thumb against the pad offered and was handed a small sealed box in return.

"Thanks, Sunny. Is Burg around?"

"I saw her about ten minutes ago. She said she was working on leads on Wheat's shooter. I don't know if she's left yet."

Another thumbprint on the box's sensor panel opened it. Greene put on his new Spec-Trons and booted them up. When the familiar, comforting heads-up display appeared, Greene felt a peace he hadn't realized he'd been missing.

Sonnenschein smoothed the front-most spike of her purple hair as she waited for him to finish this rite. "Sir, there's also a message for you. You're wanted in Dr. Ranga Rao's office."

"I'll go right now. What's going on? What did they find?"

"I don't know, sir." She looked apologetic. "They didn't say."

Greene handed her the empty security box. "Don't worry about it."

He returned to the elevators, wondering. Dr. Ranga Rao's office—this could only mean progress on the security breach. They must have found *something*, whether an insight into how the breach was achieved or a piece they were missing on Clark. By the time the elevator arrived, he was struggling to keep his speculation in check.

Greene arrived at Ranga Rao's office foyer. Janice, the COO's assistant, was at the desk there. Greene was surprised to see her, but supposed he shouldn't be. The work went on, and with Ranga Rao's passing, she was probably busier than ever.

Janice smiled up at him. "Hello, Chief. You can go right in."

"Thanks." Greene fought the urge to ask her what was happening. He would find out in a moment; impatience would only broadcast his ignorance.

The immense oak door to Ranga Rao's office, intricately carved with vinework, was set in an equally impressive oak doorframe. When Greene grasped the elegant bronze door handle, an odd sensation came over him. He felt uneasy here, out of place, much as he'd be at a cemetery. Entering the dead man's office would not be unlike walking across his grave. This thought made Greene feel silly.

He entered, and his shoes sank into the deep carpet. He'd only been in this office on a handful of occasions, and it impressed him every time. Nearly as large as Greene's entire apartment and twice as tall, the room was lavishly decorated, with several good-sized trees in planters, various flowering shrubs, and a water feature that ran the entire length of the room and contained at least a dozen fat koi. It was all real, no holograms, or so he understood.

The tall plate glass windows' auto-tint function was switched off, and with the glare from the morning sun, it took Greene a moment to notice the man behind the monolithic mahogany desk at the far end of the room.

Smiling broadly, the recently murdered Dr. Ranga Rao, dressed in a brown suit, striped shirt, and navy tie, rose from his chair behind the desk and extended a welcoming hand. "Ah, Chief Greene. It's good to see you. Please come in."

TWELVE

It was all Greene could do to keep his mouth from falling open. There stood Dr. Ranga Rao, as big as life. Greene was dumbstruck.

Hologram, he thought, fighting to get his mind working again. A hologram, it had to be a hologram.

Greene detected movement out of the corner of his eye—there was another person in the room.

From an overstuffed armchair along one wall rose a towering blond man in a blue suit. It was Wheat.

Greene's hand went to his hip for his sidearm—but it was down in his office, in his desk drawer. His entire body tensed. But Wheat only nodded to Greene and remained where he was, his hands clasped in front of him.

Greene stopped himself. Hologram, of course. What else could it be but a hologram? These men were both dead. He was about to turn around, to leave the office, to demand that Janice tell him what was going on, to hold accountable whoever was responsible for this tasteless act.

Ranga Rao spread his arms wide. "I know what you're thinking, Chief. 'Holograms, holograms, holograms. Who is tormenting me with holograms, and for what purpose?'"

Greene didn't respond. Engaging with this hologram, speaking to it, would make him look and feel foolish. His eyes flicked to Wheat, who had remained where he was.

"You do not believe." Ranga Rao came around the desk and approached him, still smiling. "And I do not blame you one bit." He turned his head and spoke to Wheat. "Didn't I tell you?"

Wary, Greene remained where he was as Ranga Rao continued to approach. He wished Juha were here.

When Ranga Rao was within arm's length of Greene, he stopped, extending his hand.

Greene didn't move.

Ranga Rao said, "Chief Greene, come. Reach out your hand and touch me."

Feeling like an idiot, Greene obediently took the offered hand. To his shock, he met not with empty air, or with the strange buzz of a solid hologram, but with warm, soft flesh. He could even feel the hard gold of Ranga Rao's ring.

Greene blinked. His bewilderment was a heavy fog on his thinking. "Dr. Ranga Rao? Is it really you?"

Ranga Rao was grinning from ear to ear now. "Yes. It is I. Do not doubt, but believe."

"What— How—" was all Greene could manage.

"Yes, I know this comes as quite a shock. Why don't you come and sit down, and I'll explain everything." Ranga Rao put his arm around Greene's shoulders—the touch, the weight of a real person—and led him to a chair opposite Ranga Rao's own.

Greene was grateful to sit down. His head was spinning.

Wheat sat down again in his chair, just inside Greene's peripheral vision. Ranga Rao resumed his place behind the desk, then leaned forward, steepling his fingers.

"Would you like some tea? Coffee?"

Greene shook his head. "No thank you."

Ranga Rao looked at him sympathetically. "I know you're confused, suspicious, perhaps even angry. So I'm just going to lay this out for you as plainly as I can. Chief, it was a drill. Everything that happened yesterday was a drill. A test, if you will. And my boy, you passed with flying colors! Absolutely flying colors. I simply couldn't be more pleased."

"A drill ..." Greene repeated, trying to wrap his mind around it. How could that be?

"I'm afraid so." Ranga Rao toyed with a stylus on his desk. "It's been in the works for some time. I don't know if you're aware, but there is a sizeable faction of this company, led by Lord-Is-My Shepherd, that was opposed to your hiring. Simply speaking, they didn't have confidence in your ability to head our company's security. They wanted someone with more experience, someone harder, someone with more of an edge."

There it was—what Greene had suspected, heard rumors of, now out on the table. But Greene was too confused, too leery of all that was happening, to feel the sting of the insult now.

Ranga Rao tapped the stylus rhythmically on the desk. "The theft of the projector, my 'murder'—these were a test of our security. Of *you*. And you exceeded every expectation. Not only did you recover the projector, not only did you apprehend the thief, but you also took down William Rubin's absolutely genuine bootlegging operation—something we suspected but had no definitive proof of. That was the icing on a most delicious cake."

Greene's brain had too much to process. "The breach ..."

"There was no breach," Ranga Rao said. "Or rather, there *was*, but it was a planned breach, all conducted securely in-house. Shepherd and I overrode the systems directly. There wasn't a thing you could have done about it, Chief."

Greene's first feeling at this news was relief. Everything he'd gone to bed worried about last night, everything he'd woken up concerned about this morning, was fiction, now washed away. But his sense of ease quickly dissolved into dread. That such a large-scale clandestine operation could go on without his knowledge—that they would put him through all of this—it was the Xiong way, he knew, but he'd never expected to be on the receiving end of that sort of treatment.

Foolish of him.

"We know you run a tight ship around here, Chief," Ranga Rao said. "But we wanted to see how you handled a crisis. And you have put every concern to rest."

Greene recovered the ability to form coherent sentences, although his voice was harder than he meant it to be. "A test, sir? People died."

Ranga Rao laughed. He reached across the desk and patted Greene with his hand. "Did they? Here I am, alive and whole. And there sits Mister Wheat, upright and in one piece. Mister Clark is in a likewise condition, I assure you."

"How?"

"As you might expect. Actors—not Rubin, of course, but Clark and Mister Wheat here. Props. Squibs." Ranga Rao turned his hands palm-up, indicating the building around them. "And holograms, of course."

Unsure what to think, what to feel, Greene found himself fighting down anger. "What about us? Juha and I almost died." He glared at Wheat. "He shot me, and not with any blanks."

Wheat remained still in his chair, holding eye contact, a placid expression on his face.

Ranga Rao took a deep breath and let it out as a heavy sigh. "Yes, it was all rather dramatic. I'm sorry for that. It couldn't be helped. I didn't want this test to be so ... over the top, but Shepherd insisted on no safeties. We couldn't allow you to get any hint that it was a drill. It's in your contract, you know."

Greene knew. A Xiong contract wasn't *quite* carte blanche, but it was within throwing distance. It was common knowledge that if you wanted affirmation in your work, or to be treated as a valued employee, or job security, you didn't work for Xiong;

Greene had known all this coming in. He'd jumped at the job because of the amazing pay and the high level of occupational prestige that came with it. Greene had known he didn't have the universal support of Xiong's powerbrokers, that they saw him as utterly replaceable—not unlike how they saw most of their employees. But this drill ... All of this, just for him? He never could have imagined it in his wildest dreams.

"Again, I am sorry for all of this, Chief," Ranga Rao said. "You'll be receiving a generous hazard bonus in your next paycheck. Very well earned."

Greene hung at the verge of speaking but couldn't decide what to say. For a moment, he and Ranga Rao simply looked at each other.

Ranga Rao interlaced his fingers. "I understand you're probably feeling confused. Possibly even betrayed."

Betrayed? Greene thought. That was putting it mildly. His employer had, in as many words, tried to kill him.

"Mister Wheat is the independent contractor we brought in to develop and execute our scenario. I assure you that none of your security staff was involved in this drill in any way. It wouldn't have been an accurate test of their abilities otherwise. Ms. Burg in particular did some very nice work on this end hunting up our trail. I don't want you to go back to your duties with any mistrust of your people whatsoever. The very last thing we want to do is undermine your leadership here."

That, at least, was something.

"You impressed a lot of people yesterday, Chief. A lot of people. I think you'll find that your standing has improved considerably, not only within your own department, but throughout the company as well."

Greene wasn't happy that this improvement had needed to happen in first place, and his pride wasn't yet ready to allow him to accept this as good news—which, as his rational mind well knew, it definitely was.

Something was tugging at Greene's mind, and he articulated it. "Sir, with respect, everything that happened yesterday—I don't see how that helps the company. The media coverage of the break-in and the murder, all the public damage that was caused..." He gave Wheat another hard look, and Wheat again ignored it. "Isn't this just a lot of bad PR for the company?"

Ranga Rao waved a hand. "Nonsense. Bad PR? Couldn't be farther from the truth. It's good PR all around."

Greene failed to conceal his puzzlement.

"Chief, consider what the public is waking up to today. Obviously we're not going to tell them that it was a drill, or that I was 'murdered.'"

"But the police were here. They think you were killed. Or were those your operatives as well?"

"No, those were indeed the real police. One of our zealous and diligent employees saw my 'body' and called them. But the police are as corrupt as they come—no offense to you or to any of our other fine security staff who have served in that capacity. Dealing with their presence merely added to our operating costs, shall we say, for this enterprise. Besides, who would believe them over us when I'm right here, warm-blooded and breathing?"

Greene wanted to ask how they'd convinced the police as far as the body was concerned, whether all it really took these days was money. But Ranga Rao had moved on.

"Now then, the good PR." Ranga Rao ticked off his points on his fingers. "One: Xiong has shown itself to be unrobbable. In the sense of getting away with it, at least. Because two: our security is the best. Three: no casualties."

"Clark looks like a casualty," Greene said.

"Yes, I suppose he would—if there were any media looking. Check the networks if you like—you won't see any stories about the grisly murder of a Xiong employee by some vicious killer, because it was staged, and no sooner had you left that scene than we cleaned it up. That leads me to—what point am I on? Four: Xiong is a good civic partner. Yes, some damage was caused to public and private property as Xiong security forces heroically brought down a dangerous criminal. And Xiong Holonautics will, of course, be more than happy to pay for that damage, to rebuild, bigger and better, to sponsor local events and promotions. And everyone will be happy with those arrangements because no one died and no one was even seriously injured."

Greene considered this logic.

"You see, Chief, we know very well that the public sees us as, to at least some extent, above the law, an independent force, a Big Brother, a bully at times. Because in the past, we have been all of those. This company has done some things I'm not proud of. But we enjoy the latitude we've achieved, and we've invested a great deal to earn it, and so there's really no sense trying to fight that perception at this point. We've decided it's better to show people that we're a force for good. A friend of Portsmith. A solution rather than a problem. And you know, most people would like to believe that anyway because we provide them with products and services that so greatly benefit their daily lives."

"All right. But isn't all of this still costing our company a lot of money?" Greene wasn't arguing, only seeking to understand.

"Reputation capital isn't your thing, Chief? Very well. Point five: social media is aflame with rumors about our amazing new technology. We started most of them, of course, but the amateur videos of you at the Galleria feed the hype. It's fantastic stuff, it truly is. As long as Xiong wins in the end, it's good to have some of that material out there on its own, spreading organically. Xiong stock is higher now than when it opened yesterday. Billions of eyes are on our company today. There's a special excitement about us. Do you see, Chief? We factored all of this in when we put our scenario together, and it's really come together marvelously."

"I see."

Yes, Greene saw. Lies. Lies and half-truths. It was Xiong multitasking at its finest: a performance evaluation, a spectacle, mayhem, a PR boost, and a stock price bump all rolled into one.

"Well, that's all, Chief," Ranga Rao said. "We've got you up to speed now. Addressed everything, I think. No loose ends? As hard as this might be for you to accept right now, it's back to business as usual going forward."

Everything resolved. Business as usual. It was extremely hard to accept. The change in Greene's thought process was slow, difficult, cumbersome. The turmoil within him must have been obvious to Ranga Rao.

"Chief, you've got a lot to process, I know. Perfectly understandable. And I'm sorry we had to put you through all that." Ranga Rao snapped his fingers. "I know: why don't you take the rest of the day off? Come back fresh tomorrow. You've earned it."

Greene nodded and stood. "Thank you, sir." Then he added, "I'm very glad you're alive, sir."

Ranga Rao rose as well and shook Greene's hand, smiling. "As am I, I assure you. Good day, Chief."

Greene turned to leave, his thoughts in chaos. Wheat hadn't budged from his chair, and it occurred to Greene that he'd never heard the man utter a single word, either today or yesterday.

He left the office, unable to reconcile his feelings of betrayal—the huge knife that Xiong had stuck in his back—with the fact that his standing within the company had never been higher. It was his pride, he figured—he'd be better off if he could get over it.

Burg was seated in Ranga Rao's office foyer, and she looked surprised to see him. "What's going on, Chief?"

Greene opened his mouth, closed it, found himself just shaking his head.

"Sir?" In her voice and her eyes were a concern and perhaps even a respect that he was unaccustomed to.

"Let's talk later, Burg. After he explains everything to you."

She looked confused. "'He'?"

By way of reply, Greene only shook his head again. He boarded the elevator, reflexively asked for Security, then corrected himself. "Lobby."

Greene used his phone to summon his car to the front of the building. His mind was racing, and he couldn't rein it in. He had, apparently, nothing to worry about—there was no breach, no shooter, no trouble of any sort. Yet he found himself worried about everything.

His mind went to the previous evening's conversation with Marlena in his office. She hadn't been as emotional as he'd expected, hadn't acted quite the way he'd supposed a newly minted widow would behave. Did she know then it was all a drill? Was she in on it with them? Surely she was. He had to assume so. He could think of no good way to ask her about it, however, without coming across as a complete ass.

Of course she was in on it. To lie and tell a woman her husband had been murdered just for a security exercise? Not even Xiong would do that to someone. Would they? After what they'd just done to Greene, he wasn't ready to rule it out entirely.

So why had Marlena come to see him, then? To conduct a sort of stealth post-test interview? To satisfy the company's curiosity about Juha, or about Greene's own views on his former partner?

The elevator opened and Greene walked through the ornate lobby, heedless of all around him, his thoughts still churning.

And Shepherd—intense and abrasive as ever, Shepherd had played his role to the hilt, even maintaining the performance on the helicopter after the mission had been completed. To get Greene's thoughts and impressions on the day's events, no doubt. Shepherd was the one he'd had to impress, Greene knew—he always had been.

Wheat had also turned in a great acting job, even if the giant man's efforts to kill him had been completely sincere. Had that really been Wheat in the body bag on the helicopter? If, as Dr. Ranga Rao had said, none of Xiong's security had been involved in the plot, it had to be. What, then? Mainprize, the doctor? Xiong's medics received some security training but weren't part of Greene's department. That had to be it—she could have given Wheat something to knock him out, slow his heart rate.

How ridiculously elaborate. Greene hoped it had all been worth it.

As he stepped outside, much to his satisfaction, his Spec-Trons tinted instantly in response to the sun's glare. It felt good to be out of that looming nest of illusions and betrayal. And here was the car.

He grasped the door handle and paused. Where was he going? Home? He didn't feel like explaining all of this to Nisha just yet. And if he went home now, his mother would ask all sorts of questions he didn't want to answer. He needed to process all of this first.

Finally, he got into the car and buckled his seatbelt. "Take me to FatAss."

THIRTEEN

Greene entered the gym and found Juha's sister Satu at the front desk, eating a salad. She looked up as the door chimed.

"Hello, and welcome to— oh, hi, Green." She smiled, showing perfect white teeth.

Greene came to the desk. "Hi, Satu." It felt good to be around someone who wasn't going to call him "Chief."

Satu leaned back in her chair and looked him over. "Looks like you survived your excitement yesterday."

She was wearing a top that was little more than a sports bra, plus yoga pants. Preoccupied as he was, Greene couldn't help but be impressed with her muscle tone.

"Juha told you all about that, I guess?"

"Juha?" She laughed. "I saw it on the news."

Greene raised an eyebrow. "He didn't tell you about it?"

"All he would say was that you two had a 'grand outing.' I think he thinks I'm going to worry about him." She shook her head. "I really don't, though, anymore—I'm past that. But as vague as he was, I imagine it was pretty crazy. Did he get shot?"

"No." It was true, even if Juha had received just about every other kind of damage imaginable.

"Did *you* get shot?"

"Yes."

"Sorry to hear that. But everybody seems fine now, so I'm not worried. Right?"

"Right."

Satu nodded. "Good. I had a feeling. I assume you're looking for my brother."

"Yes. Is he here?" Greene suddenly realized that it hadn't occurred to him to call first—that Juha might not be here, that he might be at home, or out. He needed to get his head back on straight.

But Satu stuck her thumb toward the workout room. "He should be finishing up his class right about now. You can head on in. Or you can hang out here and tell me about your adventure."

Her eyes were warm, inviting, and he wasn't sure if it was her natural friendliness and curiosity or something more. Greene would have liked to think she'd outgrown her old crush by now, but he wasn't in the mood to take chances.

"I'll go find him," Greene said.

"Nobody tells me anything!" She seemed to be half joking, half pouting.

"Later," Greene said, with no intent to follow through.

Greene went to the workout room, pushed open the door, and stepped inside, the rush of the fans carrying the mingling odors of sweat and cleaning solution to assault his senses. He stood against the back wall and did his best to ignore the smell.

Juha's program appeared to be finished. About twenty sweaty people in various states of exhaustion stood, squatted, or sat on their mats, all with their backs to him. All heads were turned toward Juha, who stood at the far end of the room, equally sweaty but as full of piss and vinegar as ever. Greene was surprised. From across the room, at least, Juha looked perfectly normal. There was no evidence of the savage beating he'd received yesterday.

"That was a good effort," Juha was saying. "But I'm going to tell you something now that you're not going to like: a lot of you are going to wake up in the morning and get on the scale and it's going to tell you the same thing it told you this morning. Or you're going to get scanned and find you've lost just a twentieth or a fifteenth of a kilo. When that happens, I'm going to ask you to do two things. The first is to not freak out. The second is that after you do freak out, don't do anything stupid. Don't give up. Nothing the scale says to you is a justification to go stuff your face with a bunch of crap. Nothing."

Juha looked around the room as he let this sink in, and his eyes met Greene's. For an instant, Juha seemed surprised. Then he winked and returned his attention to his customers.

"Are you feeling fat? Feeling thin?" Juha began to pace in front of the class. "Stop it. That's the wrong focus. That's a marketing focus."

A man held up a hand. "But this place is called 'FatAss.'"

Juha clapped his hands and pointed at him. "Exactly. If I'd called this place 'Unhealthy,' not a single one of you would have come in here. You were all successfully marketed to."

This drew a smattering of laughter.

"Get off of 'fat' and 'thin.' You need to start thinking in terms of healthy versus unhealthy. Otherwise, all of this—" he motioned to the room around him "—isn't going to work. Don't focus on the scale. Focus on your health. Focus on the process. Focus on the positive. It's a long-ass road from here to where you want to be. Yes, thin is most certainly along that road, but if you're going to stay there once you get there, this has all got to be sustainable. Be patient." He clapped his hands again. "Okay, we're done here. Satu's going to have your next session, and she's going to be getting you some information about sustainable eating. *Not* dieting. Eating foods you like, in moderation. Okay? Awesome. Go shower, you stink."

The class filed out while Juha straightened up the room.

One man stopped in front of Greene. "Hey, you're that guy from TV! That was really cool!"

Greene gave him an insipid smile, and the man departed.

Juha waited until the last had left and the door was closed to speak.

"Look at these assholes, leaving their weights out. Sweaty-ass towel on the floor. I'm going to start fining folks for this mess. Put it right in the contract."

From across the room, Greene asked, "You led the class just now?"

Juha kicked a towel into the corner. "Yeah."

"And you did all the exercises?"

"Of course. Why?"

"You got beaten half to death yesterday. Your face was swollen up like a melon. How many times did Wheat hit you in the head?"

"I don't know. Several."

"And you had that glass stuck in your face—your cheek was half torn off."

"I was there, Green. I remember. What's your point?"

"I'm just wondering how you're leading this high-intensity workout after all that."

Juha walked up to Greene, a flinty look in his eye. Up close, Greene could see that Juha still had a bit of a black eye and some telltale bruises on his neck.

"Green, do I come to your job and tell you how to oppress the peasantry? I do not. But so we can move to a less boring topic, I'll tell you that they have some good-ass steroids these days. Plus bioprinting—I was at Xiong half the night getting that complimentary bioprinting." Juha turned away and resumed picking up.

Greene was astounded. "Why did it take so long?"

The workout paraphernalia was all put away, and Juha went to the far corner and activated the floor-cleaning robot. "Because I was getting all the way fixed up. You think I'm going to turn down free bioprinting? Walk around ugly, hurt, torn up? I got shit to do, man."

Voluntarily enduring hours of direct bioprinting? Greene was agape. He thought he was past the point of being surprised by Juha; obviously, he was severely wrong.

Finished with his work, Juha joined Greene at the door. "Your docs over there know what they're doing, I'll give them that. Anyway, you probably didn't come here to marvel at my good looks, although you are of course free to do so."

"Can we talk?"

Juha studied Greene's face. "Let's go to my office."

Greene followed him out, and they stopped at the front desk. To Greene's surprise, Juha pulled Greene's Spec-Trons off his face and handed them to Satu. "Hang on to these a minute, will you? Give those Xiong boys a good show, maybe."

Greene resisted the urge to grab them back. "What are you—"

Juha only shook his head.

Satu accepted the glasses, looking confused, and put them in a desk drawer.

They went into the office, and Juha locked the door behind them.

"You got any other bugs or wires I should know about?" Juha asked. "It doesn't bother you streaming your whole life to your bosses like that?"

"It's not—" Greene began, but gave up.

Juha let down his sweaty hair and shook it out. "You know your people tried to chip me again when I was in Medical? They thought I wasn't paying attention. And then I fell asleep during the bioprinting, and they chipped me anyway. Those bastards thought they were pretty sneaky. I didn't say anything. I had it taken out right away. I know a guy—don't ask, you wouldn't like it. I attached it to the cleaning bot. Anyway, sit down. You want something to drink?"

Greene shook his head, sat on the loveseat in the corner, and tried to relax.

Juha opened the mini-fridge and took out a full two-liter bottle of diet soda, then sat in his desk chair. "No? I've got some of that zero-calorie beer, too."

"I'm good."

The soda hissed as Juha unscrewed the cap, and he took a deep drink from the big bottle, holding it with two hands like a toddler with milk. Then he leaned back and put his tennis-shoe-clad feet up on the desk.

"Okay, go. This is about yesterday, I assume."

Greene took a deep breath. "It was a drill. All of it. Everything that happened was a drill."

Juha's eyebrows shot up. "Bullshit it was. I still get paid, right?"

"Yes."

Greene proceeded to relate a concise version of the morning's events. When he'd finished, Juha appeared thoughtful. Not angry, not resentful, not surprised—merely thoughtful.

Juha scratched his head, took a long pull on the soda bottle, and belched violently. "Okay, I think I've got a handle on it. But tell me this: when I kicked that asshole in his balls yesterday, was that his real balls?"

Greene considered this. "I guess it must have been."

"Ah." Juha looked up at the ceiling, satisfaction on his face. "That's all right then."

After a moment of silence, Greene said, "Is that it?"

Juha played with the half-empty soda bottle, squeezing it, making irritating crackling noises with it. "Well ... it would explain why Wheat brought the projector right to us at Clark's apartment. You can tell whoever scripted yesterday's little adventure that that was a contrived plot point. Just lazy writing."

Greene failed to restrain an exasperated sigh.

Juha put down the soda bottle and turned both hands palm-up. "Green, you work for Xiong Holonautics. Why would you be surprised that they would do you like that? They're an evil empire. That's just how they operate. You know that."

"They're not evil," Greene replied, finding himself defensive. "Not ..." He trailed off.

"'Not anymore,' you want to say, right? I get it. I don't think you're right, but I get it, and anyway, 'neutral empire' doesn't have the same ring to it."

Greene tensed. This wasn't going as he had expected—although he wasn't sure exactly what he'd been expecting. As far as he concerned, Juha was just rambling.

Juha picked up the bottle again and studied him again with that look of uninvested curiosity he always seemed to wear.

Greene was never quite sure whether it was feigned or genuine, but it was offputting.

"You were genuinely surprised to hear it, weren't you?" Juha asked. "You were. Wow. Green, I thought you knew better."

Greene scowled. "What are you getting at? You didn't know it was a drill, either."

"Of course not. That's not the point." Juha put his feet down and leaned toward Greene. "Somebody they hired tried to kill you, and you're feeling betrayed. So what? You've got to expect that, right, working for Xiong? Water is wet. Bears shit in the woods, or so I am told. Listen, nobody loves Xiong—and they're not a place that's really ever been interested in fostering employee loyalty, am I right? But from what you've told me, it sounds like they're actually on your side, at least, so you're doing better than most."

Greene found himself fighting down anger even as he realized that Juha was just affirming thoughts he'd already had.

"Why did you come here, Green?" Juha asked. "You're a big boy. You don't need me to validate your feelings."

Unexpectedly, these words took Greene back ten years to his time as the Portsmith Police Department's youngest detective, gifted but painfully raw. Juha, the streetwise veteran, had taken him under his wing. Greene remembered the unrelenting jokes from his squadmates about how "green" he was, and he felt a nostalgic appreciation for Juha that covered his annoyance.

But yesterday had been much different from their old police days. Yesterday, Juha had deferred to Greene in all matters, a marked change from their seven years together on the force.

Why *had* Greene come here?

"Because ... because we went through it together."

Juha considered this answer, seemed to approve. "All right, that's fair. But what are you looking for from me?"

"I just needed to talk about it with someone."

Juha flicked a wayward lock of hair out of his face. "You wanted to come in here and have me say, 'Oh, those fucking bastards, how the hell could they do something like that to us-slash-you? I can't believe it!' because that's what you're feeling, right?"

"Maybe."

"Oh, those fucking bastards. Except, like I said, I *do* believe it." Juha guzzled soda again, belched again. "You made a deal with the devil when you signed your contract with Xiong. No, no, calm down; I've got no problem with that—if you're making anywhere close to what I think you're making, it was a very good deal."

"But I'm not part of—"

Juha waved a hand at him. "Am I talking or are you talking? Shut the hell up a minute. I know, I know, you're doing what you can to clean up the corporate culture over there, to try to get your goody-goodiness to take root in that fortress of shady dealings. It's noble, it really is. Best of luck to you with that."

Greene felt like Juha was dancing around a point he couldn't see. "So what's my problem?"

"This is where I tell you it's the goody-goodiness, right?" Juha had a glint in his eye. "Except that it's not. Correct me if I'm wrong, but Xiong hired you primarily for image. There are plenty of older, wiser, and way more experienced security specialists out there. Hell, on paper, I'm more qualified for your job than you are. No, calm down, I'm just making a point. Now, obviously they wouldn't have hired you if they thought you would suck at your job, so you've got that going for you at the very least. Image, though: what they really wanted was your squeaky-clean morals, youthful good looks, and cute non-lethal weapons."

Greene felt as if he'd been slapped. But Juha was right. Xiong's agenda had trumped his qualifications, and by a wide margin—his meeting with the resurrected Dr. Ranga Rao had made that abundantly clear.

Greene sighed. His pride had taken as bad a beating in the last day as Juha's face. "Okay, let's say you're right. So?"

Juha shrugged. "So get your expectations more in line with reality and you'll enjoy your life a lot better. It cuts out a lot of that crushing disappointment you seem to be struggling with right now. Look, Xiong does their corporate shenanigans and makes billions, and meanwhile you go along and throw your four or five starfish back into the ocean, or however the hell that cheeseball story goes, and then you can go home and feel like you made a difference. Everybody wins."

"You don't think that's just a little jaded?"

Juha made a face that clearly indicated he was humoring Greene. "Same old Green. So damn sensitive. No. I don't think it's jaded, and the longer you think about it, the less you will, too. Look at you—you're sitting there thinking, 'On, I can't trust people there anymore.' That's wrong. Wrong, wrong, wrong. You never should have trusted those people in the first place."

Greene crossed his arms, fighting the temptation to sulk.

Juha glanced at the wall clock. "I've got another class in a couple minutes, so let me get to the takeaway. Sure, yesterday sucked, and I totally get why you think it's worse that it was a drill. But the best thing for you to do is to put it behind you and move on with your life. Nobody died, you said, so there's really no excuse not to. Learn your life lesson and be done with it." Juha rose, found a towel, and wiped the sweat from his chair.

"Put it behind me—that's basically what Dr. Ranga Rao said to me."

Juha walked over to a blue recycling bin overflowing with plastic two-liter containers and balanced his now-empty soda bottle on top. "Well, there you go. A man's got to know his place in the world. Life's too hard to take things so personally."

"Even when it's personal?"

Juha tied up his hair again. "*Especially* when it's personal. Let's see ... four o'clock. High-intensity interval training. This one's the truth, let me tell you: you start doing some of this, you might be able to actually keep up with me in the field. Want to come try it? This time of day, it'll mostly be a bunch of rich housewives trying to out-do, out-impress, and out-wardrobe each other, but you'd be all right."

"No thanks," said Greene, wondering how Juha was going to do all those jumping jacks and pushups and whatnot with two liters of fizzy soda in his stomach.

Juha shrugged. "Your loss. Anyway, good talk. Feel free to let yourself out. I'm going to go take a piss."

Greene prepared to rise, but stopped—he still wasn't sure where to go from here. "Is it okay if I hang out here for a little while? Is that weird?"

"It's a little bit weird, but sure, you're welcome to."

"Thanks."

"It's been good to see you again, Green." Juha left, closing the door behind him.

Greene took off his jacket and hung it on a chair, then settled into the loveseat, trying to calm his mind.

Juha was right, he knew. About everything. If only he could accept it. But something about the whole thing felt off, felt wrong, and he couldn't put his finger on it.

Maybe it was his sudden profound mistrust of Xiong. Maybe it was the holograms. He was new to them, sure, but it was clear that they were a technology that cultivated suspicion by their very nature.

Maybe it was, as Juha had said, Greene's feeling foolish for having trusted Xiong in the first place—his struggle with pride and ego. He remembered interviewing with Xiong, what, four months ago. He'd actually interviewed for the deputy position— the job Burg had now—not with any real expectation of getting it, but to check out Xiong from the inside, to get the experience. The only shock bigger than being called back to interview for the top job was actually getting it. He'd been so proud of himself— much prouder, clearly, than he had any right to be.

Greene began to feel drowsy, and he soon found himself slipping off his shoes. He lay down on the loveseat, his legs up over the far armrest.

His thoughts went to Marlena, the grieving widow—or not. Juha, the torch-carrier, didn't appear to be bothered by anything Greene had told him—but Juha made a point to never appear bothered by anything. In any case, if things really were back to normal, what Marlena did or didn't know had minimal bearing on Greene's life going forward.

Greene draped an arm across his eyes and, without meaning to, fell asleep.

Greene's phone rang, and he jerked upright. He was sweating, his heart racing. He was in darkness, and for a moment, he had no idea where he was.

He fumbled for his phone. The brightness of the screen hurt his eyes. *Marlena Ranga Rao, VP IT*, it said.

Greene put it to his ear. "Hello?"

He heard several labored breaths. Then: "Chief Greene?" The words were in an undertone, barely audible.

Greene put a finger in his other ear even though Juha's office was quiet. "Mrs. Ranga Rao?"

He heard a ragged gasp for air. "Chief. Help me. I—"

The call ended.

Greene stuffed his feet into his shoes and stumbled out into the glaring brightness of the FatAss lobby, pulling up his phone's tracking function.

It searched for her position. She wasn't at Xiong Tower, or at the Ranga Rao penthouse.

He tried to focus, to bring himself to alertness. If she was in trouble but wasn't at Xiong Tower, why had she called him instead of the police or an ambulance?

Juha sat at the front desk, wearing a fresh T-shirt and baggy athletic shorts. He had showered recently, and his long, damp hair hung loose to his shoulders.

He turned as Greene approached. "Wow, you were out. That was like two hours. Why don't you just go home and go to bed? You've had your Xiong car sitting right in front of my place half the day, scaring off my customers and probably giving them bad ideas about what kind of holographic shenanigans we might be up to in here."

"Marlena Ranga Rao is in trouble." It was an invitation.

Juha raised an eyebrow. "Is this another drill?"

That thought had occurred to Greene as well. "I don't know." He jerked open the desk drawer Satu had stored his Spec-Trons in and retrieved them. "Either way, I have to go."

Juha jumped up from his chair. "Awesome, let's do this. Adventure, ho!"

FOURTEEN

With Juha right behind him, Greene went to his car in quick strides, all momentum, starting to feel stiff again. His Power-Through was in his jacket, which he'd left in Juha's office.

They got into the car, and Greene checked his tracking program again. Marlena wasn't in Portsmith at all, but fifty kilometers north, outside the city proper.

He sent the information to the car. "Take us."

The car didn't respond.

Greene scowled. "Take us to these coordinates."

The car remained inert.

Juha rolled his eyes. "You didn't charge it?"

"It says full charge." Greene clenched his teeth and set the car to manual, and the steering column emerged. But the motor wouldn't start.

Juha unclipped his seatbelt and climbed out. "Screw this piece of crap, we'll take mine."

Greene pounded his fist against the wheel and followed.

"Across the street." Juha wound his way deftly through the heavy traffic.

Greene had a more difficult time of it—his personal traffic credentials didn't seem to be working properly—and by the time he'd caught up, Juha was stopped at a sleek late-model royal blue luxury coupe.

Greene thought of Juha's rathole of an apartment, his deliberately cavalier manner of dress, and his general disregard for appearances. "This is *your* Grandlux? You aren't stealing this, right?"

Juha rolled his eyes. "Manners. Got to spend my money on something, right? Plus if I have a mid-life crisis, I'm all set."

This from a man who'd gone to Mars, lost eighty kilos, and started a gym.

Juha appeared to have the same thought. "Shut up, Green, you don't know what I'm capable of. Just get in the car."

Greene did so.

Juha started the car and it said, "Greetings, Lord of the Earth. Happy Thursday to you." Its voice was sultry, but not distastefully so, and frighteningly chipper.

Greene fed the coordinates of Marlena's phone into the navigation system.

Juha buckled his seatbelt. "Hello, darling. Shall we?"

"I would be delighted," the car said, then pulled out into the street.

Greene looked at Juha, eyebrow raised.

"What. We all need a little affirmation in our lives," Juha said.

Juha's car traveled the crowded street with agonizing slowness, and it took Greene a moment to realize why: no traffic credentials. It had been a long time since he'd ridden in a car that didn't order the autodrives around him to give the right of way. And he didn't like it. He was spoiled.

Greene tried to run his credentials through the car's computer. He'd never tried this on a third-party car, but as he understood it, it was a relatively straightforward process.

"Where's that Xiong privilege?" Juha asked.

"I'm working on it."

It wasn't taking. Greene tried again to send the credentials, but they wouldn't engage.

Juha raised his eyebrows. "None of your shit is working?"

"I don't know what the problem is."

"Car, you're letting Greene here have his way with you, aren't you?"

"He's a real gentleman. It's the highlight of my day," the car said.

Juha frowned. "You didn't get fired after all?"

Greene shrugged. "Not to my knowledge." There was nothing more infuriating than technology that failed to work. Greene squirmed in his seat, determined not to let his frustration show. "Maybe there's a problem with the network."

Juha, as he so often did, seemed to see right through him, to the issue at hand. "Do we need to go faster?"

"If possible." Greene looked out at the dense traffic oozing through the street like sludge. What was Juha going to do, bash his way through?

"Let me take over," Juha told the car.

"Be gentle," said the car, and the steering column emerged.

"Baby, I always am." Juha glanced at Greene. "What's going on with Marlena? What kind of trouble is she in?"

"I don't know. She didn't say."

"But you're worried."

"Yes." Greene realized he was squeezing his phone too hard, and he set it on his lap. "I'm worried."

"Say no more." Juha steered the car into the middle of the street's three crowded lanes. "Traffic credentials, please."

"I told you, they aren't—" Greene broke off when he realized Juha wasn't talking to him.

"Traffic credentials activated," said the car. "Let me run free!"

A second later, the cars ahead of them began to change lanes, merging to the left and right, giving them a clear path.

"Run, baby." Juha floored the accelerator and winked at Greene. "You treat her like a lady and she'll always give you what you need."

Greene was astounded. This level of traffic priority would cost twice what the car was worth—a quarter-million gigs, maybe. "Credentials. Where did you get traffic credentials?"

"Well, you know ... I always like to be prepared."

The traffic ahead melted away. Greene glanced over at the speedometer. They were blazing down Portsmith's cramped urban streets at 120 kilometers an hour—faster than Greene had ever managed with his Xiong credentials.

"These are emergency service credentials, aren't they?" Greene said. "Police. Of course." Completely illegal for a civilian to have—not that that meant anything anymore. Greene had no idea why he still let Juha surprise him. "You kept them somehow?"

Juha laughed. "You know as well as I do you can't keep them when you leave. But I still have a few connections in this town."

That was fine, Greene figured, as long as they didn't get stopped. As Xiong, he wasn't particularly worried about that, and he didn't think Juha was, either.

Juha was still smiling. "Look at us, Green: driving fast, chasing bad guys, you fussing at me and worrying about everything—two days in a row! It's just like old times."

Greene snorted.

"So why is your shit not working? A network problem? Like a security problem?"

Greene stared out the window. "If it was a security problem, someone would have called me."

"Unless it was another drill."

"Maybe." Greene didn't even want to think about that possibility.

"Or unless you really did get fired."

"You're not helping."

Greene called Marlena. He waited impatiently as it rang, but she didn't answer. He tried again, hoping against reason that she would answer this time. But she didn't.

He settled back in his seat, feeling antsy. As fast as they were going, the trip seemed to be taking forever. What had happened to her? What would they find?

Maybe it was nothing, something minor. Maybe being out of the city had interfered with her phone service. Maybe this would all be much ado about nothing.

But Greene didn't believe that. Away from Xiong Tower, why had she called *him*? Greene had never been one to ever expect the best outcome in any case. And here he was, completely unarmed, feeling ill prepared for whatever it was they were heading toward.

He turned to Juha. "I don't suppose you have a gun."

Juha looked surprised. "Of course I have a gun. What do you think? My mother didn't raise any foolish children."

When they'd crossed the strait and were out of the city, Juha put the car back on autodrive and pulled a pistol from under his seat. He inspected it thoroughly, then tucked it into the elastic waistband of his shorts.

Greene called Burg. "Have you heard anything from Mrs. Ranga Rao?"

"No, nothing since she and Dr. Ranga Rao left on their trip."

"Trip?"

"You're headed right toward them." Burg sounded confused.

Them. Greene swallowed his impatience. "What trip, Burg?"

"The Ranga Raos left the tower around five. Said they were going home to pick up a few items and then spend the weekend away from the city. They've got a cabin out there, you know."

Greene didn't know. "I just got a call from Mrs. Ranga Rao. She sounded like she was in trouble. But the call got cut off, and I can't get a hold of her. Are they at the cabin?"

"Just a second. No. They're about five kilometers from it. But they're not moving. What do you think is happening?"

"I have no idea. You haven't gotten any signals from their car?"

"Not a wreck signal, if that's what you mean. Do you want me to send a team?"

"No. We're almost there. We'll check it out. But put a team on standby, all right?"

"Understood."

Juha's car passed through Portsmith's suburbs. The highway began to ascend gently, then narrowed to two lanes each way.

Thick groves of trees appeared abruptly, clearly marking the delineation between Hollow Hills Recreational Forest and the privately held land surrounding it.

Twilight had fallen. Greene looked out the rear windshield. There was very little traffic atop these forested hills, and the view of the Portsmith skyline, just beginning to light up for the evening, was spectacular. Even from here, Greene could see, kilometers away, the golden bear of Xiong Tower, the silver serpentine dragon that continually circled Algary Applications' twisting glass skyscraper, and, closer, Crestridge's garish neon zeppelin. He should bring Nisha out here more often, he thought.

Juha had spent much of the trip peering at his phone, a serious expression on his face. Now he rapped the dashboard display with a knuckle. "We're a klick out from your signal." He resumed manual drive.

Greene brought his mind back to the task at hand. He clenched his fists, tense, mind exploring every terrible possibility, and stared at the car's display. "Here. It should be right here."

Juha pulled onto the shoulder and stopped the car. "Taillights ahead of us."

It was a van, moving away from them, the only other vehicle on the road.

His insides twisting, Greene got out of the car. In the dusk, he could make out a gully by the side of the road. His tracking program indicated that Marlena's phone lay that way.

Using the less-than-sufficient light from his phone, Greene slipped down the embankment into knee-high grass, wishing he had his security uniform and boots on rather than these slacks and dress shoes.

When he regained his footing, Greene shone his light around.

"Wait!" Juha called. He was still above, with the car. "Pan it back!"

Greene did so, and gasped at what he saw.

An expensive sedan had smashed nose-first into a large tree.

"Car, darling, point your lights at that wreck, will you please?" Juha said.

"It would be my pleasure," said the car, which repositioned itself to accommodate the request.

Greene sprinted to the wreck as light flooded the scene. He saw glints of shattered glass and fresh red blood splashed on flattened green grass.

He reached the passenger side of the car, trying to take in everything as quickly as possible: the front door open, its glass cracked; the empty seat, speckled with blood and glass; a bloody handprint on the interior door panel; the purse on the floor; the seatbelt, cut away as with a knife. The airbags on this side had not deployed.

Then Juha was there, yanking at the driver's door, pitting all his strength against the bent doorframe.

He got it open, then let out a sigh of irritation. "Oh, for fuck's sake."

The driver's seat was occupied. Slumped against the steering column was Dr. Ranga Rao, still strapped into his seat, soaked with blood, a deflated airbag covering his torso. A galvanized steel signpost had punctured the windshield and impaled his chest.

"Jesus," Greene said.

Juha stuck his head into the car, seemingly unfazed by his proximity to the carnage, and locked eyes with Greene. "Just so we're on the same page here, this is your Dr. Ranga Rao, right? The guy whose murder we solved yesterday?"

Greene could only nod.

"The guy you talked to this morning."

Greene nodded again.

"And he doesn't have a twin brother or anything like that?"

"He's an only child."

Juha threw up his hands. "So what the hell is going on? This dude is like Schrodinger's fucking cat. Is he alive? Is he dead? Who the hell can keep track?"

Greene swallowed hard. "Do you see any holograms here?"

"None."

Greene handed his phone across the top of the car. "Can you scan him?"

"Scan him? Look at this guy. He seems pretty damn dead to me. Then again, I guess he seemed pretty dead yesterday, too." Juha took the phone and scanned Ranga Rao's body. "Yeah, I think it's going to stick this time."

Juha muttered something to the corpse—the only word Greene got was "Marlena"—and then straightened and passed Greene his phone.

Greene called Burg, who answered immediately. He instructed her to send the helicopter and a medical team. "Have them ready for trouble," he said, and ended the call.

Greene considered the scene again. "Marlena's airbags didn't deploy, but she got away from the crash."

"Or was taken away." Juha clapped his hands together. "Okay, let's go find her."

Greene felt uncomfortable about calling out for her, although he couldn't identify a reason why. He pulled his tracker's display up on his Spec-Trons. Marlena—or her phone, at least—was less than a stone's throw away, toward the woods. He waded through the tall grass, following the signal, apprehensive about what he might find.

He reached the spot and knelt, shining his phone's light, half-feeling his way.

"What is it?" Juha asked from right behind him. "What did you find?" It was the closest thing to anxiety Greene had ever heard in Juha's voice.

Greene's hand closed over something cold and smooth: Marlena's phone. He straightened.

"That's not good," Juha said. "Not good at all. You don't flee the scene *away* from the road." He cupped his hands around his mouth and shouted, "Marlena!"

There was no reply. In the still night, the only sounds were those made by the wildlife and the wind in the trees.

Juha brushed grass from his shorts. "Damn it."

Greene watched dust particles filter through the beams of Juha's headlights. "We didn't get a wreck signal," he said as he realized it. "That car is fully Xiong-credentialed. We should have gotten a wreck signal the minute this happened."

"Obviously, somebody is jerking us around, and I don't goddamn like it."

"What do you think?"

Juha shrugged. "Maybe she hurt her head and came out of the wreck confused. Maybe somebody ran them off the road and took her, threw her phone out here. Not a lot of sense in speculating at this point, though, if you've got some more Xiong tricks up your sleeve."

Greene did indeed. He switched his tracker from her phone to her chip—which he should have done in the first place.

In the instant it took the tracker to lock onto her chip, Greene felt a bolt of terror that it was going to show him somewhere far away, kilometers away.

But it didn't. Marlena Ranga Rao wasn't more than a hundred meters from them. She was farther into the woods, though, and it was now pitch dark, with only sporadic light from the moon and stars trickling through the clouds.

Greene nodded toward the forest. "This way. Do you have any kind of light in your car?"

"Just my phone. I wasn't expecting to hike through the forest with you playing boy scout. Do you want to wait for reinforcements?"

Greene switched his Spec-Trons to night vision. "No."

"Good, me neither. Let's go."

They started off side by side, with Greene focusing on the tracker and Juha shining his light on the ground immediately before them.

Greene stumbled in a depression hidden by the grass and nearly turned his ankle. "I wish we had the drone."

"What drone?"

"The aerial drone in the trunk of my car. It's got infrared. It'd be nice to have. If I'd thought about it ..."

They reached the tree line and entered the woods. Greene, intent on his heads-up display, held his free hand ahead of him to ward off tree branches.

"And I wish I'd worn some pants," Juha said. "I'm getting scratched all to hell. Listen to you—you're way too conscientious, just like always. Too diligent. If you aren't perfect, you're not happy, and you *can't* be perfect, so you're never happy. Why would you have brought it? How could you have anticipated this?"

Maybe Juha was right, but it didn't ease the knot of anxiety that Greene couldn't seem to get rid of.

Greene tripped again, pitching forward, and he had to put a hand on the ground to keep from landing on his face.

Juha helped him up. "Come on man, have you never been in nature before?"

"It's been a long time." Greene's hand felt sticky. He stopped to peer at it, pushing his Spec-Trons up to the top of his head and turning on his phone light. His hand was bloody.

"Now what did you do?" Juha got in close, shone his own light on Greene's hand. "I can't take you anywhere."

A chill ran through Greene. "It's not mine."

As one, they squatted, training their lights on the ground.

The grass was spattered with blood in an approximate line along the path they were taking.

"Not good," said Juha. "How far?"

Greene pulled his Spec-Trons back down. "Not far."

They were up again, moving faster, shoving their way through brush and branches.

Greene stopped under an immense white pine. "This is the spot."

They shone their lights around the area. Marlena wasn't there.

Juha peered upward, perhaps on the off chance that she'd wandered away from that catastrophic car wreck and climbed a tree. Greene gave him a look, and he shrugged. "Just being thorough."

Greene turned his attention downward. A brief search revealed another spatter of blood leading deeper into the woods.

Greene was bewildered. The blood went on, but the tracker signal ended here. Marlena should be *here*.

Then he saw it.

A still-wet splash of blood, unsettlingly large, soaking fallen leaves and pine needles. And in the center, a bloody disc of skin almost four centimeters across.

"Juha."

"What? What'd you— Oh, fuck me, what is that?"

Greene consulted his display again, although there could be no doubt. "It's Marlena's chip."

For a moment, they could only stare at it.

When Juha spoke, his voice was as calm, as even, as controlled as ever. "God motherfucking damn it. Somebody cut that out of her, Green." He began to shake his head continuously, rhythmically. "That means she's gone. Somebody's taken her."

Why? burned in Greene's mind. If someone had abducted Marlena, that meant the crash had been deliberately caused. But why such a risky ambush? If this had been done by one of Xiong's competitors, why hadn't there been a better effort to take Dr. Ranga Rao, a far more valuable asset than Marlena, alive?

Greene realized Juha was just standing there, looking at him. "We can keep following the blood trail," Greene said.

Juha nodded.

Greene switched off the tracker and the night vision and fixed his light on the bloody ground. They continued on, leaving Marlena's chip and flesh behind them. Although there was more blood from this point, the trail was difficult to keep to because of all the underbrush, and the going was slow.

Greene shook his head as he walked. It had been over an hour since Marlena had called him. It was night, they were on foot and badly equipped, and whoever had taken Marlena was surely long gone. But what choice did they have? There was nothing else to be done.

They trudged through the forest for what felt like an hour but was probably closer to ten minutes. Greene's pants were torn in several places, and he imagined his shoes were ruined as well.

In the middle of a tiny clearing, Greene lost the trail, and they stopped. His Spec-Trons indicated that they'd traveled about a kilometer from Juha's car.

"Do you see anything?" Greene asked.

"No. Maybe they bandaged her." Juha looked up. "Maybe they airlifted her out of here. Helicopter, rappel rope—there's enough space between the trees for it. That'd be a pro operation, though."

"I suspect it was a pro operation in any case," Greene said.

Juha walked slowly around the edge of the clearing, shining his light, looking for any sign of the trail. "I'm not much of a tracker. I guess there's really nothing else we can do except make our way back and wait for the cavalry."

"Juha ... I'm sorry."

"Not your fault. We tried. I—" Juha jerked his head sideways. "There. Did you see that? It looked like a—"

Greene heard the flat report of a pistol. Juha grunted and went down.

Stuck in the center of the clearing, Greene threw himself to the ground, shoving his lit phone underneath him and fumbling to kill the light. He held still, his heart thudding like blows on his chest.

There were no more shots.

Juha had extinguished his light as well. Which way had the shot come from? Greene had no idea. He lay in utter silence for a moment, feeling horribly exposed, evaluating the risks of moving versus staying still.

Greene brought his darkened phone up to his lips and whispered, "Infrared."

The Spec-Trons' display changed to a rainbow scale. There, at the edge of the clearing, was the red and yellow silhouette of Juha, prone, moving slowly for cover. He couldn't see anyone else.

If their assailant had been using night vision or infrared, Greene thought, they'd be dead already. He launched himself toward Juha, half-crawling, half-running, and slid in next to him behind a pine wide enough to shield them both.

Greene willed his pulse to slow. In an undertone, he asked, "Are you hit?"

Juha had his pistol out. "In the leg. I'm okay. I think there's just one."

Greene nodded. "We can flank him."

"Good thought. I don't suppose you brought a gun."

"There's one in my car."

"Typical. All right, heat ray time! Pew pew! Maybe you can give him a mild rash. What, you don't have that either?" In the darkness, Juha was undoubtedly rolling his eyes. "You are the worst, you know that? What are you planning to do, run out there and give him a hug?"

Greene was annoyed at himself as much as at Juha's snark. "If you think it would help."

"We can try it." Juha handed Greene his pistol. "You've got two good legs. Any chance you can circle around quietly?"

Greene took it. "Not much. There's a lot of underbrush."

Juha shrugged. "Can't hold that against you. I don't have a better idea, though."

"But I'll try."

Juha placed a hand on his arm. "Green. We can wait for the cavalry."

Greene shook his head. "They'll come in like gangbusters, and we'll lose him. Lose Marlena."

"Good man. I'll give you some cover by, I don't know, telling jokes, maybe."

Greene took a deep breath and rose to a crouch. "Any idea where he is?"

"Facing the clearing, my best guess is about eleven o'clock. Have fun." Juha picked up a sturdy branch and began to thump it rhythmically against the trunk of the tree he was leaning on.

Greene made his way clockwise around the clearing, using the trees as cover, acutely mindful of every twig he broke and leaf he rustled.

Juha's tapping receded. Greene still couldn't see anyone else, and he wondered whether the gunman was anywhere near where Juha thought. He had to be getting close.

The drumming of the branch ceased, and after a moment, Greene heard an impact on leaves, much closer. He raised the pistol, honed in on the noise. There came an identical sound, and Greene realized what it was: Juha was throwing pinecones across the clearing.

Greene was just thinking that none of Juha's antics were enticing their prey in the least when he saw it: a flash of movement, a tiny sliver of red on his infrared display, at ground level. Greene squinted and made out a hand, part of a head. At last, he comprehended what he was seeing: the gunman had buried himself under a layer of forest debris.

A third pinecone thunked between them. Greene stalked closer, and now he could make out a pistol in the hand, pointed generally toward Juha.

The direct approach, Greene decided, was best. He gripped the pistol tight, ready to muzzle-thump the gunman, and charged.

At the noise of his approach, the gunman rolled toward him, divesting himself of his camouflage. The pistol came around and Greene dove, tackling, striking the shoulder of the arm holding the gun, forcing a drop.

There was a cry—a woman's voice.

She struggled against him, but Greene was on top of her now, a knee on her chest, gun pointed at her face. The Spec-Trons identified her.

Marlena Ranga Rao.

He lowered the gun, but she continued to thrash. He tossed the pistol aside and grabbed her wrists. "Marlena. Marlena, it's me. It's Chief Greene." He turned his head and yelled, "Juha! Clear! Hurry!"

Still Marlena struggled.

Juha's phone light came on and grew closer, bouncing as Juha limped over. Juha put the light in Marlena's face and she froze, eyes wide and wild. Blood from a gash across her forehead had run down the side of her face.

Greene turned her loose, shoved the light out of her face. "Mrs. Ranga Rao, it's all right."

Recognition spread slowly across her face. "Chief?"

He made himself smile. "Yes. You're safe now."

Juha's relief and concern were obvious. "She's in bad shape."

Greene scanned her with his phone. "Multiple injuries, possibly severe. We need to get her to a doctor."

Marlena reached up and clutched Greene's arm. "Raj. He—He—"

Greene's face fell before he could stop it. "Mrs. Ranga Rao, I'm sorry. He—"

"No!" Her fingers dug painfully into his arm, and she held him with a strength Greene wouldn't have thought possible. "You don't understand!"

Juha put a hand on her hair, then stroked it. "Tell us."

"It wasn't him!" Her eyes went to Juha's, then back to Greene's. "It wasn't my Raj!"

FIFTEEN

They patched Marlena up as best they could with rudimentary bandages torn from Greene's shirt.

"It's going to be all right," Greene told her. "We're going to get you back to Xiong Tower, get you to the doctor."

"No!" Her nails dug into his flesh. "Don't take me there. Take me to a hospital."

"But—"

"Promise me!"

"I promise," Greene said, having no idea why she wanted this, knowing he was certain to catch hell for it.

Marlena relaxed. She'd lost a significant amount of blood, and, exhausted from her ordeal, she seemed to allow herself to pass out as soon as she'd decided she was in safe hands. She was in no condition to walk in any case. With some difficulty, Greene fireman-carried her back to the car. Her blood trickled down his back, tickling him, then dried, making him sticky.

Juha hobbled along behind, both pistols tucked into his waistband. His wound, he said, was superficial. He'd consented to a bandage from Greene but declined all offers of assistance and refused to wait for help. He maintained the pace gamely enough.

Greene's phone chirped. It was Burg. "We're here. I see you're close."

"Thank you. We're clear, I think. We're on the way back. Send two to help—Mrs. Ranga Rao is badly hurt. I want you to be ready to take off the instant we get back. To the nearest hospital, not to Xiong Tower."

"But sir, that's not protocol—"

Greene hardened his voice. "A hospital, Burg, do you copy?"

"Yes, sir." She ended the call.

Greene turned to Juha. "So what do you think happened?" The question had consumed Greene's thoughts since the moment they'd found her. He knew what he thought; he wanted a second opinion.

"Somebody ran them off the road, tried to take her. She fled from them, possibly fighting her way free, and then cut out her own chip so they couldn't track her." The satisfaction in Juha's voice was unmistakable. "She's a hell of a woman."

"That sounds pretty close," Greene said. Except ... why cut the chip out? A competitor shouldn't have been able to track her using it, but Greene supposed it couldn't be ruled out. And what had she meant about Dr. Ranga Rao—"it wasn't my Raj"? It buzzed around his mind like a mosquito.

Greene heard rustling ahead of them, saw flashes of light, and then three members of Xiong Security appeared, carrying bullpup carbines with mounted flashlights.

One was Burg. She looked surprised to see Juha, and not entirely pleased.

The other two shouldered their weapons, then eased Marlena from Greene's shoulders and carried her off toward the road.

Greene nodded at Juha. "Go on."

Juha raised an eyebrow, but he accompanied them without objection.

Greene stretched his back as he and Burg walked together. "I want a full flight of drones, infrared. I don't think we're going to find anything, though. You're going to take over here. I'll accompany the helicopter to the hospital. I want a guard on Mrs. Ranga Rao at all times—send a team over there."

Burg face darkened. "Sir, standard procedure is to treat her in the tower with the company doctor."

So much for whatever goodwill he'd built with her yesterday.

"I know what standard procedure is, Burg."

"Then why, sir?" It was a demand.

Greene stopped walking, and she stopped as well, glaring at him. He glared back, finding himself content to stand here in the middle of the forest and stare her down all night if necessary.

After a moment, though, she nodded brusquely. "Yes, sir."

Greene was slowly discovering that standing up to her, matching force for force, was the way to get through to her, and that his typical more diplomatic approach might actually be counterproductive.

They resumed walking and soon reached the gully beside the road. Juha's car's lights were still on, still pointed at the wreck. Down the road, the Xiong helicopter loomed, blocking all traffic. Half a dozen Xiong security people swarmed around the Ranga Raos' shattered car.

Obedience won, Greene was now free to do his job. "Burg," he said softly, and she stopped again, not bothering to hide her frustration. "She asked specifically for a hospital. She cut out her own chip."

Burg's brow furrowed. "Shit, why?"

"I don't know yet."

"You think we have a breach?"

"I don't know. Could be."

She nodded curtly. "I understand." There was more respect in her voice now.

"And Burg ..." He couldn't think of a good way to phrase what he wanted to say. "This might sound stupid. I want you to take a good look at Dr. Ranga Rao's body. Make sure to your unshakable satisfaction that it's him and that he's dead."

They exchanged a look, and Greene recalled that he hadn't had a chance to talk through the resurrection of Dr. Ranga Rao with her.

But she appeared to be having similar thoughts. "I understand."

The helicopter was waiting. Greene climbed aboard, joining Juha, the unconscious Marlena, a medic, and two of his staff in the cabin. He pulled the door closed behind him, and the helicopter lifted off.

He turned first to the medic—it was Mainprize, the tiny young doctor who seemed to always be chewing gum. "Is she going to make it?"

Mainprize shrugged. "No reason she shouldn't."

Greene was handed a container of wet wipes and a black Xiong T-shirt that was too big for him. As he cleaned himself up, he addressed his security people.

"There was an attempt on Mrs. Ranga Rao's life tonight. On her request, we're taking her to a hospital, not to Xiong Tower. You two are her security detail until Deputy Chief Burg relieves you. Mrs. Ranga Rao is never to be out of your sight. *Never.* Don't let anyone tell you otherwise. If she goes into surgery, one of you is in the room, watching. The other is outside, checking the ID of everyone who enters. Get connected to the hospital database and keep your Spec-Trons on the entire time. Doctors, nurses, I don't care—you make sure they are who they're supposed to be. Any questions?"

They had none. These were good people. They knew their jobs.

Juha was quiet, leaning against the bulkhead, gazing unabashedly at Marlena.

Greene stared out the window at Portsmith below. At night, the city was a twinkling neon rainbow, a shifting kaleidoscope of real and holographic activity. It was never dark in Portsmith.

He allowed his eyes to unfocus, his thoughts to return to the crash—to the death of Dr. Ranga Rao. There was no question the man was dead. How odd—how ironic—that this should happen just a day after Ranga Rao's simulated death. Tragic.

Could it be a coincidence? Greene had a hard time believing so, even though there was nothing to link the two days' events except the death—*deaths*—of Dr. Ranga Rao. In Greene's experience, coincidences—especially big coincidences—just didn't happen.

He was still in the dark about a great deal, and the countless niggling details that tugged at him fled into the shadowy recesses of his mind when he tried to take hold of them.

Greene sighed, wishing he had some better clothes. An afternoon off, and now another long night. He'd be sleeping in his office—if he got any sleep.

The helicopter descended to the pad atop St. Osteen Memorial Hospital, and the medical staff swarmed around Marlena and Juha, bearing them away with the Xiong guards in tow.

Greene followed them to the elevator and then through the labyrinthine building until the entire procession came to a halt at a set of security doors. His people were being held up by the paramedics. Which meant that Marlena's treatment was being held up.

As Greene strode forward, he heard Juha say, "You don't want to mess with these guys, man. It's not going to end well for you."

Greene produced his credentials and set them all straight, and the two guards plus Mainprize were admitted to the emergency ward.

He took Mainprize by the arm as she passed him. "I'm going to join you shortly. If she comes to before that, you let me know that very minute. Understand?"

"Yes, sir."

Greene retreated to the waiting area, which was more crowded than he cared for. He needed to call Nisha, to bulldoze their dinner plan, and this was about as much downtime as he was likely to get.

He called, and she answered immediately.

"Hi, baby. I might not be home tonight. Work. I'm sorry."

"Are you all right? Has something happened?"

Greene forced warmth into his voice. "I'm fine. In no danger. I'll fill you in later."

Nisha was annoyed—but she was also at least somewhat accustomed to this. "Your mom's made biryani. She's not going to be happy."

Greene wandered out of the waiting area and turned down a vacant corridor. "I thought we were supposed to go over to the Brodens' tonight."

"Signe canceled."

"Again?"

"She said she wasn't feeling well, but I was talking to Frances at the studio and *she* said that Signe's projectors are out again. I understand you don't want to have company over if your décor's not working, but why not just say so? I think it's because they only have that old Crestridge—you know it has trouble running this year's lines—and I think she's embarrassed to tell me that. Because of you, obviously."

"Obviously," Greene answered dutifully.

Nisha wasn't getting out enough these days—that, too, was obvious. In spite of his arguments that she was pregnant, not an invalid, Nisha was too accommodating of Greene's mother, who would have had Nisha in bed twenty hours a day if it were up to her.

At least Nisha had gotten to go down to the art studio today. If only he'd been able to—

Greene's train of thought was broken as he turned a corner and nearly collided with Shepherd.

"I'll see you later. I love you. Bye," Greene said to Nisha, as quickly as he could get the words out, then ended the call without waiting for her response. He jammed the phone into his pocket and straightened, aware of how terrible he must look in shredded slacks and an ill-fitting T-shirt. Shepherd, in contrast, was immaculate as always, trim and elegant in an obscenely expensive suit.

Shepherd had gotten there astonishingly quickly, Greene thought. That was portentous.

He reminded himself that he was now in the CTO's good graces, such as they were, but the man still made him nervous. For Shepherd to be here at the hospital himself, so fast, could mean only disaster.

But he'd done nothing wrong, Greene assured himself. A four-minute call to your wife's not against company policy.

Greene gave Shepherd his full attention. "Sir."

"Chief Greene." Shepherd snapped his fingers, spun on his heel, and set off briskly down the hall.

Greene fell into step behind him. "Sir, Dr. Ranga Rao—"

Shepherd nodded. "Yes, he's dead. For real, this time. A tragedy."

Greene followed Shepherd back to the double doors to the emergency ward. Shepherd pushed through them and entered a vacant treatment room.

"Sit," Shepherd said, so Greene did, selecting the rolling stool over the bed or the lone chair.

Shepherd disabled the automatic door and then sat in the chair. He reached into a jacket pocket and produced a small device—a portable holographic projector. He placed it on the bed and activated it, and the wide glass panes of the door became black, each bearing the overlaid X-H Xiong emblem. Shepherd then produced a second device, which he also activated—a sonic scrambler, effective against various types of electronic eavesdropping.

This done, Shepherd turned his withering glare—he didn't really seem to have any other kind of look—on Greene. Greene wished his stool were taller—it was bad enough having Shepherd looking down on him figuratively.

"You're operating under the assumption that this was an attack by one of our competitors?" Shepherd asked.

"Yes, sir. I need to talk with Mrs. Ranga Rao, of course, and we'll pull the data from the recorder in Dr. Ranga Rao's car. We ought to have a lot better idea of what happened in a few hours."

"And why didn't you take Mrs. Ranga Rao back to Xiong Tower for medical care? She's a Xiong employee."

"She asked to be brought here. And based on what she's said—" Greene hesitated, because she had actually said very little, and he had no evidence. "I'm concerned we might have a breach."

Shepherd raised an eyebrow. "An internal security breach."

"Yes, sir."

"An interesting hypothesis. I'm sure you will fully explore that possibility." Shepherd leaned toward Greene, looming. "But first: Karjalainen. Why is he here?"

This seeming non sequitur caught Greene off guard. "He was shot while we were—"

Shepherd shook his head. "Why was he *there*?"

"He was helping me. He—"

"Why?"

"My car wouldn't start."

Shepherd studied Greene through narrowed eyelids. "And he just swooped in, to the rescue?"

"I was there already. At his gym."

"Why?"

This line of questioning, the incredulity—it was too much. "Dr. Ranga Rao told me to take the afternoon off. Sir—"

Shepherd was shaking his head again, slowly. "Chief, you will bear with me, I trust." His voice was granite, and there could be only one response.

"Yes, sir."

"Your car wouldn't start."

Greene forced himself to hold Shepherd's gaze. "Yes, sir. My traffic credentials weren't working, either. I figured there was some sort of network problem."

Shepherd shrugged. "To my knowledge, there have been none. So you took Karjalainen's car."

"Yes."

"And yet you got to the scene fast enough."

"He had his own credentials." Although it could scarcely be kept a secret, Greene didn't like sharing this. It felt like ... snitching.

"Interesting. And Karjalainen was with you when the car didn't start?"

"Yes."

"And your credentials didn't work in his car, either?"

"That's right."

"And what did you think about that?"

Greene tried to conceal his irritation. "As I said, sir, I thought it might be a network problem. I didn't give it too much further thought since he had his own credentials and because we were rushing to help Mrs. Ranga Rao."

Shepherd held up a hand. "All right, Chief. I believe you."

Believe? "Sir, I might be of more help to you here if you told me what the problem is."

Shepherd leaned forward, rested his elbows on his knees, and steepled his fingers. "Listen to me very carefully. While you were off today, we uncovered something I think you'll find quite interesting. Your friend Juha Karjalainen received a payment of 100,000 gigayuan today from Algary Applications."

Greene opened his mouth, then remembered who he was speaking to. He swallowed hard. "How did we find out? And when did it happen?"

"This morning. A deposit right into his account. Not from Algary, of course—they wouldn't do anything so stupid—but from a shell corporation they've been linked to."

"Respectfully, why are we in his bank account, sir?"

The tiniest hint of a smile tugged at Shepherd's mouth. "Because that's our business. Just as everything related to what we do is our business."

Greene tried to process the news of this payoff. Juha was capable of a lot of things, but corporate espionage? "He signed his NDA. We paid him."

Shepherd laughed, harsh and short. "And they paid him ten times as much. That's how this business works. You know if we call them out on it, Algary will try to find ways around the NDA, or fight it directly."

Greene massaged the bridge of his nose. "A hundred grand. For what? He didn't get the plans to the prototype—there's no way he could have. What could he possibly give them worth that much money?"

"No," Shepherd said, "he didn't get the plans. But he's been in our facilities. He's seen all our systems, and he knows all about our prototype—exactly what it is and what it does."

"What use could that be? There's no way he could have the slightest clue how it works."

"Perhaps it's a down payment on future services."

"Sir?"

Shepherd leaned back in his chair, stretched, and winced, then rubbed his neck. "Your friend isn't much for authority, is he?"

On a certain level, that was absolutely true. But Greene didn't know how best to answer the question. "Are you all right, sir?"

Shepherd crossed his legs, a pretense of relaxing. "Yes, thank you. I overdid it at the gym today is all. It's been a long couple of days for everyone. Now then, Karjalainen was extremely helpful yesterday, wouldn't you say? And he went well above and beyond the call of duty after the tragedy this evening with the Ranga Raos. He's been most accommodating. When you were police officers together, was he ever so accommodating?"

"No," Greene admitted. "But he was my superior officer."

"And now? He's just another of your security minions?"

Greene hesitated. "He's my friend."

"We know he's been in contact with Algary. He was with you for most of the day yesterday and a good bit of today. Was he on his phone at all during those times?"

"He's often on his phone," Greene replied. "Just like most people."

Shepherd gave Greene a pointed look. "I know this is hard for you, Chief. But here's the picture I'm seeing. Your friend Karjalainen was helpful throughout the drill yesterday. Very helpful. Algary took note and made a move. And lo and behold, here we are today and Karjalainen is being very helpful again, this time without any financial incentive from us—giving you rides, being a shoulder to lean on, and taking bullets for you. Why should he be so interested in the Ranga Raos?"

Because he's in love with Marlena. Uneasiness was a sharp stone in Greene's stomach. "You think he was involved in Dr. Ranga Rao's murder? Why would he be involved and then turn around and help me?"

Shepherd leaned forward and flicked a speck from his diamond-toed shoes. "Involved? Not directly. Not actively. Not for 100,000. And I'm certain he has an alibi—he's clever enough. But I have no doubt he knew about it. I think he disabled your car and your credentials, yes."

Greene had been asleep for several hours—Juha would have had plenty of time.

"But I think Algary's plot is of a subtler nature," Shepherd continued. "Why would Karjalainen be so helpful? Any number of reasons. To throw off any suspicion of his involvement, or to build your trust, or to create mistrust of us."

Why would he be so helpful? Because Juha was his friend, Greene thought—or had thought.

Greene twisted his wedding ring on his finger. "That's a lot of trouble to go to."

"I agree. Perhaps Algary is going to make a play for you, the rising star, the celebrity."

"Celebrity?"

"The media will forget about you by next week, but yes, in the technology world, you're a bit of a star now, believe it or not. I want you to be prepared when Algary comes for you."

"But— I have a contract."

Shepherd laughed again, without humor. "There are a lot of ways around a contract, and a lot of ways you could wind up in their pocket." It was a statement and a threat.

This was a wound to Greene's pride. "I mean that I will honor my contract, sir. My loyalty is to this company. I won't betray it."

"You could be the last honorable man in Portsmith." There might have been genuine warmth in Shepherd's face now, or a reasonable facsimile thereof. "Don't worry, Chief. I'm on your side. And I know you're on ours. I know you'll do the right thing."

Greene took a deep breath and let it out slowly. "What do you want me to do?"

"I want you to keep it friendly with Karjalainen. Don't let on that you know about any of this. Make a pretense of going along with him. Maybe we can find out what he and Algary are up to. But I don't want him in Xiong Tower again, and I don't want him involved in any more operations. Unless we talk about it first."

"Yes, sir."

The men's phones chirped simultaneously. Greene looked at his: Burg had sent them the data pulled from the Ranga Rao car's computer.

Greene glanced at Shepherd, who nodded, then returned his attention to his own phone. Greene pulled up the data on his Spec-Trons and began to skim the information, part of him yearning to find something of use before Shepherd did.

He soon found an item of interest. "Dr. Ranga Rao spent the entire trip on autodrive—until they entered the forest. Then he put the car on manual. He was driving when the wreck happened."

As Greene looked for the car's front and rear video feeds, someone rapped on the glass of the door of the treatment room.

Shepherd was still looking at his phone. "It's one of yours."

Greene rose and switched off the projector. The black panels on the door vanished, revealing the young, lean Xiong security man standing outside. Greene opened the door.

Reich looked at Greene, then at Shepherd, then back to Greene, seemingly unsure of whom to address. Greene gave him a little nod, and Reich turned to Shepherd.

"Mrs. Ranga Rao is awake, sir. They've moved her to the security ward. The doctor says she has a mild concussion but that you can speak with her now for a short time."

Shepherd was out of his seat in an instant, retrieving his devices. "Let's go."

SIXTEEN

When they reached Marlena's hospital room, Shepherd placed a firm hand on Greene's shoulder and another on Reich's. In an undertone, he asked, "Where's Karjalainen?"

"Still being treated, sir," Reich said.

Shepherd nodded. "When he's released, he's going to come up here. He's going to want to see Mrs. Ranga Rao. I don't want you to let him in. Tell him anything you want, do whatever you need."

"Yes, sir."

Shepherd looked at Greene. "You have no objection, Chief?"

Greene set his jaw. "No, sir."

"Very good." Shepherd told Reich to wait in the hall, and then he and Greene entered the room.

Greene always found hospital rooms gloomy places. The unnatural tint of the light, the drabness of the wall paint, the awful artificial wood grain of the cabinetry—it would really benefit from some holographic sprucing up, Greene thought. He longed to throw open the outmoded pastel curtains, to admit the light of the Portsmith night in all its multicolored splendor, but Shepherd was here, and this wasn't something Greene was willing to spend a single gig of his recently accrued status capital on.

Marlena lay propped up in the bed. Her hair and forehead were swathed in bandages, as was the forearm from which she'd dug out her Xiong chip. Her arms were yellow with bruises. She wore a neck brace and a nasal cannula for oxygen. IV lines ran from her arm to drip bags on a pole near the bed. Her eyes locked on to Greene's, then Shepherd's. Her face was marred with worry.

Shepherd stood at the foot of the bed, arms clasped, an ill-fitting expression of sympathy on his face. "I'm sorry, Mrs. Ranga Rao. Your husband didn't make it. He was a good man. The greatest mind Xiong Holonautics has had in two decades."

Marlena's lips thinned. Her hands closed into fists, her knuckles white. "That was not my husband."

"Mrs. Ranga Rao, I'm sorry. I'm sure this is hard to hear, but I have the report from Deputy Chief Burg here." He took out his phone and read from it. "Birthmark on right shoulder. Gold fillings on teeth 26 and 27. Scar on right knee. Body confirmed to be Rajendra Ranga Rao."

Marlena tried to shake her head but with the neck brace could only twist her chin. Her eyes burned into Shepherd. "Yes, Raj has those marks. But I'm not talking about the body. I'm talking about the man who was in the car with me. *That* man was not my husband. My husband died yesterday morning, at Xiong Tower, in the testing area."

Greene's mouth almost fell open. He collected himself quickly and went to her side, sitting gingerly on the edge of the bed. "Mrs. Ranga Rao, why don't you tell us what happened from the beginning?"

His presence seemed to have a calming effect on her. "Oh, Chief. I'm glad you're here. I— I shot someone, didn't I?"

He patted her hand. "You shot Juha. In the leg. But he'll be fine."

"Thank him for me, if you see him. And tell him I'm sorry."

Greene nodded. "Now, Mrs. Ranga Rao, the body we found at the wreck was your husband's. We have no doubt of that. Are you saying there was a different man in the car with you before the crash?"

"Yes! ... No." Marlena opened and closed her fists in frustration. "It *looked* like Raj. It *sounded* like Raj. But he wasn't acting like Raj. His mannerisms weren't quite right. The way he talked wasn't quite right. It was like ... like someone was *pretending* to be Raj."

Greene looked up at Shepherd, who rolled his eyes.

Shepherd sat in the chair next to the bed. "Mrs. Ranga Rao—Marlena—I know your husband was having a challenging time lately. I can tell you that he was strongly opposed to the drill we ran yesterday. And he'd been under a lot of stress lately with the new projector, hadn't he? Isn't that why you two were taking this trip?"

Marlena appeared to consider his words, weighing what she wanted to say against Xiong's new power structure. Dr. Ranga Rao had been Shepherd's superior, but now he was gone—and Shepherd was *her* superior.

"Go ahead," Shepherd said, another bad smile on his face. "Say whatever you want. My top concern right now is getting to the bottom of all this."

She looked like she wanted to spit at him. "That drill yesterday—if it *was* a drill—I knew you were behind it. Never mind how much of an asshole you are for pushing that through on Raj—you're an asshole for putting me through it. And Chief Greene. But especially me."

Greene admired her willingness to speak her mind—to say things he too had thought. He appreciated her standing up for him, but of particular interest was the implication that she hadn't been in on the drill, that her visit to his office and their conversation had been genuine.

He couldn't help himself. "You weren't aware of the drill?"

"No! And it wasn't a drill, I told you that already. I got a call from Raj—or somebody pretending to be Raj—at 9 o'clock last night, saying he was alive. I about had a heart attack."

Shepherd sighed quietly. "I'm sorry you had to go through that."

Marlena clucked her tongue at him. "No, you're not. You're a cold-hearted bastard who would torture his own mother if you thought it would raise the Xiong stock price half a gig. Don't you look at me like that; you said I could say what I wanted."

Greene's curiosity was piqued beyond restraint. "Mrs. Ranga Rao, what do you think happened yesterday?"

Shepherd snapped his fingers twice. "There'll be plenty of time for speculation later. Right now, I want to hear about this evening."

Marlena fumbled for her water cup, and Greene helped her with it. When she'd finished drinking, she said, "Thank you, Chief. Raj went to work early yesterday morning, and everything was fine." She gave Shepherd a pointed look, as if daring him to interrupt her. "Since that time—since last night, which was the first time I'd talked to him, when I was told it was a drill, he'd been acting strange. Last night, this morning, this evening."

Shepherd's incredulity was obvious. "Give us a concrete, specific way you think Dr. Ranga Rao was not himself."

"I'll give you one. Right before the crash, he tried to unbuckle my seatbelt. I was looking out the window, at the trees. And he must have thought I wasn't paying attention. I asked him what he was doing. He didn't answer. And do you know what he did? He drove that car off the road himself and into the tree. It wasn't an accident. It wasn't an attack—that came later. He crashed that car into that tree on purpose—to kill me."

"And why would he want to do that?" Shepherd asked, as if speaking to a small child.

"To make it look like an accident. Because I figured out he wasn't Raj."

"Tell me about the attack," Shepherd said.

Marlena furrowed her brow, concentrating. It must have caused her pain, because she brought a hand to her forehead.

"I'm sorry," Greene said. "This is the last thing we need from you, and then we'll let you rest."

She nodded. "There was the wreck. Blood in my eyes. Raj wasn't moving. I had to cut myself out. There was a van. There were other people there—right away, they were there. Dressed in gray, dark gray."

"We saw a van near the crash," Greene said. "It was leaving as we were arriving, moving away from Portsmith. We didn't see anything suspicious, though. Then what happened?"

"I had the knife and the gun in my purse—because of the imposter—and I managed to escape into the woods. I shot at them, but I don't think I hit anyone. Then Chief Greene found me. I don't know how long that was."

"Did you get a good look at the body?" Greene asked.

"No. There was blood. I was shaken up. The van was there right away."

There was a knock on the door, and Reich entered. "The doctor's outside, sir. He wants to know if you're almost done."

Shepherd looked at Marlena. "Anything else?"

Marlena tried again, unsuccessfully, to shake her head. "I can't think of anything else that would help."

"We'll have a guard outside the entire time you're here," Greene said. "If you remember anything else, you can tell one of them, or have them call me directly."

"Thank you, Chief."

Greene followed Shepherd into the hall, where they were flagged down by a white-haired doctor carrying a tablet. *Pole, Asher A., M.D.* appeared on Greene's heads-up display.

"Are you the Xiong Corporation?" Pole asked.

Shepherd nodded. "We are."

With Dr. Ranga Rao dead, Xiong had de facto medical power of attorney for Marlena, at least in the short term. It didn't do to think too hard about the ramifications of that, Greene decided.

"She should make a full recovery," Pole said. "We'll get her wounds printed up well enough that she ought to be able to go home by tomorrow, assuming her head injury cooperates."

"We were told she had a concussion," Shepherd said. "That means she could be experiencing some confusion? Some short-term memory problems?"

"That's possible, yes. Did she display these symptoms to you just now?"

"I think that's safe to say," Shepherd said with a sidelong look at Greene.

"Thank you for letting me know." Pole consulted his tablet. "Oh, and we have a Mr. Karjalainen downstairs who would like to know if your corporation will be covering his bioprinting. Normally, that's a matter for Billing, but he says he doesn't want it if you're not going to pay for it."

Shepherd rolled his eyes, naked disdain on his face. "Yes, we'll cover it."

"Very good," Pole said, and departed.

"Walk with me," Shepherd said to Greene, and set off toward the elevator.

Greene followed him down the hospital corridors in silence. Shepherd was no doubt trying to process the astonishing things they'd heard, just as Greene was.

Greene's thoughts returned to Juha. Was he capable of killing Dr. Ranga Rao to "free up" Marlena? Greene thought about the wild, unpredictable, borderline-sociopathic streak Juha had always had. He thought about the death of Hana, Juha's wife, and the suspicions he'd harbored—and still harbored, he admitted to himself. Yes, Greene decided, Juha was capable.

Of course, that by no means meant that Juha would, or did, or would even want to do it. And the circumstances didn't fit— they were backward, even if the outcome favored Juha: Dr. Ranga Rao's airbag should have been the one disabled and Marlena's left intact.

No, Greene decided, Juha wouldn't have been involved in something like that, not if he cared for Marlena half as much as Greene suspected. He mentally absolved Juha of that crime.

But Juha was not absolved of disabling Greene's car, as Shepherd had alleged. Greene realized that when he'd first stepped into Juha's bacon-and-incense-clouded apartment yesterday morning, he'd automatically put the same faith in the man that he'd had when Juha had been his superior officer. A lot could change—and had changed—in three years.

Greene shook his head. He didn't *want* to believe Juha would betray him like that—although Juha, he knew, wouldn't see it nearly so personally. Greene was scraping for reasons to excuse him and coming up with little. Only when he'd seen the hard evidence of the bank transfer from Algary would he be able to settle the issue in his mind.

Greene and Shepherd rode the elevator up to the roof. The Xiong helicopter was still there on the pad, on standby. The pilot leaned against its side, puffing on an herbal cylinder.

Shepherd took a deep breath of the night air. "That's better."

Greene appreciated the breeze, but the smell of the city it bore up to them—a hundred odors mingled together—was not an entirely pleasant one, even with the strides Portsmith had made on air pollution in the last decade.

Shepherd went to the railing at the edge of the roof, and Greene joined him. Portsmith stretched to the horizon, a seemingly infinite hive abuzz with color and activity. The sight of the city's full splendor always helped put Greene at ease, although he was never quite sure why. Perhaps because it reminded him that no matter what he did—whether he succeeded or failed—in this city of twelve million people, he was an insignificant speck.

In a hundred years, Portsmith would still be here, but Greene would be dead, and no one would remember him or how this fiasco he was currently embroiled in had turned out. The notion was both comforting and depressing.

In the meantime, however, he would struggle on. He forced the fey thoughts out of his mind.

Shepherd sighed. "A 'mild' concussion? I don't think she's right in the head. 'It's a drill,' 'It's not a drill.' And she hates me, but I knew that already. What do you think, Chief?"

"We have Dr. Ranga Rao's body," Greene said. "That fact in and of itself seems to negate all of her assertions about yesterday. However ... she's convinced that there was an imposter."

Shepherd leaned on the railing, chin to fist. "An imposter from, say, Algary, do you think? That would be a monumental achievement on their part. I'm going to need a bit of convincing. You spoke with Dr. Ranga Rao yesterday—did you notice anything unusual about him then?"

Greene racked his brain and came up with nothing—but he'd been in a state of shock the entire time. "No, sir."

"Do you think you spoke to an imposter or to the real Dr. Ranga Rao?"

Greene hesitated. "I really can't say. If it *was* an imposter, it was an exceptional performance."

Shepherd nodded. "From what I'm hearing from you and from Burg, this sounds like a pretty straightforward attack by Algary or Crestridge or whoever the hell. An attack that was thwarted by her resilience. What evidence do we have to the contrary?"

"Her airbags didn't deploy—none of them."

"You will no doubt determine the cause of that. Anything else?"

Greene thought. "Just the account she gave us."

Shepherd looked Greene in the eye. "She has a concussion, and I think she may also be having a nervous breakdown. She did lose her husband twice in two days. Find me some evidence, some real evidence, that what she's told us is the truth. Right now, I'd rather focus on the external forces at work here. I can see those a lot more clearly."

"Yes, sir," Greene said. "However ... I don't think it would be wise to rule an imposter out. I hope I'm wrong."

Shepherd sighed. "I hope you're wrong, too, Chief. Otherwise, it means we have a gaping security breach."

"But even if we set aside the idea that someone was impersonating Dr. Ranga Rao inside Xiong Tower, it's still possible that they could have gotten to him outside the building, at his home."

"I imagine so. But think about what you're saying. Are you seriously contemplating the idea that there was some kind of doppelgänger behind the wheel of the car? You found Ranga Rao's body there—and it was undeniably him."

This gave Greene pause. "What about the men in the van? Do you believe her on that?"

"You mean, was the wreck an accident or an attack? I say the latter. In which case, yes, I believe her."

Greene suddenly felt very tired. "I agree. But if it was an attack, we don't have much to go on. Even if we can determine the registration on the van from the car's cameras, it's likely to be forged or stolen."

"True. But we've also got Karjalainen, don't we?"

Back to this. "You're convinced he's involved." It was a foolish thing for Greene to say. Shepherd had already made his views abundantly clear.

Shepherd shook his head. "Chief Greene, why didn't your car start? Why didn't your traffic credentials work?"

Greene conceded the point. "What exactly is my objective here, sir?"

"Xiong Security's objective is to determine who killed our chief operating officer. The stronger the evidence, the harsher our reprisal can be. Burg can take point on that for the moment. Your job is to stay sociable with Karjalainen, let him lead you along, see where he wants to take you."

Greene didn't like it, not one bit. Again, Burg was being given the lead position on the investigation, and this on top of the fact that meanwhile, Greene was expected to play spy games with a man who, up until about an hour ago, he had trusted—mostly. He found it utterly distasteful, and he didn't think he was going to be particularly good at it, either.

But once more, he was taking things personally, he realized. Burg was experienced. She knew her business. She was a good officer. Greene was feeling insecure again, threatened. Shepherd preferred Burg; that was simply a fact he was going to have to learn to live with.

Shepherd cleared his throat. "That will be all, Chief. Why don't you go check on our mutual friend?"

Greene refused to let weakness show. "Yes, sir."

He made his way back to the elevator, wondering idly whether things would have played out any differently if he'd stayed at the crash scene and sent Burg to the hospital instead.

Probably not.

Juha wasn't difficult to find—he was in the waiting area outside the security ward, chatting with a heavy orderly, his business card in his hand.

"Hey, man," he said to Greene, "are we through here? Do you want to go get something to eat, or are you still on the clock?"

Greene looked at Juha with new eyes. Greene had always thought of Juha, oxymoronically, as unpredictable but reliable. Now that trust had been replaced with suspicion. Shepherd was asking him to pick up cobras.

But there was nothing to be done for it now, Greene thought. "Yeah, we can get something to eat."

"Are you okay?" Juha asked. "You look like crap."

Greene forced emotion from his face. "I'm just tired. I've got a lot on my mind."

As they headed for the exit, Juha said, "I wonder if this Ranga Rao dude will get murdered tomorrow, too. Go for the hat trick."

Greene found smoldering hostility flaring up. "Some of us care that he's dead."

"Hey, I care. I do. Just, you know, not like that."

Greene found himself overanalyzing every word that came out of Juha's mouth. Was this snark? Innuendo? Both?

"Anyway, how's Marlena? They wouldn't let me in to see her."

"Healing. She'll recover. She told me to tell you she was sorry for shooting you."

Juha waved a hand. "You can hardly see the limp anyway. I'll come back tomorrow, get it printed up the rest of the way—I'll be good by Saturday."

Juha's coupe was waiting for them at the hospital's circle drive. Xiong had sent it—no doubt infested with every possible electronic bug.

"So where are we going to eat?" Juha asked.

"Doesn't matter."

Juha went around to his side, opened his door, and paused. "Feel free to say no, but what if we went back to your place? I haven't seen your family in a long time, and there's something I need to talk to you about. We can pick something up."

Well, Greene thought, that was fast.

He didn't like the idea of letting Juha into his house, not now. And if he agreed, he'd have to have the place swept for bugs right away. But how could he refuse, apart from a feeble excuse about how late it was?

"All right," Greene said. He thought of his mother's biryani, wondered how it would fit with Juha's bizarre dietary practices, decided that wasn't his problem. "We have food."

Juha grinned. "Awesome."

They got into the car and Juha started it up. "Hello, old girl."

"Greetings, Lord of the Earth," the car said in its sultry voice.

Juha buckled his seatbelt. "All right, baby, take us to Green's house. How many e-diseases did they give you?"

The car pulled out of the drive. "Seven that I know of."

Juha rolled his eyes. "It's always some damn thing, eh? Do you have any idea how much it's going to cost me to get all that shit taken out? What else have you got, darling? Audio transmitter, of course, and phone tap. Telemetry?"

"Yes."

"Are my traffic credentials still there?"

"They are," said the car.

"But with remote override, right?"

"It appears so."

"Bomb?"

"Not to my knowledge. Dear me, I hope not."

Juha shrugged. "Well, that's something. You know, Green, dealing with you Xiong people is very nearly more trouble than it's worth."

SEVENTEEN

Greene stared vacantly out the car window as the city flew past, trying—and surely failing—to anticipate how their conversation was going to go. Dread lurked on his shoulder.

Juha slouched in his seat, his feet up on the dashboard. His phone rang.

"Let me take this. It's a rich client, possible investor. Hey, boss. It's close to midnight, you know that? No, it's cool, what's up?" His brow furrowed as the client spoke. "Okay. And? You drank a regular soda because you thought it was diet. That's it? What should you do? The treadmill? I guess, if you want to, sure. I don't think you need to worry about it though."

When he got off the phone, Juha said, "Some of my people are so uptight, you know? And then I've got other ones who are the complete opposite, people who don't know what the hell a treat is. They think because they come to my place and jump around for twenty minutes and get sweaty they can go and have a damn treat every damn day. Five hundred, eight hundred calories. You heard all that crap I was telling them back at FatAss, right? About moderation and whatnot, empowering them and such? 'Hurray for your tiny baby steps!'"

Greene didn't feel like talking about this, but he forced himself to be conversational. "It sounded reasonable. Sensible."

"Yeah, that's because I have to be careful. Mr. Positive, all the time—that's me. I'm not allowed to shame anybody. Shaming people causes stress, I'm told, and then people eat more and gain more weight, which is probably good for business but also a bunch of weak-minded bullshit if you ask me. They're all dumbasses, every one of them. Our society coddles the obese, you know that? Enabling. The people who are fat and happy, I have no problem with, enjoy your life. But these other people, getting their feelings hurt all the time ... 'Oh, fat shaming, my feelings!' Man, fuck your fat feelings. Shame is a personal problem. Take responsibility for your raggedy ass and get your shit together."

Greene's eyebrows went up. Where was all this coming from?

Juha shook his head. "I hate some of these people. Not because they're fat—you're not less of a person for being fat—ha, see what I did there?—but because they're so weak-minded. Some of these people can't get their shit together to even the slightest extent. You aren't capable of keeping yourself in a condition where you can walk up a flight of steps without your heart racing? You aren't sufficiently motivated to not eat yourself to death before your kids are grown? You don't care about yourself enough to look in the mirror and say, 'Maybe I should do something about this'? Get the fuck out of here."

It was the most conversational, even-toned tirade Greene had ever heard, and yet the animosity—hate projected both outward and inward—came across clearly.

Into Greene's mind leapt a powerful feeling that Juha had murdered Hana after all. The way Juha buried his emotions, the way he displayed that meticulously cavalier attitude toward every aspect of life made it easy for people to misjudge him—which was just how Juha liked it, Greene knew. And Greene had certainly misjudged him.

Juha was still looking at him, so Greene felt compelled to say something. "You're ... a closet obesity bigot."

Juha considered this a moment. "Yeah. That seems fair. I'll tell you a secret. I talk this and that about moderation, food-as-fuel, healthy relationships with food, and if these people get on board with that, great. But personally, I can't do moderation. Food and I cannot be allies. We cannot peacefully coexist. Each struggles continuously for mastery over the other."

"Seems like you've won."

"For now. But the battle is eternal. Look at this." Juha pinched the loose skin on his neck. "See this?" He pushed up one sleeve and jiggled the fold of sagging skin there. "When I was getting the graphics done for FatAss, my marketing guy told me I should get all this extra skin removed. That it would make me more attractive, be better for business. I told him no, obviously. I didn't let them alter the images, either."

"Why?"

There was an unusual seriousness in Juha's voice. "I need to see it every day. It reminds me of what I've been, of the things I've done. It reminds me that the shit we do has consequences."

Greene realized he had severely underestimated the extent to which Juha's abundant internalized hate was directed at Juha himself.

The car arrived at Greene's apartment. They exited, and Juha dismissed the car to Greene's garage.

"I like your building," Juha said. "It's straightforward. No holograms, no frills. Like you."

The front doors slid open before them and Greene froze. A handful of reporters still lingered in the lobby, blocking their path to the elevator.

"These kids have too much free time," Juha said. "You need some help?"

Greene shook his head. "Straightforward. No frills."

The reporters had seen him by now, and they descended upon him, practically falling over each other.

"Mr. Greene, can you comment on—"

"How does it feel to have—"

"What is Xiong Holonautics' new technology, and how does it—"

Greene strode into their midst, not stopping, not making eye contact. "I'm very pleased to have fulfilled my obligations both to Xiong Holonautics and to the city of Portsmith in protecting the company's rightful interests with zero civilian casualties."

The elevator door opened as Greene approached, and he stepped aboard, Juha right behind. The media pressed around the door, straining against their limits.

"Chief, that's yesterday's headline. What about—"

"The car wreck in Hollow Hills—a Xiong presence was seen out there, and rumor has it that—"

Greene turned and gave them his best winning smile as the doors closed. As soon as they were out of sight, he let it drop.

Juha shook his head. "You should have let me talk to them. I could have told them all about FatAss."

The elevator took them up. As they walked down the hall, Greene found himself becoming anxious again about what Juha was going to say. It was obvious he had something significant in mind.

Play along, Shepherd had said.

Greene went through the security checks, the door opened, and they entered. Ahead, the living room was dark, and he wondered whether Nisha and his mother had gone to bed. No; he could hear them in the kitchen.

The lights activated as they stepped into the living room. Something was amiss; it took Greene only a fraction of a second to spot it.

On the coffee table, a bundle of explosives and wires, a digital reading counting down from 5 ... 4 ... 3 ...

Beside him, Juha said, "Green, it's—"

2 ... 1 ...

Greene threw himself on top of Juha, knocking him to the tile floor and slamming the air out of both of them.

A blinding flash of light stunned Greene ... and that was all, or seemed to be. He sat up, surprised to find himself, the living room, and the coffee table utterly intact.

"—a hologram," Juha finished, when he could breathe again.

Greene stood, leaving Juha to fend for himself. A holographic bomb, run through the living room's projector system.

Juha hauled himself up and made a show of putting his hair back in place. "That was a hell of a thing."

Greene turned on him, a hard look in his eye. "Why did you want to come back here, Juha?"

"So you could fracture my ribs, of course. Damn, you're heavy. Maybe you ought to come by FatAss on your day off."

Greene maintained the stare.

"What?" Juha said. "Oh, you're serious. I wouldn't prank you like that; I know you have no sense of humor. It wasn't even a good prank anyway. I mean, it fooled you, but come on—did you ever see a bomb that looked like that in real life, with the red numbers and everything? That was the most generic movie bomb of all time."

Greene seethed, his teeth clenched so hard he thought they might break. To come into his house, to threaten his family, his wife, his unborn daughter—this was across the line.

"Somebody's obviously trying to warn you off of ... something," Juha said. "Dirty pool, I say, coming in your house like that."

The message had come through loud and clear. If someone could reprogram Greene's projector, they could do quite a bit more as well.

Juha shook his head. "Threatening your family ... that is a profoundly asshole move."

The urge to knock Juha back down was acute. Greene took a deep breath, but it was no use. This was just too much. He surrendered to his fury, clenched his fist, and took aim at Juha's jaw.

The kitchen door opened and Nisha called, "Green? Is that you?"

Greene froze, opened his hand, and let out a half-choked "Yes."

"One sec!" Greene heard the clink of dishes in the dining room, and then Nisha came into the living room. "Wow! Juha! Green was right! You look like a totally different person!"

Juha went to her and kissed her on the cheek. "A better one, I hope." He motioned to her belly. "Look at you. You look wonderful. I hope we're not keeping you up too late."

"No, we're kind of used to it by now." Nisha gave Greene a faux-snide look he was in no mood to appreciate.

Nisha had no idea what had just happened, Greene realized. No idea that there was any danger.

Juha looked back at Greene and winked.

Then Mother was there. "Well, Green-kutty, it's good they finally let you come home. What happened to your clothes? Who's this? I thought—"

Grinning, Juha flung his arms around her. "Hello, Auntie. You've been eating well."

"Juha? This is Juha?" She was looking at Greene.

He nodded, all his efforts concentrated on hiding his rage. The idea of Juha being involved with the holographic bomb and then making nice with his family like this was almost more than he could bear.

Mother looked Juha up and down. "You're starving! No one is feeding you! Do you not have any money?"

Juha laughed. "I'm starving myself. It's been great."

"Well, you're not starving yourself tonight." She led him into the dining room.

Greene took this opportunity to pull Nisha aside. "Has anybody been in the house today?"

She gave him a scrutinizing look. "No. Why?"

He shook his head, forced a smile. "Nothing."

"Obviously, it's not nothing. But you can tell me everything when we don't have company. Just tell me this: should I be worried?"

Greene looked at her and loved her. "No. Not yet. Let's go eat."

That she went without pressing further was a testament to her faith in him to do his job—to keep her safe. Wondering whether he was up to the task, Greene joined the others at the dining table.

Mother's goat biryani was excellent, as usual, but Greene ate without really tasting it, head down, lost in thought. When Mother asked why he was so morose, he told her only that it had been another long day.

Juha, in contrast, was as chatty as could be, picking up with Nisha and Mother as if he'd seen them the week prior. He didn't mention Xiong or Dr. Ranga Rao or the accident once, or the fact that he'd been shot; instead, he regaled them with the tedium of life on Mars, of the current state of genetically modified pig farming, and of the excitement of his new gym. At one point, he produced a FatAss card and gave it to Mother.

Juha had taken a relatively small portion of food, which he disguised by spreading his rice around to cover his entire plate. And he talked so much that he ate it extremely slowly, thus seeming to fill both Mother's desire to keep him eating and his peculiar caloric restrictions.

After Juha had told one too many old police stories that made Greene look bad, dinner ended. Mother went to wash up the dishes. Nisha went to bed. Greene and Juha returned to the living room and sat across the coffee table from one another.

Juha took out his phone. "Sonic scrambler on."

"Sonic scrambler active," said the phone.

Juha set it on the coffee table. "I don't want Xiong to hear this."

Greene raised an eyebrow. "I'm Xiong, Juha."

"Yes, you are ... but you're not, really. Not in the way I mean."

Greene recalled what Shepherd had said about Juha trying to earn his trust. He began erecting mental defenses.

"Fine," Greene said. "Go ahead."

Juha leaned forward, elbows on knees. "Somebody put some money in my account today. Cripple Creek Computing, a company I've never heard of. I'm talking a *lot* of money—a hundred thousand gigs. I think someone's trying to set me up for something. I have no idea what, but I figure it's got to be related to what's been happening the last two days."

Greene was nearly agape. All the angles, all the tricks he'd anticipated, and here was something he'd never expected. Juha, so charming, always trying to stay a step ahead.

"Cripple Creek is an Algary company," Greene said.

"Algary? Why would those guys be— Wait a minute. You already knew about this, didn't you? Damn. That means the money's from Xiong!"

Greene scowled at this weak attempt. "Hardly. It just means we know what's going on."

"You do? Of course you do—you're Xiong, after all. So tell me—I'm the last one to know anything these days."

Greene just stared at him, unwilling to make a fool of himself by explaining to Juha what he no doubt already knew.

Juha looked puzzled for a moment. Then he said, "You're suspicious of me! You think I took a payoff from whoever it was you said!" He laughed. "Well done, I didn't even realize."

"Didn't you?"

"Take a payoff? From who? For what?"

Greene's voice was hard. "Why didn't my car start today?"

"Because it's an Estados-made piece of shit? What am I, a mechanic?" Juha leaned back in his chair, apparently as unflapped as ever. "Your face is going to freeze that way, man. Think about what you're saying. I didn't tell you to come to FatAss today. You came on your own."

Yes, that was true. But it was also something Juha could have readily anticipated.

Juha shook his head. "You really think Algary is paying me to fuck with your company."

"It looks that way, yes." Greene held up his phone. "You think Xiong put that money in your account? I have access to all our financial records."

Juha waved a hand. "Don't waste your time. If the money's from Xiong, it'll be from one of your off-the-books accounts. I'm sure you don't have a handle on all of them."

"Why would Xiong even do that, Juha?" Greene asked.

"I don't know. Why would I put a holographic bomb in your house? To threaten you? That's weak. Look at me, I'm sitting in your house right now. I could kill you and your whole family if I wanted to, and you couldn't stop me."

Greene's face was death.

"Okay, sorry, under the circumstances, that didn't come out well." Juha rose. "You obviously believe what you're saying, or close enough to it, so I'm going to say good night. You think about it, come to your senses, and we'll talk later. But let me leave you with this: I think we're both getting played. I'm sorry they fooled you, whoever 'they' is. I hope none of us ends up getting murdered over it. Please thank Nisha and your mom again for dinner for me."

Juha went to the door and let himself out.

Greene remained in his chair, feeling utterly adrift. He'd expected ... well, not *this*. Could Juha be telling the truth? If so, then what in the world was going on?

He sat in the living room, grappling with the question, until he finally fell asleep.

When Greene got to work in the morning, Max Fill, who'd apparently been lurking in the lobby, pounced immediately.

"You gave the media a statement! Why?" Fill wailed. "Why are you talking to them when you haven't even come to see me yet?"

Greene strode toward the elevators, Fill at his heels. "I didn't give them a statement. They've been camped outside my house for two days. I didn't even stop walking."

"So you don't extend them any courtesies you don't extend to me either—that's gratifying to know. Nevertheless, the fact remains that this company is in dire need of your services in this regard. If you won't cooperate, I'll have to turn to Deputy Chief Burg, and she wasn't even involved—never mind that she's much less photogenic than you. I mean, she's attractive enough, but have you ever seen her smile, even once?"

Burg? Greene had little patience for PR's pandering, but if there was a chance to keep afloat over Burg in just one area ...

"I'll try to stop by this afternoon."

"Thank you, Chief, that's much appreciated," Fill said, and blessedly left him.

Burg's full report was waiting for Greene in his office. It contained nothing terribly unexpected. There was some footage of the van, which had no visible tags or distinctive markings. They'd found some bootprints in the woods, but no blood at the scene that didn't belong to either of the Ranga Raos or to Juha. Marlena's airbags hadn't been tampered with physically, which meant they'd been turned off electronically. Of greatest interest was the fact that nothing seemed to have forced the car off the road—no external force, in any case.

That meant either that the wreck had been an accident, that the car's computer had been reprogrammed, or, as Marlena had claimed, that a Ranga Rao doppelgänger had deliberately crashed the car with himself inside it. All things considered, reprogramming seemed like the safest bet.

IT confirmed this hunch. In place of the full report Greene was expecting was only a brief note stating that someone had installed a rather beefy lockout program on the car's computer and that IT thought they should be in by the afternoon, with the report to follow as soon as possible.

Greene was confident that these findings would give him the lead they needed, a target for Xiong Security's next move. Until then ...

His desk phone rang, an unlisted number. Greene felt a flash of anxiety as he picked it up.

"Chief Greene?" A woman's voice.

"Yes?"

"This is Marlena Ranga Rao. I need to speak with you right away."

"I have some time. I'll come by the hospital."

"I'm not at the hospital. I left."

"Oh." Greene was momentarily confused. "I thought you weren't getting discharged until this afternoon."

"I wasn't. I ... escaped. Meet me at the plaza across the street from the tower. Come right away. Don't tell anyone."

His mind locked onto the word *escaped*, and he thought again about her head injury. But what else could he do but go see her?

"All right," Greene said, and ended the call.

At this point, he was too lost even to speculate.

Greene rose, went to the door, and then turned back. He changed out of his suit and into his security uniform. He buckled on his tactical vest. He strapped on his heat ray and, after a moment of consideration, his conventional pistol as well. Thus equipped to be as minimally unprepared as possible, he grabbed his Spec-Trons and headed down.

Out of habit, Greene stepped immediately into the street, trusting in his credentials to stop and divert the crossing traffic. He made it across without incident, but in light of recent events, he thought, maybe he ought not to do that anymore.

The plaza's projectors were in the midst of displaying an unsettlingly graphic commercial for thigh-chafing powder.

Greene walked through the plaza, and at the sight of his uniform, passersby moved out of his way just as the cars had. Today, he didn't mind a bit.

The ad ended, and a sports broadcast resumed. Greene found himself on a soccer pitch, with holographic players running around and through him.

He found Marlena sitting at the fountain at the center of the plaza, dressed in jeans and a button-up shirt that was distractingly snug on her, the long sleeves covering her wounds. A bandage covered half her forehead. Greene sat down next to her.

"Thanks for coming, Chief." Her shirt was newly bought—it still had the creases from its in-store fold.

"Why are you here, Marlena?" The formality had disappeared, and Greene wasn't sure where it had gone.

The use of her first name didn't seem to bother her. "It's easy to get out. Only hard to get in."

"Why—how—did you 'escape'? My people were supposed to be protecting you. And since you came all the way down here, why didn't you just come to my office? Why are you out here and not in the tower? What safer place could there be for you than in the tower?"

"Did you find the imposter?" she asked. "Did you find out who's gotten inside the company?"

Greene sighed. "I haven't seen any actual evidence of an imposter."

"Have you looked? You think I'm crazy, don't you? Chief, if you won't listen to me, then no one will."

"We're working on it. We have evidence that someone tampered with the car's computer."

"See? There you go."

"That could have been any number of people. Whoever reprogrammed your car without being detected was a pro, but it would be relatively easy for someone to get at it. We hope to know more by this afternoon, and then we'll be able to act."

"You don't believe me. Why? Because I got hit in the head?"

No, Greene thought, because you're avoiding secure facilities, making outlandish claims unsupported by evidence, and generally acting like a crazy person.

She clasped her hands together. "I don't know what else to say to you, Chief. If you won't help me, I'll just have to try to figure this out on my own."

Ah, he'd always been a soft touch. That was probably why he was in this situation in the first place.

"All right," Greene said. "I'll look into it. I promise."

Marlena squeezed his hand. "Thank you."

"Meanwhile, where are you going to be?" If she wouldn't come into Xiong Tower, she probably wouldn't go home, either.

"I'll be around."

Greene didn't like the sound of that, but Marlena was already on her feet, walking away from him, away from Xiong Tower. Soon she had disappeared into the crowd.

He headed back to the tower, passing heedlessly through the soccer match. He had an idea. It might be impossible to prove all of Marlena's wild allegations, but maybe he could disprove some of them. It was something to do, at least, while he waited for IT's report.

Greene went to Medical. He passed the clinic and found Mainprize at the lab computer. She was wearing a white button-up medical suit covered in pockets. She looked up when he entered and quickly disguised her look of irritation at the interruption.

In spite of her demeanor, Greene was glad to find her. Of all Xiong's medical staff, she'd been most involved in the events of the last several days. He gave her a moment to resign herself to the indefinite cessation of her work.

She cracked her gum. "Yes, Chief?"

"You have Dr. Ranga Rao's body here, correct?"

"Yes."

"What can you tell me about it?"

"He's dead." She shrugged. "They brought him down last night, cleaned him up, and put him in the drawer. I haven't been in there today."

Greene tried to be patient. "Check your records, please. Surely you all ran some tests."

Mainprize pulled up the file. "We did a blood test and checked his dental records. Identity confirmed. That's all I've got."

"That's it?"

"That's it. We didn't get an order for an autopsy. He was impaled by a road sign, right? Not very mysterious. You'd really think they would have gotten holographic road signs put up out there by now."

Something was tickling Greene's brain, something he couldn't articulate. "I'd like to see the body."

Mainprize shrugged, then rose. "Let's go take a look."

Greene followed her to the morgue. In his three-plus months with the company, he'd never visited it. It was a small room, barely more than a closet, with six drawers. The room was spotless, all stainless steel and white tile. His stomach knotted as he thought about why this company had an onsite morgue in the first place.

The security door opened for Mainprize, who didn't appear to be the least bit squeamish as she pulled open a drawer and removed the shroud from the body within.

In death, Ranga Rao's face displayed a serenity that Greene found rather incongruous given the gaping wound in his chest.

Gum popped. "What are you looking for here, Chief?"

Greene wasn't exactly sure. "You can't tell me anything about the wound?"

"He died from it." Mainprize was obviously humoring him but wasn't succeeding in keeping the sarcasm out of her voice. "Massive chest trauma tends to have that effect on people."

"Both times," Greene said.

"What?"

"What happened on Wednesday?"

Her crinkled brow indicated that she wasn't following.

"Wednesday, Mainprize. When we thought Dr. Ranga Rao had been murdered upstairs. In the kill house. Was there or was there not a body? The police were here—there must have been."

"Right, right. Yes, the body came down. We put it in here. Later, we were told that it was a drill, that the body had been borrowed from the city morgue and made up to look like Dr. Ranga Rao."

"Do you still have that body?"

"No." She went to a wall panel and pulled up the records. "It was taken away on Wednesday night."

"Taken by whom?"

She shrugged. "By whoever arranged for it in the first place, presumably. It was Shepherd's drill, right? What's this all about? Is anything wrong?"

No, on the face of things, nothing seemed to be wrong—apart from Shepherd's tasteless grave robbing.

An idea flashed into Greene's mind. "That body had a massive chest wound, too, yes?"

"Obviously."

"Is there any chance this could be the same body?"

"I don't see how that's— Well, I guess it's theoretically possible. We didn't look at Wednesday's body closely. We just sort of chucked it in here because we were all busy with the crisis. I don't think anybody looked at it closely enough to see if it was really made up or not, if that's what you're getting at."

Greene raised an eyebrow. "You didn't even look at it?"

"I'm a busy woman, Chief," Mainprize said, defensive. "The cause of death wasn't in doubt."

"It's all right," Greene said. "I'm not criticizing you. It's just been a strange couple of days. Thanks for your help. I'll let you get back to work."

"Don't worry about it, Chief."

She followed him out.

On the way, Greene asked, "Just out of curiosity, what happened with Wheat once we got back?"

She snapped her gum. "Yes, we had him. I'm pretty sure they took him away the same time they took the other corpse."

Greene froze. "You had his body?"

"Yes."

"His *dead* body."

"We brought him straight down here off the helicopter."

He turned to face her. "And he was definitely dead? It was his body, you're sure?"

Mainprize looked at him like he was crazy. "Chief, I was there with you when he was shot. The bullet tore out his carotid artery—there was blood everywhere, remember? He died at the scene. You saw it and I saw it."

Yes, he had seen it. A Ranga Rao double was an implausible enough idea, but a Wheat double as well? That was too incredible. If Wheat was dead, the Wheat he'd seen in Ranga Rao's office had to have been a hologram. But why?

"Did they explain to you how this fatality fit within the context of a drill?"

Mainprize shrugged. "Not my department. I didn't ask. Kind of figured it was a botched hit on Shepherd. And if not, this company has certainly run drills with higher body counts, back before you got here. But now you've got me curious. What's this all about?"

Greene was still sifting through the data. He felt like the answer was close—it had to be close.

"Was Juha Karjalainen down here at any point?"

She went to the log. "He was down for treatment on Wednesday night, but he didn't go anywhere he wasn't supposed to be. We keep things locked down pretty tight here, Chief."

Greene nodded. "What about Marlena Ranga Rao?"

"She was down to view the body on Wednesday morning. She was here for about ten minutes."

"And there are no holographic projectors in this area?"

"That's right. None in the whole department."

"Thanks, Doctor."

Greene left and went directly to his office, feeling like he'd forgotten something. On the way, he found himself starting to believe that somehow, Marlena was right after all.

EIGHTEEN

Greene closed the door to his office, sat down at his desk, and pulled up Thursday's security records. Many sections of Xiong Tower had no cameras, but every Xiong employee was chipped.

He zeroed in on his own chip and ran through Thursday morning: entering the building, going up to the Armory, to his own office, and then to Ranga Rao's office. The system would show him by the chips exactly who had been in the office with him.

There was no record for Wheat, which made sense. Wheat, he'd decided, had been a hologram—and even if he wasn't, then he was an outside contractor on a mostly-off-the-books operation.

Greene ran the facial recognition program for Wheat on the footage for all Xiong Tower entrances over the last two days and received no results. Unsurprising.

He called the Security desk and got Sonnenschein. "I need you to get whoever's around and go through the records manually and see whether Bavarian Wheat or anybody with his build entered or left Xiong Tower in the last forty-eight hours."

"Yes, sir."

Greene ended the call, chewing his lip. It seemed unlikely in any case. He remembered what he'd wanted to ask Mainprize about, and he called Medical.

"Medical. Mainprize."

"I need you to go take a good look at the body you've got down there and tell me exactly what caused the chest wound. Do it now and call me back as soon as you figure it out. Please."

"All right, Chief."

Ranga Rao wasn't showing up on the record, either. But he wasn't a hologram—Greene had touched a living man, he had no doubt about it. An imposter, as Marlena had said?

Not necessarily, he realized. Thanks to Xiong Holonautics' clandestine and unscrupulous business practices and policies, it *could* have been the real Ranga Rao. For decades, the bottom line had been the only thing that mattered to Xiong Holonautics, and the company's most powerful executives had always had somewhat more latitude, legally speaking, with which to pursue the company's goals. The rank and file were constantly under the watchful eye of Xiong's higher-ups, but the movements of those upper-level executives weren't tracked, either in or outside of Xiong Tower.

But they were chipped. Greene knew they were chipped. At least, he took it on faith that they were chipped—for their own protection if not for accountability. But for the chief of security not to have access to that data—how ridiculous for Greene to need authorization just to do his job. It spoke volumes about the level of internal mistrust that had existed—and still existed—within the company.

Greene shook his head. Remember where you are, he told himself. If you wanted checks and balances, you wouldn't have taken this job.

He had to get that data. It would answer a lot of questions, and it should settle for good the most pressing one: who he'd spoken with, whose hand he'd shaken yesterday in Ranga Rao's office.

Shepherd could get him what he needed. The CTO wouldn't appreciate Greene continuing to chase this imposter angle, but Greene felt they'd moved well beyond unsubstantiated speculation. He had to know.

He was reaching for the phone to call Shepherd's office when it rang—Medical.

Gum popped. "The wound is super clean, Chief," Mainprize said. "If you're asking me to pick between an old metal pole and a hologram, I'm going hologram all the way."

"Thank you very much," Greene said, and disconnected.

So Dr. Ranga Rao had been murdered on Wednesday morning after all. And then ... What? Someone had taken the body from the morgue, kept it fresh, crashed the car on Thursday, and then placed the body in the car?

It fit, he supposed. Such a stunt would have required complex logistics, utter secrecy, and Xiong security authorization, but it fit.

Greene still had no idea as to the why of it, but he could think of only one man with the wherewithal to pull off that sort of operation: Lord-Is-My-Shepherd.

Greene put his head in his hands. "Oh, God."

Shepherd had to be involved, was probably the mastermind, with Wheat working under him.

If Ranga Rao really had been murdered on Wednesday, it seemed reasonable to assume that the projector had really been stolen and that nothing that had occurred that entire day had been a drill.

Shepherd could have pulled it off. Shepherd could have disabled Greene's car and deactivated his credentials to keep him from interfering with the wreck. Shepherd could have put that money into Juha's account. Shepherd could have engineered the car crash, and what must have been a botched attempt on Marlena's life.

But why? Beyond his motive for killing Dr. Ranga Rao, what was the motive for the ruse? Why was it necessary for Ranga Rao to "live" one more day? Surely not simply for PR and the stock price, as the doppelgänger had said. If the ruse had been directed only outward, to the public, such a thing would make sense. But there was too much internal deception for that to be plausible—far too much.

Shepherd must have had a plan in place on Wednesday, a plan that Greene and Juha had somehow thwarted—and by doing so sent Shepherd scrambling. The more Greene thought about yesterday's events—the false Ranga Rao, the news about the "drill," the crash—the more they seemed reactive rather than proactive, a plot put together on the fly. The ruse involved too many lies to stand up under scrutiny, or for more than a day or two—it had worked thus far primarily because Shepherd had managed to keep Greene and everyone else off balance.

And because he'd taken advantage of the company's dutiful, obedient, eager-to-please chief of security.

In all, it was a tremendous accomplishment. The amount of power Shepherd had to be able to wield to pull it off—he was without question the most dangerous man in the company, perhaps in all of Portsmith.

Sitting in his office, in the midst of the best corporate security force in the city, in the headquarters of one of Portsmith's most powerful corporations, Greene felt suddenly unsafe. Unseen eyes pricked the back of his neck. He feared for the safety of his wife, his mother, his unborn daughter. He didn't dare call to warn them, either with his cell phone or the office phone. Where could he tell them to go, in any case?

Shepherd's throw-everything-at-the-wall approach was unsustainable—he had to have a very short-term goal. Greene had to act immediately.

But what did he actually have? More than enough rope to hang himself with, for certain, but it boiled down to little more than circumstantial evidence pointing at Shepherd, and no real motive. It wasn't enough. As with a raging bear, Greene had to bring Shepherd down on the first shot. He wouldn't get a second.

Greene's immediate priority hadn't changed: he needed proof of who he'd talked to in Ranga Rao's office. But who could he trust?

Garcinia was his best bet. If he could trust anyone, it was her. And if anybody could get him quietly into the C-level security, she could.

He jumped to his feet, then froze. He'd almost blown the entire operation. He pulled off his Spec-Trons. Surely Shepherd could—and undoubtedly had—used them to track Greene's activity. Greene had, unwittingly, been sabotaging his own efforts all along. No wonder Shepherd had been so able to stay so consistently ahead of him.

Greene switched the Spec-Trons off, stuffed them in a drawer, found his sonic scrambler, and left the office.

He found the elderly head of R&D in her personal lab, a sleek, spare room with a full array of holographic projectors and cameras mounted on the ceiling. The many tables were piled with devices and components.

When Garcinia saw him, she put down the machine she was tinkering with and wiped her hands on her large-pocketed white coat. "Oh, hello, dear. You look like you're ready for action. What can I do for you?"

"I need your help. Is there somewhere we can talk?"

She turned her hands palm-up. "This room is as good as any."

"Somewhere private. Somewhere without cameras."

"Hm? Oh. How mysterious! Come this way."

"Bring your tablet," Greene said. "Leave your Spec-Trons."

She complied, then led him down the hall to a storage room. When the hall was clear, they stepped inside. Garcinia sat down on a parts crate, beaming with anticipation.

Greene felt a bit foolish, sneaking around like this. He squatted, facing her, and activated his sonic scrambler.

"I need access to C-level security," he told her.

"Oh. Is that all?" She looked disappointed. "I'm not even the right person for you to be talking to. Wait, is this about Raj?"

Greene hesitated. Could he really trust her?

Be serious, he told himself. Why else was he hiding in a closet with her? He had to take a leap of faith at some point if he was going to get anywhere—and this seemed like the safest leap to make.

"Yes, it's about Dr. Ranga Rao. About his murder."

"Murder? But the car accident ..."

Greene shook his head. "Murder. I need you to help me prove it."

"Oh, dear. The last several days have been rather bewildering, I must say. You should really be talking to Shepherd, you know. He can authorize everything you need."

"Yes, I know. But I'm not sure getting that authorization from him is going to be possible."

"Well, there are others, too. I wish I could help you, dear, but—"

Greene held up a hand. "I need *undetectable* access. You've been with this company for what, thirty years? You've been in our computer systems that whole time. You could get me in there without anyone knowing, couldn't you? You could access that data for me right now, couldn't you?"

"Well ..."

He took that as a yes. "This is a legitimate security issue. Our executives are chipped for security and I'm the chief of security and I'm trying to get to the bottom of an internal security matter. You were close to Dr. Ranga Rao, weren't you?"

"Oh, yes. We worked together for nearly ten years. He was a wonderful man."

"Then help me catch his killer. I'm convinced he was murdered. If he was, his killer—or the man who hired the killer, I should say—is still at large. In this building. I need your help to prove it."

Garcinia knit her brow. "How terrible. Of course I want to help you if that's the case, but we should go talk to—" She clapped her hands suddenly. "Shepherd! It was Shepherd, wasn't it? That pompous ass! He's the reason we're hiding in this closet, isn't it?"

"Yes." Greene relaxed slightly. Any doubts he had about Garcinia had been put to rest.

"Tell me what you need," Garcinia said.

"I've just been down in the morgue. It looks like Dr. Ranga Rao was killed on Wednesday, by the projector, like we all originally thought, and not in the car crash. But on Thursday, I got called into his office, and he was there."

"A hologram?"

"No. He shook my hand. It was a real hand. He was wearing a real ring. Do we have any technology that can replicate that feeling?"

Garcinia shook her head immediately. "Not remotely."

"That's what I thought. That's why I need the C-level access—so I can prove it wasn't Dr. Ranga Rao I was talking to."

She mulled this over for the better part of a minute before saying, "Oh, very well. I'll need a little bit if you don't want anyone finding out what we're up to."

She went to work on her tablet for what felt to Greene like an hour but was probably closer to five minutes.

"Ready," she said at last.

At Greene's direction, Garcinia pulled up yesterday's security record for Ranga Rao's office. She held the tablet so Greene could see it. "So this is where you came into the office ..." Greene could see himself, a blip at the doorway. The blip moved into the room. "And this is what it looks like with the C-level authorization." A second blip appeared in the spot corresponding to behind the desk. "Ah, there we are."

Greene squinted at the screen, surprised. "Is that Dr. Ranga Rao? How is that possible? Could someone have been using his chip, his signal?"

"No." Garcinia's voice was grim. "It's not him. It's Shepherd."

Greene's train of thought hitched. "How is that possible?"

"Shepherd must have projected Ranga Rao over himself. They have similar heights, you know, similar builds."

Greene grabbed a crate. He needed to sit down. "But I didn't see any ghosting. He was up, he was moving around, he was waving his arms."

"None? You didn't notice anything amiss?"

"Nothing." Although, Greene admitted to himself, he'd been so utterly shocked to see Dr. Ranga Rao alive that he might not have noticed anything like that.

"He must have been using a facial projector, then," Garcinia said.

Greene blinked. "A what?"

"It looks like a collar, with some bits on the shoulders as well to make the hologram three-dimensional. It doesn't project onto the face, exactly, but in front of it, around it. If it's properly calibrated, it can do a face with no ghosting with ... what are we up to? Sixty-two-point-seven percent reliability, I want to say. I'd have to check the file. Not wonderful, but it's coming along."

This tugged at Greene's brain. It sounded familiar. Shepherd had mentioned it, on the helicopter. "He told me that technology wasn't ready yet."

Garcinia hugged the tablet to her chest. "It's not. We have a barely workable prototype. It's been a pet project of Shepherd's for a while now. But it isn't nearly good enough to use reliably—in fact it's one of the areas we're lagging behind Algary."

Greene rubbed his face with both hands. "Why don't I know about this?"

She shrugged. At Xiong Holonautics, it was a question that didn't really require an answer.

"Is it just another projector?" Greene asked. "I mean, is the tech standard? It's not solid, not any kind of hologram I've never seen before?"

"Not significantly, no."

"Then why is it so secret?"

"Ah." Garcinia frowned. "That's because if you think about it, there really are no scrupulous uses for it. Not a single one. Its only purpose is deceit. What can you use it for besides fooling people? Even public knowledge of it would result in total mistrust of our company. I'm sure you can imagine. No, I think we're fine with Algary moving first on this one."

Greene could indeed. Mistrust of the company, within the company, outside the company, throughout the city. Chaos would erupt until appropriate ID countermeasures could be universally implemented. The effects on Xiorg's almighty bottom line would be disastrous.

And Shepherd had such a device. Greene's mind sprinted from implication to implication, starting from Wednesday morning and running up to the present. There had been no drill. Dr. Ranga Rao had been murdered by the projector in the kill house, which meant that the projector really had been stolen. Wheat's accomplice Lewis And Clark was really dead, and so was Wheat himself. Shepherd must have had the bodies disposed of.

Greene took the tablet from Garcinia and went through Shepherd's activity over the last two days. The man appeared to have spent considerable time on Wednesday and Thursday impersonating Dr. Ranga Rao.

"Shepherd was driving the Ranga Rao car," Greene said. "He must have been. He crashed it deliberately, trying to kill Marlena and make it look like an accident, because she suspected him. And then he put the real body in the car."

"That's quite a feat," Garcinia said.

Greene leaned back against the wall and felt all the air go out of him. "Everything that man has said to me in the last forty-eight hours has been a lie. Every word of it. This is catastrophic. It could not be worse."

"And yet you recovered the prototype and caught the murderer in spite of all his efforts," Garcinia said. "That's really quite something."

Greene supposed it was. "I'm not sure what good that's done, though, since Shepherd's essentially had free run of the place for the last two days. But why? Why would he go to these elaborate lengths?"

"Maybe it wasn't about Dr. Ranga Rao. Maybe it was about the projector, about stealing the prototype."

Greene considered this, then shook his head. "He's the CTO. He doesn't need to conduct a physical raid of the company to get what he wants. Why would he need to go to all that trouble? He went to a stupid, foolish amount of trouble. Maybe he couldn't just walk out the door with the prototype, but he has access to all the specs for it, to everything you'd need to build another one. Those plans could be worth half a billion gigayuan."

"Then why?"

Greene scratched his chin. "I don't know. I think Dr. Ranga Rao was the reason. The projector was either icing on the cake or it was stolen to throw us off the scent."

"A half-billion-gigayuan red herring?"

Greene shrugged. "What I don't understand is, why all the lies? Why pretend it was a drill? To buy an extra day? And why impersonate Dr. Ranga Rao? That's a desperate move. Not safe, not smart. That's why he ended up having to try to kill Marlena."

"He was off-plan."

"I had the same thought."

Garcinia stroked her chin. "It was your adorable friend, I think."

Juha. They never would have taken down Wheat without Juha, and they wouldn't have recovered the projector either.

And what would have happened then? Greene could think of one possibility: he, Greene, would have been blamed for the entire fiasco and fired. Shepherd would have been able to clean house in Security as much as he wanted to ensure that there were no further investigations. Xiong would have taken a hit, but Shepherd would have had the opportunity to consolidate his power within the company even further.

Was that right? Greene couldn't say. Killing Ranga Rao was a brash move, too brash for a simple power play for someone already as high-ranking as Shepherd. But Greene felt like he was in the ballpark.

"Where's Shepherd now?"

Garcinia consulted her tablet. "In his office."

"I don't suppose you can get into his personal records? Find out what he's been doing the last couple days?"

She had a twinkle in her eye. "Give me a little bit of credit, will you?" Garcinia went to work. "All my years here ... you're right, Chief, I have back doors all over the place. Look at me, a harmless little old lady. Nobody here takes me seriously as a player because I don't care about power, and I make no secret of that. I love creating. I love technology. I'm happy doing those things. But working for this company, you learn to protect yourself. You learn that very quickly."

Greene thought that might be the best advice he'd ever heard.

"Now then, Shepherd, what do you have for me?" Garcinia pursed her lips. "Tsk. That firewall is so last year. And you're keeping it all in a sandbox; well, that's no trouble. Dear me, is this our standard security suite? Our intrusion detection is, frankly, underwhelming. Well, there are our data. Now let's see if my decryption key is worth a damn."

While she worked, Greene made himself take slow, deep breaths. Even with evidence on his side, the prospect of walking into Shepherd's office and escorting him to a holding cell was daunting. He wondered if it would go half as simply as he imagined. Nothing ever seemed to.

Garcinia cleared her throat. "Here we are. Do you want the short version or the long version?"

Greene snapped back into focus. "I want to know what hard evidence we have."

"Well, there are messages he sent to intermediaries on Wednesday when our stock plummeted to buy up a ton of it. And he's been moving company assets around quite a bit lately. Looks like he's been at it for some time—he's pulled nearly every patent we have at one point or another. He's really stepped it up in the last two days, though—by an order of magnitude, almost. Much less discrete. It's almost like a snatch and grab. Why settle for five million gigayuan in compensation when you can run off with the whole billion-gig cookie jar? Going to go overseas, Shepherd, maybe go into business for yourself?"

"You think he's getting ready to bolt," Greene said. "Then all this business with Dr. Ranga Rao was just to keep us busy."

"It looks that way. And probably to get access to Raj's home files. But yes, Wednesday afternoon was when he really stepped it up."

"Wednesday afternoon ..." Greene tried to make sense of it. "That was when we recovered the prototype. But so what? Even if we hadn't recovered it, he could have put the blame on Wheat; Shepherd would be in no trouble himself."

"It must have something to do with Wheat, then."

"Maybe. Maybe if we hadn't caught Wheat, we wouldn't be in this situation."

"What do you mean?"

Greene recalled something Juha had said yesterday at FatAss. "Wheat brought the projector right to Clark's house, right to us. Juha thought it was awfully convenient. I think he was right. I think Shepherd knew what I was going to do. Wheat was supposed to kill us. Or else we were meant to get the projector back and Wheat was meant to escape. I was going to let him go. But Juha chased after him. Shepherd couldn't have us interrogating Wheat, giving him away. So he had to eliminate him. He could have had a sniper or maybe he just used the solid projector—it was right there on the helicopter. Of course we were going to investigate Wheat's killing, and then we were going to find the trail back to Shepherd." Greene shook his head. "What better way to get us off the trail than to tell us it was a drill? With 'Dr. Ranga Rao' there to tell me so himself, how could I think otherwise?"

"Don't be hard on yourself, dear. You've done more than anyone could have expected." Garcinia smiled. "More than Shepherd expected, to be sure. Are these data enough for you?"

Greene made himself return her smile. "It's more than enough. Thank you for your help."

He had one thing left to do before he went to collect Shepherd. He had a number in his phone he had never called, never dared to call, and he wasn't sure what would happen when he did.

He pulled it up now: *Xiong Xiuquan, President, Xiong Holonautics*.

Greene had never met Mr. Xiong, never even seen him. He had no idea if the man was in Xiong Tower, in Portsmith, or, as Juha had joked, whether he really existed at all.

Greene switched off the sonic scrambler and called the number. After a moment, a small old-style translucent blue-scale hologram appeared on the face of the phone courtesy of its rudimentary projector.

The hologram was the head of a middle-aged man with a flawless face and strong features. Greene had no doubt he was looking at a construct, a program, and not at a real person.

"Chief of Security Green Pacha Greene," said the head. "Proceed."

Greene gave a concise account of Shepherd's activities.

There was no emotion on the construct's face or in its voice. "What evidence do you have of these allegations?"

Greene nodded to Garcinia, and she transmitted the data to his phone.

"One moment." The construct closed its eyes, then opened them again. "It is sufficient. You are fully authorized to take whatever action is necessary to protect this company and its interests. Do your duty, Chief Greene."

"Yes, sir," Greene said, but the construct had already vanished.

"How interesting," Garcinia said. "What are you going to do, Chief?"

Greene stood. "I'm going to go get Shepherd."

NINETEEN

Greene stepped out of the supply room, and his phone rang. To his surprise, it was Juha.

Greene answered it. "This isn't really the best time." He owed Juha an apology, would give it to him later.

"Hey, man, I've been trying to get a hold of you for like ten minutes," Juha said. "I'm downstairs. I need to talk to you and they won't let me in the building."

Greene wanted to tell Juha to go away, to go home, but he stopped himself. "I'll be down in a minute," he said, and ended the call.

"Let me come with you," Garcinia said. "It might be good for you to have a reliable witness. Plus if this is all true and Shepherd killed Raj, then I want to see his smug face when you nail him."

"Come on," Greene said, and they went downstairs.

Juha sat on the floor just inside the front door like a derelict in jeans and a T-shirt, his backpack beside him, undoing and redoing his ponytail. Marlena stood beside him, focused on her phone.

The two security guards at the checkpoint nodded deferentially to Greene as he passed.

Juha nodded at him. "Hey, man. We were just talking about you." Greene took Juha's hand and pulled him to his feet. "Listen, as you know, I still have a lot of connections around town. I've been doing some legwork, trying to figure out where that money came from. It's not from Algary. I think I can prove that to you if you'll hear me out."

"I know. I'm sorry. I've just found out. It was Shepherd. Everything was Shepherd."

Marlena gasped. "I knew it. I told you, I knew it."

Juha looked Greene over: tactical gear, heat ray, pistol. "And you're about to go bust his ass, aren't you?" He elbowed Marlena. "We got here just in time."

"No, you can't—" Greene stopped. Why couldn't they? The more the merrier. "Fine, let's go."

He turned around, headed back toward the elevators, and was stopped at the checkpoint.

"I'm sorry, sir," said one guard, Rich Lather, in a state of obvious anxiety. "He's not allowed in."

Greene tried not to show his impatience. "I'm ordering you to let him through."

Lather looked as if he desperately wanted to be somewhere else. "I can't, sir. The entrance ban comes directly from Mr. Shepherd."

Juha sidled up to Greene and whispered, "Just whip out that heat ray and shoot him. He'll get over it."

Greene shoved Juha away. He was in the midst of clenching his fists and setting his teeth when he stopped himself. Why should he be frustrated? He had the full authorization of Mr. Xiong himself.

Greene looked up and up at the hulking Lather, met his gaze. "Check the order again."

Lather shrugged apologetically, a cascade of rippling muscle. "We just checked it five minutes ago, sir. I'm sorry, sir. You know that Mr. Shepherd has the power to—"

"I have the power. Check it again or you're fired."

Lather's eyebrows went up. He exchanged glances with the other guard, shrugged again, and then went to look.

He returned wearing a confused expression. "Huh. Okay, Chief. Sorry about that. He's clear now. You can go on ahead."

"Thank you. Now listen. We have ... a situation. I'm about to lock down the building. No one in or out. Especially out. *No one*, do you understand? Lock the doors when you get the order. I don't want to have to close the front blast doors; that always makes the news."

"Yes, sir, but why—"

Greene waved this away. He didn't like talking to his people like they were children, but he didn't have time for this now. "Do you understand me?"

"Yes, Chief."

Greene led the others to the center of the glorious Xiong Tower lobby, where he gave the lockdown orders with his phone and then called Burg.

"I'm ordering a full quiet lockdown, Burg. Nobody in, nobody out, no alarm. I want security at every exit. Every single one."

"What's happening?" Burg asked.

"I'm taking Shepherd into custody."

"What? Why?" Burg's shock was apparent in her voice.

Garcinia touched Greene's arm. "Shepherd has left his office."

Greene nodded acknowledgment. "I will be glad to explain that to you later."

There was silence for a moment, then a huff. "Fine."

Greene ended the call and turned to Garcinia. "Where's Shepherd going?"

Garcinia consulted her tablet. "He's on the elevator. Going up."

Juha thumped Greene in the arm. "You didn't lock down the elevator?"

"I'm trying not to tip our hand," Greene said.

"Well, let's go get his ass, then."

"Elevator or no, he can't get out of the building under lockdown," Green said.

"Don't put it past him," Marlena said.

"He's stopped," Garcinia announced. "He's in the kill house."

Greene nodded. "He's going to try to override the elevators to the roof."

"Looks like you tipped your hand after all, boss," Juha said.

"He must have gotten the lockdown signal. All right, let's go."

As they headed toward the elevators, Garcinia seized Greene's arm in a surprisingly firm grip. "Chief ... yesterday, that room received a full installation of solid projectors. They cover ninety-seven percent of the floor area."

"Wonderful." Greene attempted to shut down power to that floor with his phone. It wasn't working.

Garcinia peered over his shoulder at the screen. "He must have countermeasures in place."

Greene attempted to revoke Shepherd's access to Xiong's systems. This, too, failed. "More than you know."

"Protect yourself," Garcinia said. "Number one rule around here."

"Shit," Juha said. "That place'll be a deathtrap. If he's in control of all of those projectors, he'll be like a goddamn wizard. There's no telling what we'd be walking into. Dude could conjure up some automated gun turrets, an army, a fucking herd of furious unicorns."

"We can't wait him out," Greene said. "He's got too much control of the system. I'd be surprised if he isn't able to override the elevators eventually. Sooner rather than later." He called Burg again. "I need a team to the roof. Have the helicopter take off, just get it away from the tower. And have a full security team meet me at the Armory, assault gear."

"He'll have his own helicopter," Juha said. "Probably on autopilot. I would."

Greene agreed.

"Look here," Garcinia said, and they huddled around her tablet. "This is the floor plan of the kill house. Here are the main elevators; that's where we'll be going up. For safety, there's about a five-meter arc that the projectors don't cover. Here are the elevators to the roof; there's the same kind of safety zone there.

The projectors don't cover these areas, so we won't have to worry about getting blasted the instant the elevator doors open, but beyond that, I'd imagine it could be quite dangerous. Everywhere else in the room is covered by the solid projectors."

"Can you shut the projectors down?" Greene asked.

"Of course ... eventually. Shepherd has some new systems in place I'm not familiar with."

"Before he overrides the elevator controls?"

Garcinia looked downcast. "I can't promise that."

"Is there any other way to shut him down?" Juha asked.

"Quickly?" Garcinia shook her head. "Not unless you want to cut power to the entire building."

Greene shook his head. "That would cause as many or more problems as it would solve."

"You've got a room that dangerous and you don't have any kind of shutdown override?" Juha asked.

"Of course we do," Garcinia replied. "But he's managed to lock us out of it somehow."

Juha shrugged. "It's always some damn thing, eh?"

"Let's go," Greene said.

They went to the elevators. One set of doors opened, and Max Fill stepped off. "Ah, Chief, I'm looking forward to your visit to my—"

Greene stepped onto the elevator. "I'll reschedule."

"But— I—"

Juha patted Fill on the chest as he passed. "PR, right? Relax, buddy. Go take a long lunch. You're really going to earn your money tomorrow."

"What? Chief!"

The elevator doors closed on Fill.

"Armory," Greene said, and the elevator bore the four of them up.

A security team of six was already in the Armory when they got there, getting outfitted with liquid body armor, ballistic helmets, and the standard Xiong bullpup carbines.

Kingjack, the quartermaster, met them. "Chief. What's happening?"

Garcinia patted his arm. "Shepherd is evil and we're going to go kick his ass."

Kingjack blinked. "What?"

"I'll fill you in later," Greene said. "Give me the same loadout. Burg has already been here?"

"Already left. With light gear, though. I don't think she's going to as fun a party as you are." Kingjack smiled. "You sure you don't want any of these non-lethal options? We've got plenty."

"Not this time." Greene looked over his team. "This isn't riot control or a fleeing suspect. This is a cornered animal."

One of Kingjack's people brought Greene his gear, and he began to strap it on. "Juha, get what you need."

Juha shook his head. "I don't want to wear all that stuff. Cuts down on mobility."

"Don't be stupid. You know what we're getting into."

Juha returned his gaze. "I know exactly what we're getting into. You remember what happened to Clark? Projector cut him clean in half. I don't think any amount of armor would have helped that poor bastard. What I want is some grenades. Can I get some grenades?"

Greene raised an eyebrow. "What are you going to do with grenades?"

"I like to be prepared is all."

"Prepared for what?"

Juha sighed. "I don't know exactly, but I don't want to get up there and then we get into a situation and I'm like 'Shit, man, I wish I had some grenades.' What are you worried about? I'm sure this place has great insurance."

Greene turned to Garcinia. "What would a hand grenade do to a force field?"

"Disrupt it completely," Garcinia replied. "But only for a few seconds. If the projectors are undamaged, the force field would be good as new almost immediately."

"If force fields are up, you won't have room to throw them," Greene said.

Juha rolled his eyes. "I don't want to throw them. I just want to have them. Just forget it—you're so overprotective."

Greene nodded to Kingjack. "Give him a couple of grenades. Some flashbangs or something."

"Sweet." Juha went across the room with Kingjack to get them.

Fully armored, Greene slung his carbine across his front. "Garcinia, what about those force field jackhammers?"

"I only have two so far. I could go get them, but ..."

"Yes?"

"They're small, experimental. There are too many projectors up there. The overall strength of the fields will be too strong."

"Might as well, just in case."

Garcinia nodded. "I'll have someone bring them up."

Now Greene turned his attention to Marlena, who was being helped into a vest by Juha. "You don't have to come," he said. "It could be dangerous."

She gave him a hard look. "I'm coming."

Why did he bother? "Fine."

Neither could Garcinia be dissuaded.

"But you can combat his systems from anywhere in the building," Greene said.

She shook her head. "He's shut down all the cameras up there. I'll have a better time of it if I can actually see what he's doing—and if by some chance you can get me into the kill house control room, I'll really be able to shut him down. In any case, I'll do what I can for you."

Greene assented. The old woman looked ridiculous in armor, but she seemed quite happy with it.

At last, they took the elevator up.

"We're going to give Shepherd a chance to surrender," Greene told his team. "One chance. If he doesn't, then it's weapons free. Please understand that he's going to be extremely dangerous. I want him alive if possible, but not at the expense of any of your lives. Is that understood?"

The six nodded.

Garcinia poked Greene in the arm. "Shepherd's disrupting his signal."

"Hold elevator." The car stopped. "What does that mean?"

She shook her head. "It means that I can't tell you where exactly in the kill house he is."

"Hide and seek," Juha said. "Good times. I'm going to have the worst migraine after this, I bet."

"Resume elevator. You've all gone through some degree of holographic training," Greene said to his team. "This will not be like that. The projectors throughout the kill house can now project force fields. When the doors open, it will be faster, more confusing, and more dangerous than you are expecting. I want you to secure the safety zone and stay within it until I give the signal."

Greene had no idea what to expect when the doors opened. It occurred to him to tell his people to be ready for anything, but that would be a profoundly stupid thing to say. It was impossible.

Instead, he said, "Let's go."

Greene hit the button, and the doors opened. He sprinted out of the elevator, gun ready, and stopped at the thick black-and-yellow curved stripe that marked the limit of the no-force-field zone. What he saw surprised him.

There were no holographic gun turrets, no automated soldiers, no rabid fantasy creatures. Greene could identify no holograms of any kind.

At the far end of the enormous room, at the top of the stairs to the control center, stood Shepherd, resplendently dressed. His face was placid; his arms were clasped behind his back. Smirking, he radiated condescension and arrogance down upon them.

"Have you come out as against a robber, with swords and clubs to capture me?" Shepherd said. "Did you think I was going to hide from the likes of you? With whom, exactly, do you think you are fucking?"

Greene adjusted his helmet. "This is your one chance to surrender, Shepherd."

Shepherd sneered.

Beside Greene, Juha said, "That's not him. It's a hologram."

Then where was Shepherd? Greene turned back to his group, looked them over: Garcinia and Marlena back by the elevator, Juha and the seven members of Greene's security team in position across the safety zone.

Seven?

Juha had followed his gaze, was already moving. At the other end of the safety zone, a man in a Xiong security uniform whom Greene didn't recognize was bringing his carbine to his shoulder.

As Greene dropped to the floor and brought his weapon to bear, the man fired several bursts. Greene was aware of grunts, blood, bodies hitting the floor. Juha sprinted toward the shooter from five o'clock, going for a low tackle. There was a splash of blood, and he cried out. Other gunfire followed from Greene's people.

Juha was in Greene's line of fire. The shooter tried to sidestep Juha's takedown, but Juha got a bloody hand on the man's collar as he fell, taking the ghost of the man's face with him.

Shepherd, magazine empty, threw down his gun and stepped across the safety stripe, the remnants of the face projector collar around his neck. He took a small device from his breast pocket.

Before Greene could think about what he was doing, he rolled across the striped line and into the force field area.

There was a loud, tangible buzz, and the air flickered with energy as force fields came into being all around the safety zone, reaching from ceiling to floor. Greene's carbine was on the tape, and the force field cut it cleanly in half as it activated. His team's bullets ricocheted harmlessly off the field in front of Shepherd.

Greene and Shepherd were in the force field area together, but on opposite ends of the safety zone, with a field between them.

Greene spared a look at the others. Everyone was down, but he couldn't tell at a glance who had been shot.

Juha sat up, clutching his bloody left hand, which was missing its ring finger. He turned to look at Shepherd. "I am going to shoot you in your holographic fucking face for this."

Shepherd's smirk became a scowl when he saw Greene was inside with him. He sprinted for the control room.

Greene hauled himself up and pursued, drawing his pistol. He called back, "Hold the elevator and get the medics up here!"

He wasn't going to be able to overtake Shepherd before he made it to the control room. He drew up and took aim with his pistol. "Shepherd, stop!"

Shepherd paid no heed. Greene fired.

The bullet sizzled off a force field somewhere between them. Shepherd's boots clanged on the metal staircase to the control room.

"Damn it," Greene muttered. He reached the force field and stopped, feeling it out. It seemed to run the entire width of the room.

"Green, we can't break through to you," Juha called from behind him.

"There are too many projectors," Garcinia said. "Shepherd's cycling the fields. Every time one goes down, a fresh one comes right up."

Shepherd was in the window of the control room now, at the panel. He spoke into the microphone. "An impressive effort, Chief Greene. Very impressive indeed. But surely you didn't think I wouldn't have my own contingency plans. You can't keep me locked out. I practically run this company."

"Not for long," Greene said.

With a loud hum, the projectors above him activated.

Too bad I won't be around to see it, Greene thought. Trapped in here, by himself, at the mercy of Shepherd's projections—he was in for it now.

"Green!" Juha called. "I have an idea. I can help lock down the roof. Let me have your security authorization."

Greene took out his phone with his free hand. "You aren't chipped; I can't give it to you. Hang on." He addressed the phone. "Give full security access to Marlena Ranga Rao."

Greene glanced back at the safety zone. Juha was pulling Marlena by the hand back toward the elevators. Garcinia worked furiously at her tablet. Four of Greene's people were down; only one was moving. A fifth crouched over her; the last stood, weapon ready, watching Greene helplessly.

Juha waved his maimed hand as the elevator doors closed. "Thanks, man. Try not to die. Marlena, call R&D and tell them to—"

And then Greene had no more time to spare for any of them.

Where could he go? The maze? It was mostly plywood; Shepherd could flatten it with the projectors in a matter of minutes. But those were minutes Greene wouldn't have out here in the open.

Greene broke for the maze. He got five meters before he slammed into a force field wall that flashed a sparkling blue on impact. He reversed course, collided with a second. Just as Wheat had done when they'd had Clark, Shepherd had boxed him in. The next force field would cut Greene in half.

It flashed into existence some twenty meters away, waist high, moving toward him with incredible speed.

Greene dropped to the floor and saw another force field plane, parallel to the first, only centimeters off the ground. He tried to scramble out of its course, but the other fields constrained him.

Greene braced for the end.

It didn't come. Instead, centimeters from his face, there was a flash of pink, a dazzling explosion of energy, a tremendous crackling sound. A collision of force fields.

"I've gotten a couple of the projectors away from him!" Garcinia shouted. "You should be able to move around a bit now, but try to stay in the middle of the room."

Greene rose, still clutching his pistol, which might have been a water gun for all the good it would do him against these force fields. Even with Garcinia on his side, he felt like a sitting duck.

Shepherd caused a new hologram to form, a long, slender cone, pale blue, rotating in space. He launched it at Greene.

"Move!" Garcinia cried, and Greene dove to the side, half-expecting to slam face-first into an energy wall. He landed cleanly and rolled into a crouch.

The cone punctured Garcinia's wall in a firework of crackling light, disrupting both fields.

More cones formed, spinning, flying. Garcinia blocked them all with fields of her own.

Greene raised his arm against the brightness, beginning to hope he might yet survive. He detected movement out of the corner of his eye, looked around, and saw ... himself. Or rather, himselves. Garcinia had made four duplicates of him, synced to his movements.

"Might buy you a few seconds," Garcinia called.

Greene was glad to have them. The space in front of him, behind him, above him, beside him—the entire massive kill house, it seemed—had become a swirling, blinding maelstrom of piercing cones. They all fired as one. Reflexively, futilely, Greene shielded his face with his arms.

Garcinia was up to the task. Energy enveloped Greene, encased him in a glowing roseate egg that held against the onslaught. Every strike sent out a blazing flare of light, forcing Greene to shut his eyes.

Finally, the impacts stopped. The buzz of the shield ceased. The projectors went quiet.

Greene remained tensed, but nothing more was forthcoming. He opened his eyes. His duplicates had been obliterated. The kill house was still.

Shepherd was no doubt searching the system for something new. The projectors had nearly unlimited power, but Shepherd was constrained by what he could find in the system or whip up on the spot—the man was capable with the technology, but he didn't seem to be particularly familiar with the software. Plus his attention was divided between killing Greene, overriding the security lockdown, and fending off Garcinia's cyberattacks.

Greene backed toward the safety zone, his eyes locked on the control room.

"Fantastic work so far," he said to Garcinia. "How are we doing?"

"Oh, quite well, quite well." She was in her element, entirely unfazed by the mayhem in front of her. "You're still in one piece, and I'm only a few minutes away from taking control of the entire system. Ah, there's one more projector for us now."

Greene tugged on the strap of his helmet. "How many is that?"

"Five. To his eleven. Progress, dear."

"And Shepherd's override?"

"I'm afraid I haven't been able to do much about that. Whatever he's using is really quite something. He doesn't have long to go, either. It's going to be close."

Greene looked back, saw a security officer standing there on the other side of the force field. Purple hair peeked out from under the helmet—it was Sonnenschein. Her carbine clenched in white-knuckled fists, she was clearly frustrated at her inability to provide assistance. Behind her, the medical staff had arrived.

"Report," Greene said.

"Three dead here, sir, two wounded," Sonnenschein said. "And Deputy Chief Burg says she can't get to the roof."

"Why?"

"There's some kind of security measure in place. They can't get the blast door to open."

Greene took out his phone. "Retract all blast doors."

"Error," said the phone. "Main door to roof jammed. Utility door to roof jammed."

"I'm sure they're both not really jammed," Garcinia said without looking up from her tablet. "Shepherd's probably fooled the system somehow. It's a pretty clever way around your authorization."

"Make sure Burg's got engineers on the way," Greene said. "We don't have long. Otherwise call our copter back, have it land in the plaza. We can get a team up that way."

"Yes, sir," Sonnenschein said.

The projectors above began to hum as they powered up again. Greene tensed in anticipation of Shepherd's new trick. As long as it had taken the man, it ought to be quite something.

Energy—an incredible amount—coalesced into the shape of an immense creature. An enormous lion, three meters high at the shoulder. The mane framed a face that suggested human features. The creature thrashed its tail—the tail of a scorpion, ending in a stinger the size of Greene's torso—and unfurled leathery bat wings that seemed to stretch the entire width of the kill house.

Greene fell back against the force field that separated him from safety. "You've got to be kidding me."

"Just a moment, dear," Garcinia said. "Remain calm."

If Shepherd had been going for intimidation, he'd succeeded completely.

"A dragon," Greene said. "Why is there a dragon?"

"It's a manticore, dear," Garcinia said.

"How does he have it?"

"It's from our fantasy adventure line of programs. I didn't realize we'd gotten so far in integrating the line with our solid technology just yet ... but that's the future, you know."

The manticore locked its eyes on Greene, tucked its wings, and stalked toward him. He had nowhere to go.

"Let's see now," Garcinia said.

A pink wall of energy appeared immediately in front of the monster, and it stopped. The manticore's scorpion tail whipped, smashing through the wall, dispersing the energy. The creature continued its advance, intact and undamaged.

"I was afraid of that," Garcinia said. "It looks like Shepherd's figured out how to concentrate the energy.

Greene raised his pistol and fired several shots at it, then stopped when he realized his gun was completely useless.

"Here, dear, see what you can do with this," Garcinia said.

At Greene's feet materialized a riot shield and a medieval broadsword.

Greene looked at them. "You're joking."

"Please think holographically, Chief. That sword, for example, is made of energy, and is sharp to a point measurable on a molecular level. Like the cones Shepherd was throwing around just now. It should be enough to disrupt that creature's fields."

Greene was skeptical, but nothing more was forthcoming from Garcinia, and the manticore was closing.

The colossal projection was accompanied by unsettling sound effects. The manticore's immense padded paws thudded on the floor. Slavering, the beast bared three rows of teeth like daggers and let out a low, rumbling growl.

Greene stooped, dropped his pistol, and picked up the holographic weapons. They felt strange in his hands—they buzzed and vibrated, making his arms tingle, and they had no real weight.

"Remember, all you have to do is survive for a few more minutes," Garcinia said.

She made it sound so easy.

And then the manticore was upon him, sweeping its tail. Greene leapt out of the way and backed toward the center of the room, seeking space to maneuver.

He raised his sword and felt ludicrous. He had no idea how to fight with a sword—but against a monster like this, maybe it didn't matter.

The manticore pounced, swatting at him with razor claws. Greene got his shield up, but the impact of the blow knocked him onto his back.

The manticore was above Greene now, its paw descending rapidly toward his head. With no time to try to dodge, Greene raised the sword to meet the enormous paw, hoping, trusting that Garcinia was right.

The sword hit the paw in a crackle of light. The force of the impact ran all the way up Greene's arm, and everything went dark.

Confused and disoriented but uninjured, Greene leapt to his feet and backed away—*through* the manticore's leg. Then he understood: he had destroyed the force field in the monster's leg, but not the hologram, which had continued to move according to its program.

Well, maybe he could whittle this thing down after all. He only had three more paws, a mouth full of giant teeth, and a massive stinging tail to contend with.

But the manticore didn't register any pain from the "wound," nor did it appear to be incapacitated in any way. And why should it? It was a hologram.

It advanced again, and Greene stood his ground, holding forth his sword with more confidence.

The manticore lunged for him with its gaping maw. Greene's sword flashed again, disrupting the force field again, and Greene found himself inside the hologram a second time. Progress.

As he emerged from within the hologram, a crushing blow on his shield from the manticore's tail sent him flying. Greene lost his grip on the sword, didn't see where it landed. He landed on his back, all the air slammed out of him.

Greene struggled to rise, but the manticore was already above him. It placed its remaining solid front paw on the lower half of his body, pinning him, sending vibrations through his legs. Its tail whipped in an overhead arc. The bulbous stinger slammed against Greene's shield, nearly jarring it from his grasp. Another blow like that might break his arm, or worse.

The tail flicked back, then came forward again, knocking Greene's shield arm away from his body and leaving him exposed.

The manticore struck a third time with its tail, directly at Greene's torso. A killing blow.

Greene strained with all the might his desperation provided and managed to flip onto his side just as the blow came.

Agony enveloped his left arm, devouring his strength. Greene tried to bring the shield back up but couldn't manage it. He didn't seem to be holding it anymore.

That was it, then. The next blow would be the last.

The tail went up, flicked twice, came down.

Greene thought fleetingly of his wife, of his unborn daughter. They hadn't picked a name ...

The sweeping tail vanished. The pressure on his legs abated. The manticore was gone.

Greene sat up, feeling light-headed. He tried to rise but couldn't seem to get his hand planted.

Then Mainprize was at his side. "Take it easy, Chief."

Greene shook his head. "Where's Shepherd?"

"He's just gone up," Garcinia said. "He overrode the lockdown about a minute ago."

Greene labored to his feet and almost passed out. There was blood, a lot of blood. Then he saw it: a severed forearm lay on the floor in a puddle of blood.

"Huh," Greene said.

Greene looked at his own left arm, which now ended just below the elbow. A frightening amount of blood poured from the wound. Reality rushed in.

"Oh, God," Greene said. "Oh, Jesus."

Mainprize was a flurry of activity beside him, swathing the stump in a bandage, covering it with some sort of sleeve, fastening it with a tourniquet just above the elbow, pulling it painfully tight.

His mangled arm tingling, Greene stumbled toward the roof access elevators, listing to the right. His center of gravity was off. He felt very cold.

Mainprize had her hand on his right shoulder, steadying him, slowing him down. "Chief, stop. I need to get you to Medical."

Greene shrugged her off. "Not until we get Shepherd."

"There's a strong likelihood you're going to go into hypovolemic shock. You've lost too much blood. You could pass out, or ... worse."

Greene set his jaw, fastened his eyes on the elevators, and made his way toward them. "Then I guess you'd better come along with me."

TWENTY

Greene felt dazed, almost drunk. He leaned against the wall of the elevator car and found Mainprize and Sonnenschein there with him.

He pulled off his helmet and let it drop to the floor. "Report."

"Burg has just obtained roof access," Sonnenschein said, clearly trying not to stare at Greene's maimed arm. "She's up to speed on what's happening—mostly. She says Karjalainen was already on the roof when she got there. Went through the utility door."

This didn't make sense. Greene mustered his wits. "How did he get through the blast door?"

"Something about a grenade. Oh, and Karjalainen said to tell you he'd 'come up with a great plan.'"

Greene tried to put his hand to his forehead, but it wasn't there anymore. The profound feeling of loss was needles in his heart.

Focus, he ordered himself. Don't think about that. Do your job. Do your duty, if only for a few minutes more.

Through the blast door? Kingjack must have given Juha plasma grenades. God. That was a conversation that had to happen later.

Mainprize jabbed a large needle into Greene's arm, and fire shot through his blood. But his head cleared somewhat, and he felt a little stronger.

"What was that?"

"It'll help keep you going," Mainprize said. "For a little while."

Greene nodded his thanks. "Gun," he said, and Sonnenschein immediately pressed her sidearm into Greene's hand.

The elevator doors opened. Pistol ready, Greene stepped out onto the roof of Xiong Tower. The sun was blinding, soporific. Overhead, Xiong's towering golden bear prowled silently in mid-air. It made Greene's head hurt.

The wind whipped around them here, two hundred stories up, and Greene struggled to keep himself steady.

Shepherd's autocopter was on the pad, its passenger door open, its stealth rotors spinning almost inaudibly. Burg and the six members of her team had formed a ring around the stairs up to the pad. Across the roof, Greene saw, the utility access stairwell was rubble.

Halfway up the stairs to the helicopter pad was Shepherd, gripping Juha by his long hair. Standing several steps below the CTO, Juha looked remarkably unperturbed given that Shepherd had a grenade in his hand. The pin was out, and Shepherd was holding the safety lever down—a dead man's switch.

Juha had a great plan? He was a hostage.

"Oh, good," Juha said to Greene. "You made it. I didn't want you to miss this."

"Where's Marlena?" Greene asked.

"Don't worry, she's safe."

Greene addressed Shepherd. "You can't really think you're going to get away with it."

Shepherd laughed. "I've already gotten away with it. Do you have any idea? I have this whole company—the designs, the specs, the schematics—all worth billions of gigayuan, Chief, billions. All I have to do is get out of here."

Juha awkwardly adjusted his position to relieve the pull on his hair. "Yeah, best of luck with that."

"Dr. Ranga Rao found out what you were doing, didn't he?" Greene said. "That's why you killed him. The theft of the projector was just to throw us off."

Shepherd wore his arrogant smirk. "I was able to keep ahead of him for quite a while—months—before he figured out exactly what he had. I knew this day was coming, and I had plenty of time to prepare. Why else do you think I hired you?"

Greene blinked. "You?"

"I needed a patsy, obviously. How else do you think someone as grossly unqualified as you could become chief of security for this company?"

In spite of everything Greene had been through, this remark stung him like a slap.

"Be fair," Juha said. "Based purely on how badly he's fucked up your plans, you've got to give him at least a 'meets expectations.'"

Shepherd jerked hard on Juha's ponytail. "Granted, things would have gone more smoothly if Wheat had killed you like he was supposed to, but my plans are just fine, thank you. The two of you have been in my way for the last two days, it's true, but I've still managed to get most of what I set out for from this company. Now tell your people to stand down."

"Don't do it," Juha said.

Shepherd looked surprised. "I will kill you. You must know that."

Juha's face was serious but untroubled. "You should have picked a hostage who gave a fuck, then."

Shepherd raised an eyebrow. "This is a plasma grenade. It would kill not only you and me, but probably all your friends here as well."

"That sounds like a personal problem," Juha said. "You know, I bet I could grab it out of your hand and toss it onto your copter before you could shoot me. That might wreck your day, huh? Shall I try?"

Shepherd twisted Juha's hair, forcing him to one knee. "Tell them to stand down."

Juha looked at Greene, caught his eye. "Don't you do any of that weak-ass crap." Then he winked.

The wink was unmistakable, a splash of cold water in Greene's face. But what did it mean? Greene didn't know, couldn't think through it. His mind was fogging over.

"You know I can't let you leave," Greene said.

"Yes, of course," Shepherd said. "Pride, duty, obligation, all of that. I grow tired of repeating myself."

Juha had a plan—that was all Greene had to work with. A plan for what? Greene had no idea. Did he trust Juha that far?

Greene decided that he did. He nodded to Burg. "Stand down."

Juha gave an almost imperceptible nod of his head at this, so slight Greene wondered if he'd imagined it.

Burg was incredulous, aghast. "But sir!"

A gust of wind made Greene totter. Sonnenschein discretely put a hand on his back to steady him.

Greene kept his eyes on Shepherd and Juha. "Stand down, I said."

Slowly, reluctantly, Burg lowered her carbine, and the rest of the security team followed suit.

"Good," Shepherd said. "Very good. Most of us may yet survive this. Now tell all your people to lay down their weapons and go back downstairs."

Juha gave another tiny nod. "Don't negotiate with terrorists," he said.

"Do it," Greene said.

Burg threw up her hands. "You've got to be shitting me."

Greene shook his head. "I said do it." If nothing else, it would get most of these people out of the blast radius of Shepherd's plasma grenade.

Burg didn't comply. "With respect, sir, what are you going to do, just let him leave and ruin this company? After everything he's done? What's your plan?"

"The plan is that nobody dies," Greene said.

"Xiong policy is to—"

"Do it, Burg."

Not bothering to hide her disgust, Burg threw down her carbine, turned, and stalked back toward the stairwell. The six members of her team followed.

"Excellent." Shepherd nodded at Sonnenschein and Mainprize. "Them, too."

"Don't do it," Juha said. "Tell this douchebag to cram it right up his ass."

Sonnenschein looked to Greene. "Sir?"

Greene nodded. "Go on." To Mainprize, he said, "I'll manage," and wondered if it was true.

Shepherd waited for them all to leave. "Down the stairs," he said. "I don't want to see anyone."

They obeyed.

Only Greene, Shepherd, and Juha remained on the roof.

"Why just me?" Greene asked. "I'm still here, I still have my gun."

Shepherd grinned. "You've taken a certain ... ownership of everything that's happened, haven't you? You feel ... responsible. To this company. It's really quite commendable." He jerked again on Juha's hair. "Your idiotic friend here is right—you aren't quite what I thought you were. If I told you to put down your gun and walk away, would you do it?"

"No."

"I thought not. Nevertheless, I have you figured well enough. Whether there was one life in the balance or ten, you'd play this the same way, so I figure we might as well keep it simple. Here I am: you have me. But you're going to let me go to save this fool's life."

"Don't forget 'and throw away your career,'" Juha said.

Greene raised his pistol and pointed it at Shepherd. He was reasonably confident he could still hit a stationary target from this distance. "Maybe."

"That's it," Juha said. "You shoot him and I'll grab the grenade out of his hand. Trust me, I know what I'm doing."

Shepherd kicked Juha in the side. "If you say another word, I'm going to put the grenade in your mouth."

Juha shrugged. "Let him go, then. I don't give a fuck. I don't own stock in this company. Bunch of clowns running things around here anyway."

Greene held his aim and began moving toward the helicopter pad. "What now, Shepherd?"

"No, no, Chief, stop right there." Shepherd tightened his grip on Juha's hair and began backing up the stairs to the pad, dragging Juha with him.

"Am I going, too?" Juha said. "That'll be fun. Can we stop for ice cream?"

On the pad, Shepherd said, "I can think of no more excruciating torture. On your knees, Karjalainen, back to me. Hands on top of your head."

Juha complied, and Shepherd released his ponytail.

Greene was confused. What was Juha's plan? Where was there room left for a plan?

Still holding the live grenade, Shepherd drew his pistol with his free hand. "Now I get on the helicopter ... and you save your friend's life. Goodbye, Chief. If it's any consolation, you almost won."

Shepherd pointed his gun at Juha and fired. Juha grunted and pitched forward, writhing on the pad. Shepherd turned and dashed for the autocopter, vaulting into the cabin. The door closed automatically behind him.

"Medic!" Greene shouted. He sprinted toward the pad, thundering up the stairs. The sudden exertion and change in elevation nearly made him black out.

The helicopter lifted off.

With some difficulty, Juha rolled over and propped himself up on his elbows, grimacing. "God damn, that hurts. Fucker gut-shot me. Just uncalled for. Shit, I think I'm going to need a new kidney."

Greene watched the helicopter ascend. Watched Shepherd succeed, escape. This would be the end of Greene's tenure at Xiong Holonautics. He found that he didn't mourn for it. He had done his best, inadequate though it had been, had done what he thought was right. He'd expected more from Juha—perhaps unfairly—but at least no one else had died.

The helicopter began to move off. It was over, Greene thought. He turned to Juha to ask him about his so-called plan.

In spite of his injuries, Juha had a wicked grin on his face. "Surely he's got the pin back in that grenade by now, right? He's over the street. Marlena, cut it!"

The helicopter vanished. For the briefest instant, Shepherd appeared to hang, suspended, in the air. Then he fell—all the way down.

Juha raised the middle finger of his bloody hand in salute. "Pride goeth, motherfucker."

Then Marlena was there on the pad with them, a tablet in her hand, and Mainprize, pressing a bandage over the wound in Juha's abdomen.

"Drugs, please," he said.

Mainprize produced a syringe and stuck Juha with it, and the strain on his face lessened.

"What a dick. I wish I could have seen his face." Juha clapped Greene on the leg. "Well done. High fives all around."

Greene felt dizzy, and he sat down. "How—"

On Juha's face, delight triumphed over pain. "You remember we were talking about how sitting on a solid hologram was like taking a rough ride in a vehicle? Well, it gave me an idea. Look there."

On top of the main access stairwell, nestled among all the conventional projectors that created the mighty Xiong bear, was the mobile solid projector, wired into the system.

"We were able to divert the real copter before Shepherd got up here," Juha said. "Then Marlena whipped up the hologram, with sound effects, even. Quality work. Only the cabin and the blades were solid—for the downwash, you know; the rest was conventional holograms. But once we got him in there ..."

Medics were swarming around them now, bearing stretchers.

"We need to get you both down to Medical right away if you want to live," Mainprize said.

"Might as well," Juha said. "I'm in a hell of a lot of pain right now."

Greene lay down on his stretcher. "Did you *let* him take that grenade from you?"

Juha allowed the medics to pick him up and place him on the other stretcher. "Well ... 'let' is a strong word. But I knew you weren't going to shoot him. I had to work around that. You played your role to the hilt, though."

"Juha, I'm sorry I—"

Juha waved this away. "It's cool, man. Don't worry about it."

The medics bore them down the steps, past Burg and her team. Burg's eyes met Greene's, and she nodded.

Marlena walked between the two stretchers. There were tears in her eyes, but she was smiling. "Thank you. Both of you. For everything."

"It was entirely my pleasure," Juha said.

She squeezed Greene's hand. "I'm glad," he said.

The medics carried them onto the main elevator. Greene looked at Juha and said, "Thank you."

"We make a good team, don't we?" Juha put his uninjured arm under his head, trying to get comfortable on the stretcher. "It's just like old times." He tapped the nearest medic on the arm with his bloody hand. "Hey, did you guys find my finger, or are you going to print me a new one?" Juha motioned to Greene's lost limb. "It's going to take a shitload of bioprinting to get you back together, too, huh? Don't worry; you get used to it."

It was true, Greene thought—his ordeal wasn't over. He still had the bioprinting to look forward to, but to regain his hand, any price was a small one.

Right now, though, he wanted to sleep. Exhaustion crashed over him like a breaker, pulling his eyelids closed.

As they rode down the elevator, Greene's mind swept back across the last three days. Good riddance to them. Killers, conspiracies, car wrecks, monsters, dismemberment—he wouldn't relive them for all the money in the world.

Juha tapped his arm. "Green."

Greene didn't open his eyes. "What?"

"I've had a great time these last few days. I just wanted to tell you that."

Yes, Greene thought, it was just like old times.

Acknowledgments

I am profoundly grateful to all those who contributed meaningfully to the development of this book:

-Divya, the mighty one.

-David Lange, chief elephant wrangler.

-Mark Darrah, Jackie King, Jennifer Mathews, Mary Coley, Naomi McDonald, and Ada Harrington, critique group of champions.

-Aaron Leatherbarrow, lover of all unworthy things.

-Emily Carry, vanquisher of the roiling miasma.

-John Cunningham, haver of opinions.

About the Author

Joshua Danker-Dake lives in Tulsa with his longsuffering wife, their three irrepressible children, and a tank full of cannibal guppies. Things he gets rather excited about include bombastic European power metal, *He-Man and the Masters of the Universe*, St. Louis Cardinals baseball, and conversations about science-based health and fitness.

Visit him online at www.dankerdake.com.

Made in the USA
Coppell, TX
25 August 2020